# Notes on a Cuff
## and Other Stories

## Mikhail Bulgakov

Translated by Roger Cockrell

ALMA CLASSICS LTD
London House
243-253 Lower Mortlake Road
Richmond
Surrey TW9 2LL
United Kingdom
www.almaclassics.com

This translation first published by Alma Classics Ltd in 2014

Translation, Introduction and Notes © Roger Cockrell, 2014

Extra Material © Alma Classics Ltd

Printed and bound by CPI Group (UK) Ltd, Croydon, CR0 4YY

ISBN: 978-1-84749-387-3

# Contents

Mikhail Bulgakov (1891–1940)

Afanasy Ivanovich Bulgakov,
Bulgakov's father

Varvara Mikhailovna Bulgakova,
Bulgakov's mother

Lyubov Belozerskaya,
Bulgakov's second wife

Yelena Shilovskaya,
Bulgakov's third wife

Bulgakov's residences on Bolshaya Sadovaya St. (above) and Nashchokinsky Pereulok (bottom left); an unfinished letter to Stalin (bottom right)

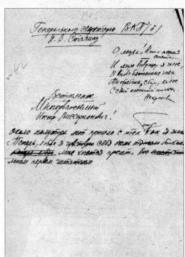

An autograph page from *The Master and Margarita*

# Introduction

"I have just one dream: to get through the winter, to survive December, which will be the most difficult month, I should imagine."* So wrote the thirty-year-old Mikhail Bulgakov to his mother on 17th November 1921, two months after he had arrived in Moscow. By this time, Bulgakov had already decided to forgo his medical career and to devote his life to literature. This decision (echoing that made by Anton Chekhov some sixty years earlier) marked the beginning of a twenty-year-long literary career characterized by poverty, conflict with the authorities and an unceasing battle with the often arbitrary restrictions of the censors. Masterpieces such as his novels *The White Guard* and *The Master and Margarita* were never to be published in the Soviet Union in his lifetime.

Despite these difficulties and hurdles, by 1926 Bulgakov was beginning to establish his position and reputation as an author – at least among his more discerning fellow writers, if not within the wider literary world. Two years earlier he had published his story 'Diaboliad' and written two remarkable novellas, *The Fatal Eggs* and *A Dog's Heart*.* By the middle of the decade Bulgakov had also published a large number of lesser-known pieces of varying quality in a range of newspapers and journals. This volume contains a selection of some of the best of these stories, all of which appeared within five years of each other in the first half of the 1920s, and many of which are translated into English for the first time.

As might be expected at this early and experimental stage in Bulgakov's career, the twelve stories presented here differ considerably in tone, range and narrative viewpoint. Six of these stories – 'Notes on a Cuff', 'A Week of Enlightenment', 'The Unusual Adventures of a Doctor', 'Psalm', 'Moonshine Lake' and 'The Murderer' – reflect, to a greater or lesser extent, Bulgakov's own personal experiences. But we should hesitate before labelling these stories "autobiographical" in the strict sense of the term. As is so often the case with Bulgakov, the boundaries between autobiography and fiction, journalism and belles-lettres are deliberately blurred. In 'Notes on a Cuff', for example, we have ostensibly a record in diary form of events in 1920 and 1921, when Bulgakov was working first as a journalist in the Caucasus and then as a literary administrator in Moscow. But the interest lies less in the authenticity or otherwise of the details than in the intriguing nature of the relationship between the real-life author and the diary's narrator, who presents himself in deprecatingly ironic and anti-heroic terms. In 'The Unusual Adventures of a Doctor', Bulgakov is undoubtedly recreating his own traumatic experiences in the civil war, but he chooses to relate his story through the semi-coherent diary of an unknown participant. 'The Murderer' may be set within a more conventional narrative framework, but it again illustrates Bulgakov's propensity to portray himself "at a distance", with the storyteller, Dr Yashvin, foreshadowing the semi-autobiographical figure of Alexei Turbin in *The White Guard*. Although the "uneducated" narrator of 'A Week of Enlightenment' can plainly not be identified with the author, the story is nonetheless directly based on Bulgakov's own firsthand observations as a journalist in Vladikavkaz. Finally, in this group, 'Psalm' and 'Moonshine Lake' are more straightforward accounts of Bulgakov's early Moscow experiences, although in their portrayal of character they both demonstrate a literary quality that places them above the usual run-of-the-mill feuilleton.

'Makar Devushkin's Story', 'A Scurvy Character', 'The Cockroach' and 'A Dissolute Man' are purely fictional. All of them feature unprepossessing characters, and all of them provide Bulgakov with an opportunity to explore the vicissitudes and foibles of human nature within the context of the new fledgling Soviet society, forming an ironic commentary on the Bolsheviks' claim that they were in the process of socially engineering a "qualitatively new era in the history of mankind".

This leaves us with two substantial pieces: 'The Fire of the Khans' and 'The Crimson Island'. Characterized at the time as "the most graphic and picturesque of all Bulgakov's stories", 'The Fire of the Khans' demonstrates Bulgakov's concern with a supremely topical issue arising from the Bolsheviks' seizure of power: whether or not a return to private ownership would be possible in Soviet Russia. Bulgakov explores this question not simply through the prince's violent and explosive (not to say incendiary) reaction to the new order that has displaced him and his way of life, but also through the relationship between servant and master in the figures of Iona and Tugai-Beg – a new twist to a familiar nineteenth-century theme.

We turn, finally, to the most idiosyncratic and exotic story in the collection, 'The Crimson Island'.* The story is a political allegory commenting on the cataclysmic events that took place in Russia during the two 1917 revolutions and their immediate aftermath, the civil war. By setting his story on the "most immense of uninhabited islands" in the Pacific Ocean, "below the 45th parallel" (could this be the South Island of New Zealand?), by the references to two of his favourite authors Jules Verne and Rudyard Kipling and by his laconic, almost throwaway conclusion, Bulgakov achieves an ironic distance that lends the narrative its particular force. Along the way, we are treated to a savage sideswipe at the archetypal emotionless and calculating Englishman in the figure of Lord Glenarvan. Yet the wider question of Bulgakov's own attitude towards the political events he is satirizing remains a matter for speculation. The story has generally been seen as an attack on the Red terror arising from Bolshevik actions during the civil war, and it is certainly true that Bulgakov was deeply antipathetic to the Bolsheviks and their cause. But in view of the eventual coming-together of the white Arabs and the red Ethiopians, he may have had another, more conciliatory aim: to reflect his often expressed view that Russia's political salvation could be assured only in the event of a coalition between all right-thinking forces, of whatever political persuasion.

The allusions to Jules Verne and Rudyard Kipling remind us of the central importance of literature in Bulgakov's life, a fact to which his diaries and letters bear witness. References to both foreign and Russian authors abound in 'Notes on a Cuff'. Yet this is not merely name-dropping: significantly the narrator's most "heroic" moment comes when he takes it upon himself to defend the reputation of the father of Russian literature Alexander Pushkin, thereby challenging the boorish philistinism of the brave new world of Soviet Russia. Many such references are explicit, but others are less direct. Take 'The Cockroach', for example: here we find an opening section that lavishes extravagant praise on a city, Moscow, only for the narrative to descend, as the story unfolds, into a shadowy world of deceit, corruption and crime. What is this if not a retelling of Nikolai Gogol's first St Petersburg story, 'Nevsky Prospect'? In 'The Crimson Island', the absurd duel between Lord Glenarvan and Michel Ardan, witnessed by an Arab crouching behind a bush, mirrors the scene in Chekhov's 'The Duel', in which the encounter between Layevsky and von Koren is seen through the eyes of the similarly concealed deacon. In 'A Week of Enlightenment', the action of the opera is presented in a crudely naive way that brings to mind Tolstoy's description of the opera in *War and Peace* – although we should of course not ignore the irony that Bulgakov's and Tolstoy's opinions of opera were diametrically opposed.

Such moments may well have been subconscious echoes rather than deliberate references but, either way, they place Bulgakov firmly within the mainstream of Russian literature. Across time, Russian authors have responded to, or reacted against, other authors in a resonant interplay of ideas, expressed either as abstractions or through the portrayal of character. It is, however, an ironic and melancholy fact that the awakening of Bulgakov's extraordinary imaginative powers in the first half of the 1920s should have coincided with the shift from a relatively relaxed cultural period to a far more repressive regime. Despite the Bolsheviks' protestations of love for pre-revolutionary Russian culture, ideological constraints prevented them from partaking fully in its rich traditions. Some, such as Trotsky, considered that this was merely a temporary condition occasioned by prevailing political circumstances. Not everyone was so sanguine: in the same year that Bulgakov moved to Moscow, Yevgeny Zamyatin expressed his fear that Russian literature would have "only one future – its past".* Bulgakov was not given to making grand statements or gestures, but few fought harder than he did to keep the flame of literature alive. The creative process, even when ending in apparent failure, remained precious. "I realized," he writes in Chapter XII of 'Notes on a Cuff', "that people who say you must never destroy what has been written are right! You can tear it up, you can burn it… You can hide it from other people. But from yourself – *never*!"

– Roger Cockrell

# Notes on a Cuff

## and Other Stories

# Notes on a Cuff

## Part 1

*To all Russian writers travelling
or voyaging, by land or by sea*

T HE CORRESPONDENT of the late-lamented newspaper
*The Russian Word*,* wearing gaiters and smoking a cigar,
grabbed the telegram from the table and, with a practised
professional eye, read it through from beginning to end in a
single second.

Automatically he scribbled "2 columns" on the side of the
telegram, but he pursed his lips into a funnel:

"Phew!" he whistled.

He fell silent for a moment. Then he ripped off a quarter-page
and dashed off the following lines:

Tiflis is some forty miles away…*
I need a car, and I need it today.

On top "Short feuilleton"; in the margin "Long primer"; underneath "The Rook".

At that he started muttering to himself, like Dickens's Jingle.*

3

"Right! So that's it!... I knew it! It looks as if I may have to scarper. Well, so be it, then! I've got six thousand lire in Rome. *Credito italiano*. That's right, isn't it? Six... And, in essence, I'm an Italian officer! Yes, sir! *Finita la commedia*!"*

And with another whistle he placed his cap on the back of his head and dashed to the door – with the telegram and the feuilleton.

"Wait!" I yelled, suddenly coming to. "Wait! What's this *credito*? What do you mean, *finita*? What's going on? Has there been some disaster?"

But he had disappeared.

I wanted to run after him... but instead I gestured dismissively and, with an apathetic grimace, I sat down on the small sofa. Hold on a moment: what's really bothering me? The mysterious *credito*? The panic? No, that's not it... Ah, yes, got it! It's my head! This is the second day I've had a headache. It's a real nuisance. Yes, my head! Then, one minute, I felt a cold shiver run up my spine. And then, the next, the opposite: I felt all dry and hot, and my forehead started sweating unpleasantly. Hammering in my temples. I've got a cold. Damn this February fog! Please don't let me get ill! Please don't let me get ill!

Everything feels odd, but that means I've got used to it all in six weeks! How wonderful after all that fog. I'm at home! Cliffs and sea in a gold frame. Books in the cupboard. Scratchy rug on the ottoman, no possibility of lying in any comfort, such a hard, hard pillow. But I'm not going to get up for anything in the world. So lazy! Can't be bothered even to raise my arm. Here I've been for the last half-hour thinking I should reach out and take an aspirin from the chair, but I don't move...

"Misha! Let me take your temperature!"

"Oh, I can't stand it!... There's nothing wrong with me!..."

My God! My God! My... y... y God! Thirty-eight point nine! It can't be typhus, can it? Surely not! Quite impossible! How could I have caught it? But what if it is typhus?! Anything you like, but

4

please not right now! That would be terrible... No, it's nothing. Just a cold. Hypochondria. I've simply caught a cold, that's all. I'll take an aspirin for the night, and I'll be right as rain in the morning!

Thirty-nine point five!

"But doctor, it can't be typhus, can it? Can it? Surely it's just influenza, isn't it? Oh, this fog!"

"Yes, yes... the fog. Deep breath, there's a good fellow... Deeper... That's it."

"Doctor, there's something I have to do. It won't take long. Is that all right?"

"Are you out of your mind?!"

The cliffs, and the sea, and the ottoman are swimming in heat. You only have to turn the pillow and lie back for it to be hot again. All right... I'll just get through one more night, and then, tomorrow, I shall be off. Away from here, on foot! And if not on foot, I'll drive. Yes, that's what I'll do! Have to keep calm. It's just some rubbishy influenza... It's good to be ill. To have a fever. To forget everything. To lie down and rest, but please, God, not right now! No time to read in this devilishly chaotic state... I would so love to be able to read right now. But what exactly? Yes: forests and mountains. But not these blasted Caucasian mountains. Our mountains, far away from here... Melnikov-Pechersky.* The snow-covered monastic retreat. The flickering light and the heated bathhouse... Yes that's exactly it: forests and mountains. I would give half a kingdom right now to be lying on a shelf in a hot bath house. I would feel better in a flash. And then... to dive naked into a snowdrift... Forests! Dense pine forests... Pines suitable for ships' masts. Peter the Great* in his green kaftan chopped down such pine trees. Thenceforth. What a splendidly, solid, official-sounding word – thence-forth! Forests, ravines, carpets of pine needles, the tiny white monastery and the chorus of nuns singing so tenderly and harmoniously:

To Thee, oh Warrior triumphant… we sing!…*

No, that's wrong! What nuns! There aren't any nuns there at all! Where *are* they now, the nuns? Black nuns, white nuns, thin nuns, straight out of Vasnetsov?…*

"Larissa Leontyevna, where are the nuns?"

"He's delirious, poor chap, delirious…"

"Nothing of the sort. I'm not delirious at all. Nuns! Surely you remember, don't you? Pass me that book – there, on the third shelf. Melnikov-Pechersky…

"Misha, you shouldn't be reading!…"

"What?! What do you mean, 'shouldn't be reading'? But I'm getting up tomorrow! I'm going to see Petrov. You don't understand. They're abandoning me! Abandoning me!"

"All right, all right! Get up then! Here's your book."

What a lovely book. It has such an old, familiar smell. But the lines become blurred and jump about all over the place. And then I remember: they forged false notes in that monastery, imperial Romanov notes. I had a memory at one time! Not nuns at all, but notes…

Sashki, my kanashki*

"Larissa Leontyevna… Larochka! You love forests and mountains, don't you? I'm going to go to a monastery. Without fail! A remote little monastery. Walled in by trees, deafened by birdsong, nobody about… I'm sick and tired of this idiotic war! I'll run away to Paris, write a novel, and then the monastery. But, just for tomorrow, Anna is to wake me at eight. You have to understand that I should have gone to see him yesterday… you have to understand!"

"I understand, I really do – just keep quiet!"

Fog. Hot, reddish-coloured fog. Forests, forests… and a gentle trickle of water from a crack in a green rock. Such a pure, crystal, stream of water snaking down the rock. You need to crawl up to it, but once there you can drink as much as you want, and then it's gone, just like that! But it's torture creeping along the pine needles, they're sticky and prickly. And then you open your eyes, and you see it's not pine needles at all, but a sheet.

"Good God! What sort of a sheet do you call this... Have you covered it in sand, or something?... I want a drink!"

"All right, just coming!..."

"Oh it's warm, awful rubbish!"

"...this is terrible. Forty point five again."

"...get me an ice pack..."

"Doctor, I demand that you send me off to Paris immediately! I don't wish to stay in Russia a moment longer... If you won't do that, then be so good as to hand me my revolv... my Browning! Larochka! Get it for me!..."

"All right. All right. We'll get it. Calm down!..."

Darkness. Light. Dark... Light. For the life of me, can't remember...

My head! My head! No nuns chorusing away, but demons trumpeting and ripping my skull with red-hot hooks. My head!

Light... dark. Light... no it's gone... it's not there any more! Nothing's terrible, and nothing matters any more. My headache's gone. Darkness and forty-one point one.....

## II

### WHAT ARE WE GOING TO DO?

THE WRITER YURY SLYOZKIN* was sitting in his plush armchair. In general, everything in the room was plush, making Yury look so out of keeping with his surroundings. His head, hairless from typhus, had exactly the appearance of the little boy's head in Mark Twain (like an egg, with a sprinkling of pepper on top). He was wearing a moth-eaten army jacket with a hole in one of the armpits. Grey puttees. One of them too long, the other too short. A cheap two-copeck pipe in his mouth. Fear and longing played leapfrog in his eyes.

"What is going to happen to us now?" I asked, not recognizing my own voice, which after the second bout of typhus had become weak, thin and desiccated.

"What? What?"

I turned over in the bed and looked glumly out of the window, where the branches, still bare, were gently swaying. And, of course, there was no answer from the amazing sky, barely touched by the fading glow of dawn. Slyozkin remained silent as well, his disfigured head nodding.

There was the rustle of a dress in the next room, and a woman's voice whispered:

"The Ingush will ransack the town this evening…"

Slyozkin turned abruptly in his armchair and corrected her:

"Not the Ingush, but the Ossetians.* And not this evening, but tomorrow morning."

In response, on the other side of the wall, there was a nervous clink of scent bottles.

"My God! Ossetians? That's awful."

"What difference does it make?"

"What do you mean 'what difference'? You obviously don't know the local customs around here. When the Ingush rob people, they just… rob. But Ossetians both rob and murder."

"Are they going to murder everybody?" Slyozkin asked in a businesslike tone, puffing at his evil-smelling pipe.

"My God! What a strange man you are! No, not everybody… I mean who would… Goodness, what am I doing? I've forgotten… We're alarming the patient."

There was the rustling of a dress. The landlady leant over me.

"I don't feel alarmed…"

"Trivial nonsense!" Slyozkin snapped. "Trivial nonsense!"

"What do you mean, 'trivial nonsense'?"

"Well, what you've just been saying… about the Ossetians and all that. Just rubbish." He emitted a puff of smoke.

My exhausted brain began to sing:

Mum, oh mum! What are we going to do?

Slyozkin smirked with just his right cheek. He thought for a moment. Then he was seized by a flash of inspiration.

"We'll start up an arts sub-department!"

"What did you say?"

"What?"

"Something about 'tarts'?"

"No, an *arts* sub-department."

"Sub?"

"Uh-huh."

"Why 'sub'?"

"Well, you see," he said shifting in his armchair, "there's the Department of Education and there's the Regional Department of Education. Department, you see, and then a sub-department. Sub. You see?"

"Sub. Grub. Barbusse. Barbos."

The landlady leapt to her feet.

"For goodness sake, don't talk to him! He's starting to get delirious again."

"Nonsense!" Yury said sternly. "Nonsense. And all these Mingrelians, these… these Imeria… what are they called? Circassians. Simply idiots."

"What do you mean?"

"They just run around about the place. Fire at the moon. They won't rob anybody."

"And what about us? What will happen to us?"

"Nothing much at all. We'll start up a…"

"Arts?"

"Uh-huh. There'll be everything: Izo. Lito. Photo. Theo."*

"I don't understand."

"Mishenka, stop talking! Doctor…"

"I'll explain later! There'll be everything. I've already planned it all. What about us? We're apolitical. We are art."

"And how will we live?"

"We'll toss money behind the rug."

"What rug?"

"Oh, in that little town where I was in charge we had a rug on our wall. On pay days my wife and I used to toss the money behind the rug. It was nerve-wracking, but we ate. Ate well. Rations."

"But what about me?"

"You'll be the head of Lito."

"Head of what?"

"Mishenka. I beg you."

## III

### THE ICON LAMP

THE NIGHT FLOWS ON. Pitch-black. Can't sleep. The light in the icon lamp flickers. Somewhere outside there's the sound of gunshots. My brain's on fire. It's foggy.

Mum, oh mum! What are we going to do?

Slyozkin's busy doing something. Piling stuff up. Photo. Izo. Lito. Theo. Theo. Izo. Liso. Tiso. Forming piles of photographic boxes. What for? Lito. Litterateurs. We're a sad bunch. Izo. Fiso. The Ingush are galloping up on horseback, their eyes flashing. Seizing hold of the boxes. Noise. Shooting at the moon. The nurse puts camphor on my feet. It stings. Third bout of typhus.

"Oh. What's going to happen now? Leave me alone. I'm going, I'm going, I'm going."

"Shh, Mishenka dear. Keep quiet!"

After the morphine injection the Ingush disappear. The velvet night sways. The divine eye of the icon lamp glimmers and trembles, and sings in a crystal voice:

"Mum, oh mum!"

# IV

## THE SUB-DEPARTMENT COMES TO TOWN

S UN! THE CAB WHEELS trail clouds of swirling dust… The building echoes with the sound of people coming and going. In a room on the third floor two cupboards with their doors broken off. Rickety tables. Three young lady typists with bright crimson lips, either clattering away on their machines, or smoking.

The writer, now taken down from his cross, sits in the very centre of the room and creates his sub-department out of the chaos. Theo. Izo. The bluish-grey faces of actors advance on him, demanding money.

The bout of typhus over for the time being, it's now dead calm. I'm shaky on my feet and nauseous, but I'm in charge. Head. Lito. I'm coping.

ArtsDepHead. Department of Education. Literature Board.

There's someone walking around among the tables. In a grey army jacket and a pair of monstrous riding breeches. Dives headfirst into groups of people who immediately scatter before him. Carves through the water like a torpedo boat. Everybody he looks at turns pale. Eyes scour the floor under the tables. Only the young lady typists remain unconcerned. Fear is alien to them.

He came up to me. His eyes drilled right through me, he removed my soul, placed it on his palm and examined it carefully. But my soul was crystal clear.

He replaced my soul and smiled graciously.

"Head of Lito?"

"Yes, head. That's right."

He moved on. He doesn't seem too bad. But nobody has any idea what he's doing here. Doesn't look like a Theo. Even less like a Lito.

A poetess has arrived. Black beret. Skirt fastened at the side, and stockings falling down. She's brought some verse.

Ta, ta, tam, tam
My heart beats like dynamite
Ta, ta, tam.

"That's pretty good. We'll... er... let's see... we'll read them at the concert."

The poetess's eyes are radiant with happiness. She's all right. But why doesn't she pull her stockings up?

# V

## CHAMBER CADET PUSHKIN*

EVERYTHING WAS GOOD. Everything was excellent. And then I spoilt everything, all because of Alexander Sergeyevich Pushkin, God rest his soul.

This is what happened:

A group of local poets had built a nest in the editorial office, under the spiral staircase. Among them there was a young man in dark-blue student's trousers, that woman poet with dynamite in her heart, some impenetrable old man who had started writing poetry in his sixtieth year and a number of others.

A bold-looking fellow with an aquiline nose and a huge revolver strapped to his waist took an indirect approach. He was the first to plunge his pen, its tip intoxicated with ink, into the hearts of survivors of the old regime – those who had gone on a nostalgic trek at last summer's gathering. Against the background of the ceaseless roar of the turbid river Terek,* he had cursed the lilac and thundered:

Enough of praising the seagulls and the moon,
Let me praise the Cheka instead.

It was effective.

Then someone gave a lecture on Gogol and Dostoevsky.* And wiped them both from the face of the earth. He had some negative things to say about Pushkin, but only in passing. And promised to give a special lecture on him. One night in June he lay into Pushkin. Attacked him for his white trousers, his "looking ahead without fear", his "court lackey and generally servile attitude", his "pseudo-revolutionary ideas and hypocrisy", for his indecent verse and his flirtatious behaviour...

I sat in the front row in that stuffy room pouring with sweat and listening to the speaker as he tore into Pushkin's white trousers. And when, having taken a drink of water to moisten his dry throat, he concluded by proposing that Pushkin be thrown into the stove, I smiled, I'm sorry to say. It was an enigmatic smile, damn it. A smile's not something to be trifled with!

"Come up and speak against that!"

"I don't feel like it."

"You lack civic courage."

"So that's what you think, is it? In that case, I will."

And so I spoke, damn it! I prepared myself for it for three days and three nights. I sat by the open window by the lamp with its red shade. On my lap lay a book written by the man with the fiery eyes.

...false wisdom gutters and shimmers
Before the immortal sun of the mind*...

Pushkin wrote:

I shall accept the insult with indifference.*

No, not with indifference! I'll show them! I'll show them! I shook my fist at the pitch-black night.

And I showed them. There was uproar amongst the group of local poets. The speaker lay flat on his back on the floor. I could see an expression of unspoken glee in everyone's eyes.
   "Finish him off! Go on, finish him off!"…

But not now!! Later…

I am a "wolf in sheep's clothing". I am a "gentleman". I am "a bourgeois yes-man".

I am no longer head of Lito. I am not head of Theo.
   I am the stray dog in the attic. I sit there, my body contorted. They'll come for me at night. I shudder…

Oh, dusty days! Oh, sweltering nights!…

And in the summer of 1920 AD someone appeared from Tiflis. A young man, thoroughly worn-down and exhausted, with the wrinkled face of an old woman, arrived and introduced himself: a poet who enjoyed a scandal. He had brought with him a little book, like a wine list. The book contained his poems.
   Forget-me-not. The rhyme: utter rot.
   I shall go out of my mind, you'll see…
   The young man hated me from the very first. Writes scandalous stuff in the newspaper (page 4, column 4). About me. And about Pushkin. Nobody else. Hates Pushkin more than me. What of it? He's already in a place where there is no…
   But I shall disappear, like a little worm.

# VI

## THE BRONZE COLLAR

H OW I HATE this damned Tiflis!
Someone else has arrived! In a bronze collar. A *bronze* collar!
Appeared like that in a journal. No, seriously!

Bronze, would you believe it!…

The writer Slyozkin has been sent packing. Despite his Russian name and the fact that his wife is pregnant. And this man, this new arrival, has now taken his place. There goes your Izo, and your Miso. And there goes your money under your rug…

# VIII

## LITTLE BOYS IN BOXES

H ALO ROUND THE MOON. Yury and I are sitting on the balcony looking up at the star-filled night. But it doesn't help. In a few hours' time the stars will have disappeared and the fiery ball of the sun will be bursting into the sky and we shall expire like beetles transfixed by pins.

Through the balcony door we can hear a thin, constant whining. Somewhere at the back of beyond, at the foot of the mountains in some strange town, in a tiny little, monstrously cramped room, a son has been born to the starving Slyozkin. He's been put in a little box by the window. The box is marked "*Mme Marie. Modes et Robes.*"*

And he lies there in his box grizzling.

"Poor little chap."

It's not him who's poor. It's us.

The mountains hem us in. Table Mountain is asleep in the moonlight. Far, far away to the north lie the limitless plains. And to the south – gorges, ravines, raging streams. And somewhere over to the west is the sea, with the shimmering Golden Horn*…

…Have you seen a fly caught in fly paper?

When the crying stops we go to the cage.

Tomatoes. A little black bread. And Georgian moonshine. Horrible stuff! Revolting! But you drink it, and you feel a little better.

And when everyone around is sleeping the sleep of the dead, the writer reads me his new story. There's nobody else about to listen to it. The night floats on. He finishes reading, carefully rolls up the manuscript and places it under his pillow. There's no desk in the room.

We whisper on until the pale light of dawn...

What names escape our dry lips! What names! Pushkin's poetry has a surprisingly calming effect on embittered spirits. No need for anger, Russian writers!...

...Truth comes only through suffering... That's absolutely right, I can assure you! But nobody will pay you any money, nobody will give you any food for knowledge of the truth. Sad, but true.

# VIII

## A PASSING BREEZE

YEVREINOV'S ARRIVED.* In an ordinary white collar. On his way to St Petersburg, from the Black Sea.

There used to be such a city, somewhere to the north.

Does it still exist? The writer laughs: he assures me that it does. But it takes ages to get there. Three years in a freight car. The whole evening my eyes rested, as they looked at the white collar. The whole evening I heard the stories of his adventures.

Writers, my brothers, in your fate...*

He sat there without any money. His things had been stolen... And the next evening, his last with us, at Slyozkin's, in the land-lady's smoke-filled sitting room, Nikolai Nikolayevich sat at the piano. With iron stoicism he endured the torture of everyone looking at him. Four male poets, a female poet and an artist (the literary group) sat there decorously and gaped at him.

Yevreinov is a versatile man:

"Now, some musical expressions…"

And immediately looking down at the keys he began. First… First he portrayed an elephant invited to play the piano, then a piano-tuner in love, then a dialogue between damask steel and gold, and finally a polka.

Within ten minutes the literary group were reduced to an utterly helpless state. They were no longer sitting down, but lying on the ground next to each other, waving their arms about and groaning…

…The man with the lively eyes has gone. And no silly expressions!

The breeze swept them along. People were flying around like leaves. Someone on his way from Kerch to Vologda, someone else from Vologda to Kerch. An unkempt Osip* arrives with a suitcase and says angrily:

"We'll never get there, that's for sure!"

Of course you won't get there if you don't know where you're going!


Yesterday Rurik Ivnev left.* From Tiflis to Moscow.

"It's better in Moscow."

He got so worn out travelling that one day he lay down by a ditch.

"I'm not going to move. Something's bound to turn up!"

And indeed, an acquaintance of his chanced to come by the ditch, took him home and fed him dinner.

Another poet, on his way from Moscow to Tiflis.

"Things are better in Tiflis."

And then a third poet – Osip Mandelshtam.* He arrived on an overcast day, holding his head high like a prince. Stunned us with his pithy sentences.

"From the Crimea. Appalling. Anybody accepting manuscripts here?"

"…but they don't pay any…" I began to say. But before I could finish my sentence, he had gone. Goodness knows where…

The writer Pilnyak.* On his way to Rostov with the flour train, dressed in a woman's blouse.

"Are things better in Rostov?"

"No, going there for a rest!!"

Total eccentric. In gold-rimmed glasses.

Serafimovich – arrived from the north.*

Tired eyes. Indistinct voice. Gives a lecture to the literary group.

"Remember that in Tolstoy* there's a handkerchief tied to a stick. One moment it's quite still, the next it starts to flutter again. As if it's alive. Once he wrote a label attacking drunkenness, to be used on a vodka bottle. Wrote one phrase. Struck out a word, wrote another one on top. After a moment's thought he struck that one out as well. And went on doing this several times. But the phrase turned out to be perfectly crafted… Nowadays people write… people write oddly!… You take something and read it once. No! No idea what it means. Once more, and still no idea. So you put it to one side…"

The literary group is sitting, *in corpore*, right by the wall. Their eyes seem to suggest that they don't understand a thing. That's their problem!

Serafimovich left… Intermission.

# IX

## THE STORY OF THE GREAT WRITERS

THE SUB-DEPARTMENT SET DESIGNER drew a picture of Anton Pavlovich Chekhov* with a crooked nose and wearing such a monstrously large pince-nez it looked like a pair of automobile goggles.

We put it onto a large easel. The set included a red pavilion, a little table with a carafe and a lamp.

I gave the opening lecture 'On Chekhov's Humour'. But whether it was because I hadn't eaten for over two days, or whether it was for some other reason, I felt a little confused. The auditorium was packed. At times I lost my way. I saw hundreds of faces swimming in front of me, packed to the rafters. It would have helped if I'd seen a smile. But the applause at the end was friendly. Despite my confused state I realized this meant I had finished. With a feeling of relief I made my way offstage. I had earned myself two thousand – now let someone else be in the firing line. On my way through to the smoking room I heard a Red Army soldier complain:

"Damn them and their humour! We come to the Caucasus and all we get is this nonsense!…"

He was absolutely right, that soldier from Tula. I shut myself away in my favourite spot, a dark corner behind the props room, and heard the sound of cheering and laughter coming from hall. The actors were terrific. Chekhov's *Surgery* had come to the rescue, together with the story about a clerk's sneeze.*

Success! A hit! Slyozkin came running into my rat-infested corner, rubbing his hands.

"Write another programme," he hissed at me.

And so after the "Evening of Chekhov's Humour" we decided to put on a "Pushkin Evening".

Yury and I lovingly put together a programme.

"That idiot can't draw," Slyozkin raged. "We'll give it to Marya Ivanovna."

I immediately had a nasty premonition – in my opinion Marya Ivanovna couldn't draw any more than I could play the violin… I had come to this conclusion as soon as she had appeared in the sub-department and announced that she had been a pupil of no less than N. (She had been appointed head of Izo on the spot.) But since I knew nothing about art I held my tongue.

Exactly half an hour before the start I went into the props room and froze to the spot… Looking out at me from a gold frame was Nozdryov.* He was astonishingly good. Insolent, protruding eyes, and even one sideboard more straggly than the other. The illusion was so strong that it seemed that at any moment he would roar with laughter and say:

"I've just come from the fair, my friend. You can congratulate me: I've gambled everything away!"

I don't know how I must have looked, but the artist was mortally offended. She blushed to her roots under her face powder and screwed up her eyes.

"You... er... evidently don't like it."

"No, really," I laughed. "It's very... nice. Very nice... It's just... the sideboards."

"What about the sideboards? So that means you've never seen Pushkin. Congratulations! And you call yourself a literary expert! Ha! So you think Pushkin should be depicted clean-shaven?"

"I'm sorry, the sideboards are fine. But Pushkin certainly never gambled at cards and, if he did, he wouldn't have cheated."

"What cards? I don't understand! I can see you're mocking me!"

"But, if you'll permit me, it's you who are mocking me. You've portrayed Pushkin with the eyes of a bandit."

"Aha... so that's it!"

She threw down her paintbrush. As she left the room she said in the doorway:

"I shall complain to the sub-department about you!"

What happened next? What happened was this: as soon as the curtains opened and the insolently grinning face of Nozdryov appeared in the darkened hall, the first burst of suppressed laughter could be heard. My God! The public had decided that, after the evening of Chekhov's humour, this was now to be one of Pushkin's humour! Bathed in cold sweat, I began to talk about the "radiance from the north shining down on the snow-covered wastes of Russian literature" while people in the room started giggling at the sideboards. Behind me loomed the figure of Nozdryov. He seemed to be muttering to me:

"If I were your boss, I would string you up on the nearest tree!"

At that I myself began to giggle, unable to hold out any longer. It was an astonishing, phenomenal success. I have never, either before or since, heard such a roar of applause. And it got even better. During the scene in which Salieri poisons Mozart,* the audience expressed its pleasure by their roars of approving laughter and their thunderous shouts of "Encore!!"

As I scuttled out of the theatre by the back entrance I dimly caught sight of the scandal-monger poet racing, notebook in hand, to the newspaper office...

I knew it! A copy of the newspaper on the kiosk, and, in the fourth column, the following:

## PUSHKIN AGAIN!

Literary specialists from the capital who have taken refuge in our local sub-department of the arts, have engaged in an objectively new attempt to corrupt the public in their presentation of their idol Pushkin. Not only did they take it upon themselves to depict this idol looking like a serf-owning landowner (which, we may suppose, he was) with sideboards...

And so on.

Good God! Please arrange that scandal-monger's death! After all, people are falling ill with typhus everywhere around here, aren't they? Why can't he get ill with it too? The cretin will get me arrested for sure.

Oh, damn that powdered doll Izo!

That's it. It's finished!... The literary evenings have been banned.

...Autumn's here and it's foul. Faces lashed by horizontal rain? And I've no idea what we're going to eat. What are we going to eat?

# X

## A PUTTEE AND A BLACK MOUSE

I'M WALKING THROUGH the puddles in the dark one evening. It's late and I'm hungry. Everything's boarded up. My socks are full of holes and my boots are in a terrible state. There is no sky. Instead there is just one huge puttee. Drunk with despair I start muttering to myself:

"Alexander Pushkin. *Lumen cœli. Sancta rosa!** And his threat is like thunder."*

Am I going out of my mind?! A shadow flees from the lamplight. I know: it's my shadow. But it's wearing a top hat, whereas I'm in a cap. As I was starving, I took my top hat to sell at the market. Some kind people bought it and made a chamber pot out of it. But I won't take my heart and my brain to be sold at the market, even if it's the last thing I do. Despair. A huge puttee above my head, and a black mouse in my heart.

# XI

## NO WORSE THAN KNUT HAMSUN*

I'm starving…

# XII

## RUN, RUN!

"A HUNDRED THOUSAND… I've got a hundred thousand roubles!" I've earned it!

It was a local assistant barrister who inspired me. He came up to me when I was sitting silently somewhere with my head in my hands and said:

"I haven't got any money either. There's just one way out: we must write a play. About the life of the local people. A revolutionary play. We'll sell it…"

I looked at him vacantly and replied:

"I can't write anything about the life of the local people, either revolutionary or counter-revolutionary. I don't know anything about their way of life. And, in general, I can't write anything. I'm tired, and I have no talent for literature."

"You're talking nonsense," he answered. "It's because you're starving. Be a man. Their way of life – that's easy! I know all about it, through and through. We'll write it together. We'll go half and half."

We started to write that very same evening. The barrister had a warm circular stove. His wife would hang out the washing on a line in the room and then serve us beetroot salad with butter and tea with saccharin. The barrister gave me typical local names, explained the local customs, and I wrote the plot. He wrote as well, and his wife would draw her chair up to us and give us advice. I very soon became convinced that they were both far better at literature than I was. But I didn't feel envious, because I had firmly convinced myself that this would be the last play I would write...

So we wrote.

He would lie blissfully by the stove and say:

"I love writing!"

And I scratched away with my pen...

A week later the three-act play was ready. When I read it to myself at night in my own unheated room, I am not ashamed to confess that I wept! On the scale of awfulness, it was something really special, something really striking! There wasn't a single line of this collective enterprise that wasn't insolently mind-numbing. I couldn't believe my eyes! What an idiot: if I wrote like that what possible hope could there be for me?! Shame looked out at me from the damp green walls and the appalling black windows. I began to tear up the manuscript. But I stopped myself. Because suddenly, in a flash of uncharacteristically miraculous lucidity, I realized that people who say you must never destroy what has been written are right! You can tear it up, you can burn it... You can hide it from other people. But from yourself – *never*! It's been done! You can't get rid of it. I had written that astonishing piece. It had been done!…

In the local literary sub-department, the play created a sensation. It was immediately bought for two hundred thousand. And two weeks later it was put on.

Daggers, bandoliers and eyes gleamed in the fog formed by the breathing of a thousand people. After the scene in the third act when the heroic horsemen had burst in and seized the police officer and the policemen, the Chechens, Kabardians and Ingush yelled:

"Got him! The bastard! Serves him right!"

And they followed the young ladies of the sub-department by shouting for the author.

In the wings they shook our hands.

"Vonderful play!"

And they invited us to their mountain village.

…Run! Run! On a hundred thousand it's possible to get away from here. Westwards, to the sea. Then by sea to France and, by dry land, to Paris!

…With the rain lashing my face and huddled up in my coat, I ran home through the little lanes for the final time…

…All you prose writers and playwrights in Paris and Berlin, just try! Try, just for fun, to write something really bad! If you are as talented as Kuprin, Bunin or Gorky* you won't succeed. I have broken the record! For collective authorship. There were three of us writing it: I, the barrister and hunger. At the beginning of '21…

# XIII

… THE TOWN DISAPPEARED into the foothills. Damn you… Tsikhidziri, Makhindzhauri, Cape Green! The magnolias are in blossom, the white flowers the size of plates. Bananas. Palm trees! A palm growing out of the ground! Seen with my own eyes, I swear! And the constant sound of the sea beating against the granite cliffs. The books haven't lied. The sun sinks into the sea. The beauty of the sea. The height of the sky. A sheer cliff wall, with creeping plants. Chakva. Tsikhidziri. Cape Green.

Where am I going? Where? I'm in my last shirt. I've got crooked letters on my cuffs. And tortuous hieroglyphs inscribed on my heart. And I've only managed to decipher one of the secret signs. It means: woe is me! Who will decipher the others for me?

I lie on the flat stones smoothed by the salt water, as if dead. I've become totally weak from hunger. My head aches from early morning to late at night. And night is here now, by the sea. I can't see it, only hear its roar. Approaching and receding. And the swish of a delayed wave. And then suddenly, from behind the cape – three-layered lights. That's the *Polatsky* on its way to the Golden Horn...

...My tears are as salty as the sea.

I saw one of the poets whose name I don't know. He was walking around the Nuri market, trying to sell the hat he was wearing. People were laughing at him.

He gave a shamefaced smile and explained that it wasn't a joke – he was selling his hat because his money had been stolen. He was lying! He had long since been without any money, and he hadn't eaten for three days... He confessed this to me later, when we were sharing a pound of Abkhazian bread. He told me he was travelling from Penza to Yalta. I was on the point of laughing when I suddenly remembered: and what about me?...

My cup has overflowed. My "new boss" arrived at twelve o'clock.

He came in and announced:

"We're going to do things differently! We don't want any of this pornographic stuff any more – *Woe from Wit* or *The Government Inspector*.* Gogol, mogol. We'll write our own plays."

Then he got in his car and drove off.

His face will always be etched on my brain.

An hour later I sold my coat at the market. The steamer was leaving that evening. He didn't want to allow me to get on board. Do you understand? Didn't let me on!

Enough. Let the Golden Horn shine. I'll never be able to get there. There is a limit to the amount of strength I have. I have none left. I'm hungry, and I'm broken! There is no blood in my brain. I'm weak and afraid. But I am not going to stay here any longer. If that's the case… that means… that means…

# XIV

## HOME

Home. By sea. And then by train. If I don't have enough money, then I'll walk. But home. My life is ruined. Home!…
To Moscow! To Moscow!!
To Moscow!!!

. . . . . . . . . . . . . . . . . . . . . . . . . . . . . . . . . . . . . . . . . . . . . . . . . .

Farewell, Tsikhindri. Farewell, Makhindzhauri. Cape Green!

# Part Two

## I

### MOSCOW ABYSS

*Twelfth Anniversary*

A BOTTOMLESS PIT of darkness. Screeching. Rumbling. The wheels start moving again, but more and more quietly. And stop. The end. The final end to end all ends. No possibility of going any farther. This is Moscow. M-o-s-c-o-w.

For a second my attention is caught by a powerful sound, coming out of the dark. Hideous sounds reverberate around the brain:

*C'est la lutte finale!... L'internationa-a-ale!*\*

And nearby, just as hoarsely and terrifyingly: "The Internationale!"

A row of carriages in the darkness. The students' carriage has gone quiet.

My mind finally made up, I jump down onto the platform. Someone's soft body slips out from under mine with a groan. Then, grabbing at the rail, I fall down even farther into the depths. My God, could it really be an abyss beneath me?

Grey figures carrying monstrous burdens on their shoulders start moving... moving...

A woman's voice:

"Oh, I can't go on!"

In the dark I can make the figure of the young medical student who has been travelling with me for three days and nights, writhing in pain.

"Please, let me take that."

27

For a moment the black abyss sways and turns green.

"How much have you got?"

"About fifty kilos... compressed flour."

Amid sparks, we lurched along in zigzags towards the lights.

Rays of lights were radiating in all directions. The strange grey snake was creeping unseen towards them. A glass dome. A long, long rumbling sound. A dazzling light. Ticket gate. Voices explode. Heavy cursing. Darkness once again. Light. Darkness. Moscow! Moscow.

The luggage cart was piled up as high as church domes, as high as the velvety stars. It crashed and rumbled along, and demonic voices in grey overalls cursed the stationary cart and the person clucking at the horse. A crowd of people followed behind the cart. And the long white coat of the medical student appeared now on my right, now on my left. But finally the wheels managed to extricate themselves from the confusion, and the bearded faces stopped flickering before our eyes. We went along the pitted roadway. Darkness everywhere. Where are we? What place is this? Doesn't matter: it's all the same. The whole of Moscow is black, black, black. The houses are silent. Looking out at us drily and coldly. Oh, ho ho. A church floats by. It looks indistinct and abandoned. It disappears into the darkness.

Two o'clock in the morning. Where are we going to find somewhere to sleep? One of the houses, that's where, one of the houses! What could be simpler?... We can knock on the door of any one of them. Let us in for the night. I can just imagine!

The medical student's voice:

"Where are you going?"

"I don't know."

"What do you mean, you don't know?"

There are kind people on this earth. Yes, the apartment manager's room right here. He's not yet back from the country. You can use his room for one night.

"Oh, thank you very much. Tomorrow I'll find some friends to stay with."

My spirits lifted a little. And the amazing thing is that the minute it became clear I had a roof over my head that night I suddenly realized I hadn't slept for three nights.

On the bridge there are two lamps breaking through the gloom. Then, from the bridge, we plunge once again into the dark. Then a street lamp. A grey fence, with a poster on it. Huge brightly-coloured letters. Ye Gods! What's that word? Tavlam. What on earth does that mean? What can it mean?

The Twelfth Anniversary of Vladimir Mayakovsky.*

The cart stopped, and they unloaded the things. I sat on a little concrete post and stared as if bewitched at the word. Oh, it was a very good word. And I, as some pathetic provincial, had snickered in the mountains at the ArtsDepHead. Oh, to hell with it! Moscow is not as terrible as it is painted. I was overcome by a burning desire to see the man himself. I have never seen him, but I know... I know. About forty, very short, bald, with glasses, very lively. Short, turned-up trousers. Employed. Non-smoker. He has a large apartment with heavily curtained doors which he shares with a lawyer, who is not a lawyer any more but the manager of some government building. He lives in his study with a non-working fireplace. Loves butter, humorous verse and a tidy room. His favourite author is Conan Doyle, and his favourite opera *Eugene Onegin*.* Cooks his own chops for himself on a primus stove. He cannot stand the lawyer, and dreams one day of being able to throw him out, getting married and setting himself up really nicely in all five rooms.

The cart creaked and shuddered, went on a little way farther, and then stopped again. Neither storm nor tempest has ever discomfited that immortal citizen Ivan Ivanych Ivanov. At one house which, in the darkness, seemed to the fearful to be fifteen or so storeys high, the cart visibly thinned out. In the pitch-black darkness a little figure darted out from the cart towards the entrance and whispered: "Dad, what about the butter?... and the lard?... and the white flour?..."

The father stood there in the gloom and muttered: "Lard, yeah; butter, yeah; white, black... yeah."

Then there was a flash of light from the infernal darkness illuminating the father's stubby little finger as he licked it and counted out twenty notes for the drayman.

There will be more storms to come. Oh yes, and they will be big storms! Everybody could die. But this dad won't die!

The cart turned into an enormous platform, on which the medical student's bag and my travel bag got lost. And we sat there, our legs dangling over the side, as we moved off into the dark depths.

## II

### HOUSE NO. 4, ENTRANCE NO. 6, 2ND FLOOR APARTMENT NO. 50, ROOM 7

I HONESTLY DON'T KNOW why I should have crossed the whole of Moscow and made my way precisely to this colossal building. The piece of paper which I had carefully brought with me from the mountain kingdom could have related to any six-storey building, or more exactly, had no relation at all to any of them.

I'm standing at the entrance to No. 6 by the gated shaft of an out-of-service lift, recovering my breath. A door. Two signs: "Apartment 50" and, more mysteriously "Art". Have to get my breath back. One way or another, my fate is about to be decided.

I pushed at the unlocked door. In the semi-dark of the hallway I could make out a huge box with papers on it and the lid of a grand piano. There was a glimpse of a smoke-filled room, full of women. A typewriter clattered briefly, then fell silent. Then a bass voice said: "Meyerhold."*

"Where can I find Lito?" I asked, resting my elbows on the wooden counter.

The woman standing by the counter gave an irritable shrug. She didn't know. Another woman didn't know either. Then I walked along a rather dark passageway, trying various doors at random. I opened one door and came across a bathroom. On another door there was a little scrap of paper. Tacked on any old how, with one edge bent back. Lit… Oh, thank God. Yes. Lito. My heart started beating again. There was a hum of voices coming from behind the door.

I closed my eyes for a second, and pictured the scene. There, in the first room, is an enormous carpet, a desk and shelves with books. Everything is solemnly quiet. A secretary is sitting at the desk – most likely one of those with a name I already knew from the literary journals. More doors. The director's office. Even more profound silence. More shelves. And, in the armchair, Maxim Gorky of course! *The Lower Depths. Mother.** Who else? The sound of more voices conversing… What if it were Bryusov and Bely?*

I knocked lightly on the door. The hum of voices stopped, and I heard a muffled voice say "Yes?" Then the voices started up again. When I tugged at the handle it came off in my hands. I froze to the spot. That was a good start to my career – I had broken it! I knocked again. "Yes! All right!"

"I can't get in!" I shouted.

A voice came through the keyhole:

"Turn the handle to the right, and then to the left. You've locked us in…"

Right, left and the door opened meekly…

## III

### I'M NUMBER ONE AFTER GORKY

I HAD COME TO THE WRONG PLACE! Lito? A simple cane chair. An empty wooden table. An open cupboard. A small upside-down table in the corner. And two people. One of them was a very young, tall man in pince-nez, with strikingly white puttees.

He was holding a battered briefcase and a bag. The other was a grey-haired old man with lively eyes that had a hint of a smile. He was wearing a Caucasian fur hat and a tattered army coat with pockets hanging down in shreds. Grey puttees and patent-leather dance shoes with bows.

With a glazed expression I looked around at the faces, and then at the walls, looking to see if there were any other doors. But there weren't any. The room with its tattered wiring led nowhere. *Tout.*\*

"Is this... Lito?"

"Yes."

"Is it possible to see the person in charge?"

"That's me," the old man answered gently.

Then he took a huge page from the Moscow newspaper on the table, tore off a quarter-sheet, sprinkled in some tobacco, made a roll-up and asked:

"Do you have a light?"

I mechanically struck a match, and then, under the gently questioning eye of the old man, I took my precious document out of my pocket.

The old man bent over the document, while I tortured myself wondering who it might possibly be... More than anybody, he looked like a clean-shaven Émile Zola.\*

Looking over the shoulder of his older colleague, the young man also read the document. When they had finished reading it, they looked at me in a rather confused way, but with respect.

"And so, what?..." began the old man.

"I would like a job in Lito."

"Wonderful! You know..."

The young man grabbed him by the arm. They started whispering...

The old man turned on his heels and grabbed a pen from the table. The young man said hastily:

"Write out an application."

I already had an application tucked away in my clothes. I handed it to them.

The old man brandished his pen. It made a cracking sound and jumped, tearing the paper. He dipped it in the inkwell, but it was dry.

"Isn't there a pencil anywhere?"

I took out a pencil and the director wrote in a slanting hand:

"Request the bearer be appointed as secretary of Lito." Signature.

I stood there for several seconds gaping open-mouthed at the flowery signature.

The young man tugged at my sleeve.

"Go upstairs. As quickly as you can, while he's still here. Quickly!"

And I flew upstairs like an arrow. Burst through a doorway, raced through a room full of women and went into the office. Someone sitting in the office took my document and scrawled "Apptd. Sec." A single letter. A flourish. He yawned and said, "Downstairs."

In a mental fog I raced back downstairs. A glimpse of a typewriter. Not a bass voice but a silvery soprano said: "Meyerhold. October Theatre…"

The young man was shouting with laughter as he moved around the old man.

"He's agreed to the appointment? Wonderful. We'll set it up. We'll set it all up!"

At that he slapped me on the shoulder.

"Chin up! It'll all be fine!"

From childhood I have never been able to stand over-familiarity, and from childhood I have always been at the receiving end of it. But now I found everything going on so overwhelming that I could only say weakly:

"But the tables… the chairs… and what about the ink?!" The young man shouted exultantly:

"They'll be here! Splendid! Everything will be here!"

And, turning towards the old man, he winked in my direction.

"What a businesslike fellow! That comment about the tables. He'll sort everything out for us!"

"Apptd. Sec." Good God! The Literary section. In Moscow. Maxim Gorky… *The Lower Depths… Scheherazade… Mother.*

The young man shook his bag, spread out a newspaper on the table and poured about five pounds of peas onto it.

"This is for you. Quarter rations."

## IV

### I GET LITO ON THE MOVE

T HE LITERARY HISTORIAN should not forget the following:
At the end of '21 there were three people in charge of literary matters in the Republic: the old man (drama; he wasn't Émile Zola of course, but someone I had never heard of); the young man (the old man's assistant, also someone I didn't know, poetry); and me (I hadn't written anything).

And the literary historian should also know: Lito had no chairs, or tables, or ink, or lamps, or books, or writers, or readers. In short: it didn't have anything.

And what about me? Well, from nowhere, I managed to get hold of an ancient mahogany desk, in which I came across an old yellowing cardboard box on which was written the following: "Ladies in low-cut ball gowns. Soldiers in frock coats with epaulettes. Civilians in full-dress uniform coats and ribbons. Students in full-dress uniform. Moscow 1899."

And there was a delicate, sweet smell. The drawer had once contained a bottle of expensive French perfume. Then a chair appeared. And, finally, a rather slow and sad young lady.

At my behest, she laid out piles of everything that was in the cupboard on the desk: leaflets on "saboteurs", twelve copies of a St Petersburg newspaper, a packet of green-and-red tickets inviting people to a congress of governors' departments. And immediately it began to look like an office. The old man and the young man were delighted. They clapped me affectionately on the shoulder and disappeared.

For hours on end I would sit there with the sad young lady. I sat at the desk, with her at the table. I read *The Three Musketeers* by the incomparable Dumas,* which I had found on the bathroom floor, while the young lady sat in silence, every so often sighing deeply and heavily.

"Why are you crying?" I asked.

She responded by starting to sob and wring her hands. Then she said:

"I've realized that I've married a thug."

I don't know if, after these two years, there is anything that could surprise me. But now... I looked at the girl in stupefaction...

"Don't cry. These things happen."

And I asked her to tell me about it.

Wiping away her tears with a handkerchief, she told me she had married a student, then had made an enlarged picture from his student card and hung it up in the sitting room. But when someone who worked for the secret service saw the photograph, he said that it wasn't Karasev at all, but Dolsky, otherwise known as Gluzman, otherwise as Senka Moment.

"Mo-ment," said the poor girl with a shudder and wiped away her tears.

"And he pushed off, I suppose? Well, good riddance."

However, three days have gone by, and nothing. Nobody has come. Nothing at all. The young lady and I...

Then it suddenly struck me: Lito had still not been brought to life. Overhead there was some sort of life going on. The trample of feet. There was also something happening on the other side of the wall. Now the muffled clatter of a typewriter, now the sound of laughter. There would be people there with smooth-shaven faces. Meyerhold was phenomenally popular in this building, but of the man himself there was no sign.

But we had nothing. No paper. Nothing. I decided to get Lito on the move.

A woman was climbing the stairs with a bundle of newspapers. On the top newspaper someone had written "Izo", in red.

"And what about 'Lito'?"

She gave me a scared look and said nothing. I went upstairs. I went up to the girl sitting under a sign which said "Secretary". When she heard what I had to say, she looked startled and glanced at her neighbour.

"Ah, yes… Lito…" the first girl said.

The other one responded:

"There is paper for them, Lidochka."

"Why didn't you send it down to them?"

They looked at me tensely.

"We didn't think you were there."

Lito is now operating. A second lot of paper arrived today from the girls above. It was brought by a woman in a dress. Together with a book: "Sign here."

I wrote an official request to the procurements department: "Request a typewriter."

"Surely you don't need a typewriter, do you?"

"I think there's nobody in this building who needs one more than I do."

The old man turned up. As did the young man. When the old man saw the typewriter, I said he needed to sign the papers. He stared at me for some time, chewing his lips.

"There's something about you. How about focusing on getting us academician rations?"

The terrorist's wife and I began to put together a payroll form. Lito had now become part of the general swing of things.

Note to my future biographer: I had been responsible for this.

# V

## THE FIRST SWALLOWS

AT II A.M. A YOUNG POET came into the office, clearly frozen to the bone. He quietly introduced himself as "Shtorn".*

"How can I help you?"

"I would like to get a job with Lito."

I opened the document headed "Staff". The document specified a total of eighteen people for Lito. I had been vaguely nurturing the following names:

Poetry teachers:

Bryusov, Bely, etc....

Prose teachers:

Gorky, Veresayev, Shmelyov, Zaytsev,* Serafimovich, etc...

But none of these people ever appeared.

And with a bold flourish I wrote on Shtorn's application: "Please appt. as instructor. Pp Director." Letter. Signature with a flourish.

"Go upstairs, catch him while he's still here."

Then a curly-haired, red-faced and very cheerful poet called Skartsev came in to the office.

"Go upstairs, catch him while he's still here."

And then an unusually morose-looking person arrived from Siberia. He was about twenty-five years old, with such a smooth, compact face that it looked as if it had been fashioned from brass.

"Go upstairs..."

But he replied:

"I'm not going anywhere."

He sat down in a corner of the room on a broken, wobbly chair, took out a quarter-sized piece of paper and began to write something in brief sentences. Clearly an experienced man.

The door opened and someone came in wearing a good-quality warm coat and a sealskin cap. He turned out to be a poet. Sasha.

The old man wrote the magic words. Sasha took a careful look around the room, pensively touched the worn dangling wire and glanced into the cupboard. Then he sighed.

He sat down next to me and asked confidentially:

"Will there be any money?"

# VI

## WE BUILD UP STEAM

T HERE WAS NO ROOM at the tables. Everyone was writing slogans, together with another newcomer, a lively, noisy person in gold-rimmed glasses, who called himself "the king of reporters". The king had arrived at a quarter to nine, on the day after we had received an advance, with the words:

"Listen, I hear you've been given some money."

And he started to work for us.

The reason for the slogans was as follows: a document had come down to us from above.

The document proposed that Lito should produce, as a matter of urgency, a series of slogans by midday on such and such a date.

In theory, the matter should have proceeded as follows: with my assistance, the old man should have issued an order or summons at every venue where it was assumed there might be writers. The slogans could be submitted in every form: written, spoken and by telegraph. Then a commission should have been set up to choose the best out of thousands of slogans and present them by midday on the relevant date. Then I, together with the office of which I was in charge (that is, the sad-looking terrorist's wife), were to make an official application for money to pay the person who had devised the slogans.

But that was the theory.

In practice what happened was this:

1) No summons was possible, as there was nobody to send it to. As far as could be seen, the only literary figures around at that time were those already mentioned, plus the king.

2) Since point no. 1 was impossible there could have been no slogans flooding in.

3) It would have been impossible to have the slogans ready by the midday of the day in question for the very good reason that the paper only arrived at 1.26 on that very same day.

4) It was not possible to put in any application for money since there was no heading for "slogans". But the old man did have a small sum of money allocated especially for "travel".

Therefore the following points arose:

a) The slogans were to be written as a matter of urgency by everybody present.

b) The monitoring group responsible for assuring complete impartiality in assessing the slogans would also have to be formed from those present.

c) The sum of fifteen thousand roubles would be paid for each of the slogans considered to be the best.

We sat down at ten to two, and the slogans were ready by three o'clock. Each of us managed to produce between five and six slogans, with the exception of the king, who wrote a total of nineteen, in both prose and verse.

The monitoring group were both fair and exacting.

I, the slogan writer, had no connection with the I, the person responsible for receiving and evaluating the quality of the slogans.

The result was that the following slogans were accepted:

Three of the old man's, together with three of the young man's and three of mine, etc., etc. That meant that each of us received forty-five thousand.

Ooh, what a wind! Here it comes, it's beginning to drizzle. A meat pie on Trubnaya Square, wet from the rain, but fantastically tasty. A tube of saccharin. Two pounds of white bread.

Caught up with Shtorn. He was also chewing on something.

# VII

## AN UNEXPECTED NIGHTMARE

I SWEAR, I'M DREAMING!!! What sorcery is this?
... Today I was two hours late arriving for work.

I turned the handle, opened the door, went in and saw that the room was empty. But not just empty! Not only were there no tables, no sad young lady, no typewriter... even the electric wires had gone. Nothing.

In other words, it had to be a dream. Understandable. Of course.

I have thought for a long time that everything around me is a mirage. A shimmering mirage. In the place where only yesterday... to hell with it, why yesterday? A hundred years ago, an infinity ago... maybe none of it had ever been there at all!... A proper Kanatchikov's dacha.*

So does that mean that the old man, the young man, the sad-looking Shtorn, the typewriter, the slogans – never existed?

But they did exist. I have not gone out of my mind. They did exist, damn it!

So where on earth had they all got to?

I walked gingerly along the semi-darkened corridor, trying to keep my eyes firmly cast down to prevent anyone immediately grabbing me and carting me off. And I now became finally convinced that something was really wrong. In the darkness, above the door leading into the lit neighbouring room, glowed the following sentence, just as in a film:

1836

ON THE TWENTY-FIFTH OF MARCH IN ST PETERSBURG AN UNUSUALLY STRANGE EVENT TOOK PLACE. THE BARBER IVAN YAKOVLEVICH...*

I didn't read any further, but slipped away in horror. I stopped when I came to the counter and, looking down at the floor with even greater determination, asked dully:

"Can you tell me please, do you know what's happened to Lito?"

An irritable, morose-looking woman with a crimson ribbon in her dark hair answered:

"What Lito?... I don't know."

I closed my eyes. Another female voice said gently:

"I'm sorry, it's not here at all. You've come to the wrong place. It's on the Volkhonka."

A cold chill immediately ran down my spine. I went out onto the landing and wiped the sweat from my brow. I decided to go back across the whole of Moscow to Razumikhin,* and to forget everything. After all, if I were to keep quiet and to say nothing, nobody would ever know anything. I would be able to camp down on Razumikhin's floor. He wouldn't get rid of me, as if I were someone who was mentally ill.

But I still maintained a faint glimmer of hope. And so I started walking and walking. That six-storey building was positively weird. It was criss-crossed by long passageways, like an ant hill, so that it was possible to traverse the entire building, from end to end, without ever going out onto the street. I walked along dark, convoluted corridors, finding myself on occasions in some niche or other, lit by red, non-economical lights and tucked behind wooden partitions. I came across anxious-looking people scurrying about. Scores of women were clattering away at typewriters. Signs flashed past. Finance. National minorities. I went through brightly lit areas, and then back again into the dark. Finally I came to an area where I looked around in stupefaction. Here there was some other domain altogether... It was stupid. The farther I went the fewer chances I seemed to have of ever finding the bewitched Lito. Hopeless. I went downstairs and out onto the street. I looked around and saw that I was by entrance no. 1.

...A vile gust of wind. Cold streams of rain once again started to gush out of the sky. I pulled my light summer cap more firmly down onto my head, and raised the collar of my coat. A few moments later and the soles of my boots had been filled with water coming through the enormous cracks in the soles. That came as a relief. I did not console myself with the thought that I could somehow get back home in a dry state. Instead of leaping from cobblestone to cobblestone, thereby prolonging my journey home, I walked straight through the puddles.

# VIII

## ENTRANCE NO. 2, GROUND FLOOR, APARTMENT 23, ROOM 40

A brightly lit sign.

> SUCH COMPLETE NONSENSE TAKES PLACE ON THIS
> EARTH. SOMETIMES THERE IS NOTHING AT ALL THAT
> SEEMS PLAUSIBLE: SUDDENLY THAT VERY SAME NOSE
> WHICH HAD BEEN TRAVELLING AROUND IN THE FORM
> OF A STATE COUNCILLOR AND WHICH HAD CAUSED SUCH
> A COMMOTION IN THE CITY, FOUND ITSELF BACK IN ITS
> PLACE, AS IF NOTHING HAD HAPPENED.*

Mornings are more sensible than evenings. That is the honest truth. When, on the following morning, I was woken up by the cold and sat down on my divan ruffling my hair, everything seemed to have become a little clearer in my mind!

Logically, had all that really happened? Yes, of course it had. After all, I could remember the date, as well as my name. It hadn't vanished into thin air. That meant I needed to find it. But what about those women in the neighbouring room? On the Volkhonka... Rubbish! Anybody could steal anything they wanted to from under their noses. I really don't know why they kept these women on. Like an Egyptian plague!

After getting dressed and having a drink of water which I had kept in a glass from the previous evening, I ate a piece of bread and one little potato, and planned my day.

Six entrances times six floors, that's a total of thirty-six. Thirty-six times two apartments equals seventy-two. Seventy-two times six equals a total of four hundred and thirty-two rooms. Was it sensible to think that I could find Lito? Yes, it was sensible. The day before I had searched horizontally, going along two complete passageways without any system. Today I would systematically search the entire building in a vertical as well as a horizontal direction. And I would find what I was looking for. Unless of course it had vanished into the fourth dimension. If it had, then that would be the end of course.

At entrance no. 2 I came face to face with... Shtorn!

Good God! Like meeting my own brother!

This is what had happened: an hour before my arrival in the office yesterday, the head of administration had come with two workmen and transferred Lito to entrance no. 2, ground floor, apartment 23, room 40.

Our place had been taken by the Music Department.

"Why?"

"I don't know. But why didn't you come yesterday? The old man was really concerned."

"For Heaven's sake! How was I to know where you had gone? You should have left a note on the door."

"Well, we thought they'd let you know."

I gritted my teeth.

"Have you seen those women? In the next room?..."

Shtorn said:

"Say no more."


# IX

## FULL STEAM AHEAD

HAVING GOT MY OWN ROOM, I felt the life blood surging back into me. They installed a light in Lito. I obtained a ribbon for the typewriter. Then a second young lady appeared. "Please appt. chief clerk."

Manuscripts began to come in from the provinces. Then another first-class young lady. A female journalist. Efficient with a good sense of humour. "Please appt. secretary to the artistic feuilletons department."

Finally, a young man from the south. A journalist. We put in an application for him to be appointed as well. But that was the last: there were no more places available. Lito was full. And work burst into life.

# X

## MONEY! MONEY!

T WELVE SACCHARIN TABLETS, and that's all.
Sheet or jacket?

Neither sight nor sound of any salary.

I went upstairs today. The young ladies met me coldly. For some reason they couldn't stand Lito.

"May I have a look at the requisition list?"

"What for?"

"I want to see if everyone has been included."

"Ask Madame Kritskaya."

Madame Kritskaya stood up, her grey bun swaying.

"It's lost," she said, growing pale.

Pause.

"And you've not said anything?"

Madame Kritskaya tearfully:

"My head's all in a whirl. What's going on here is totally incomprehensible. I've written the list seven times, and each time it's been returned. It's not right. But, in any case, you won't be getting your money. You took on someone unofficially."

To hell with them all! Nekrasov and the reformed alcoholics.*
I dashed off. Corridors again. Gloom. Light. Light. Gloom. Meyerhold. Personnel. Lamps burning in broad daylight. A grey coat. A woman in damp felt boots. Tables.

"Who's been taken on unofficially?"

Reply:

"Nobody at all."

But best of all: Lito's founder member is not on the list.

Lito *is* the old man! What? What if I myself haven't been included?! What on earth is going on?

"You probably never filled in a form."

"Not filled in a form? I've filled in four forms. I've given them to you personally. If you include those I've already written, that makes 113 in all."

"They must have got lost. Write another."

Three days went by in that way. After three days everybody's rights had been restored. New requisition lists were written.

I am against capital punishment. But if Madame Kritskaya should ever be taken off to be shot I will go and watch. Also the young lady in the sealskin cap. And Lidochka, the assistant to the chief clerk.

"Off with you! On your broomstick!"

Madame Kritskaya was left with the lists in her hands, and I can solemnly announce that she won't do anything with them. I cannot understand how that devilish bun ever managed to find herself here. Who could ever have entrusted her with any position? Fate is definitely at work here.

A week has gone by. Have been to the fourth floor, entrance no. 4. They stamped my document, but I need another one. This is the second day I've tried unsuccessfully to get hold of the head of the taxation assessment board.

Have sold one sheet.

The money won't be coming for at least two weeks.

There's been a rumour that everybody in the building will be getting 500 as an advance.

The rumour is true. Everybody's been sitting down "outside", filling out their claims sheets. For four days.

I went off with the claims for an advance. I got everything. All stamps present and correct. But, while running from the first floor to the fourth, I managed, in my rage, to bend some metal bolt that was sticking out from the wall in the corridor.

I've handed the claims in. They'll be sent off to some other building on the other side of Moscow. There they'll be checked and then returned. Then money...

The money came today. Money!

Ten minutes before I was planning to go to the cash desk, the woman on the ground floor who had to put the final stamp on the document said:

"The form's incorrect. Your claim will have to wait."

I cannot remember precisely what happened. Fog.

Apparently I yelled something extremely unpleasant along the following lines:

"Are you making fun of me?"

The woman opened her mouth.

"Oh, you're such a..."

At that I calmed down. Calmed down. I said I was over-excited. I apologized, and took back what I had said. She agreed to put in the corrections in red ink. Scrawled "Approved", and signed with a flourish.

To the cash desk. What magic words: cash desk. I couldn't believe it even when the cashier produced the notes.

Then I suddenly realized what it meant: money!

The total time taken, from the moment I had begun to write out the claims to the moment I received the money, was twenty-two days and three hours.

# XI

## HOW ONE OUGHT TO EAT

I'M ILL. I've been careless. Today I ate beetroot soup with meat, with little golden globules of fat floating around in it. Three plates of it. Three pounds of white bread in a single day. Slightly salted gherkins. When I had eaten to the full I brewed myself some tea. Four glasses with sugar. I felt tired, so I lay down and went to sleep.

I dreamt that I was Leo Tolstoy at Yasnaya Polyana.* And that I was married to Sofya Andreyevna. I was sitting upstairs in my study. I had to write something, but what exactly, I didn't know. And the whole time people came in and said that dinner was ready.

But I was afraid to go downstairs. And it was all so idiotic. I felt there had been a major misunderstanding. I hadn't written *War and Peace*, had I? The whole time I was just sitting there. And then Sofya Andreyevna herself came up the wooden staircase and said:

"Come on. It's a vegetarian dinner."

And I suddenly grew angry.

"What?! Vegetarian? Send for some meat! Make some rissoles. And a glass of vodka."

She burst into tears, and some Dukhobor* with a thick ginger beard came running into the room and said reproachfully:

"Vodka? Ay, yay, yay! What are you thinking of Lev Ivanovich?"

"What do you mean 'Lev Ivanovich'! I'm Lev Nikolayevich! Get out of my house! Out! I don't want another Dukhobor in this house."

It turned into an enormous scandal.

When I woke up I was ill and in a shattered state. It was dusk. Someone somewhere on the other side of the wall was playing a guitar.

I went up to the mirror. What did I look like! Gingery beard, white cheekbones, red eyelids. But that was nothing, compared to my eyes. Not good. Again with that gleam in them.

When your eyes gleam like that, my advice is to take care. As soon as that happens, then you must borrow some money from a bourgeois immediately, without paying it back, buy some food and eat. But don't stuff yourself all at once. Just some bouillon and white bread on day one. Gradually, step by step.

I did not like my dream either. A nasty dream.

Once again I had some tea. My mind went back to the week before. On the Monday I had eaten some potato with butter and a quarter of a pound of bread. I had drunk two glasses of tea with saccharin. On Tuesday I had had nothing to eat, but I had drunk five glasses of tea. On Wednesday I had borrowed two pounds of bread from the locksmith. I had drunk some tea, but the saccharin had run out. On Thursday I had eaten a first-class dinner. At two o'clock I had gone to some friends. A maid in a white apron had opened the door.

It's a strange feeling. It's as if all this had happened ten years ago. At three o'clock I can hear the maid beginning to lay the table in the dining room. We sit there and talk (I had shaved that morning). They curse the Bolsheviks and tell stories about how worn out they are. I can see that people are waiting for me to go. But I stay where I am.

Finally the hostess says:

"Perhaps you'll have some dinner with us? Or perhaps not?"

"Thank you. With pleasure."

So we ate. Macaroni soup with white bread, followed by meat rissoles with gherkins, then rice kasha with jam, and finally tea with jam.

I have a vile confession to make. As I was leaving, I imagined them being searched. People coming and turning the place upside down. Finding gold coins in underwear in the chest of drawers... flour and ham in the pantry... the host being led away...

It was disgusting to think such thoughts, but I had them all the same.

My advice to anyone who sits starving in his attic trying to write some feuilleton or other is not to follow the example of that sissy Knut Hamsun. Go and have dinner with those people who own seven rooms. On Friday I went out to a café and ate soup with a potato rissole, and today, Saturday, I got my salary, ate too much and fell ill.

# XII

## A THUNDERSTORM. SNOW.

THERE'S SOMETHING OMINOUS hanging in the air. I'm beginning to sense something. The cracks are beginning to appear under our Lito.

The old man came in today. Jabbing his finger up at the ceiling, above which the young ladies were concealed, he said:

"There's a plot against me."

No sooner had I heard this than I began to count up how many saccharin tablets I had left… Enough for five to six days.

The old man crashed in and announced cheerily:

"I've scuppered their plot."

As soon as he said this an old woman's head wrapped in a shawl appeared round the door.

"All of you here, sign this."

I signed.

The document said:

"Lito will be disbanded on such and such a date."

…Like a captain from his ship I was the last to leave. The order was that all our business – Nekrasov, the Reformed Alcoholic, the Famine collections,* the poems, the instructions to local branches of Lito – was to be filed away. Turning off the light myself, I left the room. And at that very moment it started to snow. Then to rain. Then neither rain nor snow, just something plastering one's face from every direction.

At times of cutbacks and when there's weather like that, Moscow is not a nice place at all. Yes, sir, it was a cutback. Other people were also being kicked out of their rooms in that appalling building.

But Madame Kritskaya, Lidochka and the sealskin hat stayed put.

# The Fire of the Khans

WHEN THE SUN had begun to set behind the Oreshnyev pine trees and the Great God Apollo the Sad had sunk into the shadows in front of the palace, the cleaner Dunka came running out of the wing of the building belonging to the museum supervisor Tatyana Mikhailovna and shouted:

"Iona Vasilych! Iona Vasilych! Come quickly. Tatyana Mikhailovna's asking for you. About the excursions. She's ill. It's her cheek!"

And pink-faced Dunka raced back to the annexe, her skirt billowing up like a bell, showing her bare calves.

The decrepit old valet Iona tossed down his broom and staggered past the ruins of the burnt-down stables overgrown with weeds to Tatyana Mikhailovna's.

The shutters in the wing were closed and, even from the entrance porch, there was a strong smell of iodine and camphor oil. Stumbling in the semi-darkness, Iona made his way towards the sound of someone quietly moaning. In the dark he could dimly make out the cat Mumka and a white hare with enormous ears on the bed. And, in the bed, one suffering eye.

"Is it your teeth?" Iona mumbled sympathetically.

"Yes," sighed the pale-faced person.

"Ooh... what a to-do..." he sympathized. "A disaster. And that Caesar does nothing but howl... 'You idiot,' I say to him, 'what are you howling about in broad daylight? Eh? It's for your dead master. That's it, isn't it? Keep quiet, you idiot. You're howling at your own head.' You need to apply chicken droppings to your cheek – they'll take away the pain, and it will be gone in no time."

"Iona, Iona Vasilych," said Tatyana Mikhailovna feebly, "we're open to the public today – it's Wednesday. But I can't come. That's the problem. You must go round with the tourists and show them everything yourself. I'll give you Dunka; she can go round with you."

"Well, all right… Excellent idea. So be it. And we'll manage by ourselves. We'll keep an eye on them. The main point is the goblets… that's the main thing. You get all sorts coming here… It won't take long: someone will put one in his pocket, and it's gone for good. Who will be held responsible? We will. A painting's something else – you can't hide one of those in your pocket. Isn't that right?"

"Dunyasha will go with you; she'll watch from the back of the group. And in case they start asking about me, you can tell them that the museum supervisor is ill."

"All right. All right. But chicken droppings for you. Doctors would just whip the tooth out, ripping open the cheek. They did that to someone once, Fyodor from Oreshnyev, and he went and died on them. That was before your time. His dog also howled for him in the yard."

Tatyana Mikhailovna gave a brief groan and said:

"Go on, off you go, Iona Vasilich. Someone may have arrived already."

Iona opened the heavy metal gate, with its white sign that said:

PALACE MUSEUM
KHAN HEADQUARTERS

Open Wednesdays, Fridays and Sundays
6 to 8 p.m.

And, at 6.30, the tourists arrived on the local train from Moscow. First, a whole group of about twenty high-spirited young people.

Among them were youths in khaki shirts, and girls without hats, some wearing white sailors' blouses, some in brightly-coloured cardigans. Some were in sandals without socks, some in black down-at-heel shoes; the youths in blunt-toed high boots.

Amongst this group of young people there was an older man of about forty, who immediately caught Iona's attention. He was wearing nothing apart from a pair of pale coffee-coloured short trousers, not reaching his knees, fastened around the waist by a belt with a metal clip saying "Secondary Modern School no. 1", and a pair of pince-nez on his nose, stuck together with violet-coloured sealing wax. His hunched bare back was covered in an ancient brown-coloured rash, and his legs were different in shape – the right one was thicker than the left, and both shins were marked by knotted veins.

The young people were behaving as if there was nothing surprising in the fact that this older man was travelling in the train with them and was part of the excursion group. But old, mournful Iona found it both striking and surprising.

The naked man walked together with a group of girls from the gates to the palace, his head flung back. One moustache was jauntily cocked into the air, and his beard was trimmed as if belonging to an educated man. The young people around Iona twittered away like a flock of birds, and laughed the whole time, so that Iona became thoroughly confused and upset, his thoughts anxiously centred on the goblets. He winked meaningfully at Dunka, indicating the naked man. Her cheeks were ready to burst at the sight of the man, with his different-sized legs. And just at this moment, as ill luck would have it, Caesar appeared from nowhere. Allowing everyone else to walk by without hindrance, he started barking at the naked man in an especially hoarse, senile and malicious way, choking and coughing. Then he began to emit excruciating, heart-rending howls.

"Pff, blasted animal," Iona thought angrily and absent-mindedly, cocking an eye at the uninvited guest – "look what the devil's brought in. What's he howling at anyway? If anyone's about to die, let it be that naked chap."

As there was a group of five well-bred visitors following immediately behind the crowd of young people, he had to give Caesar's ribs a right walloping with his keys. The group included a red-faced lady with a large stomach, looking irritably at the naked man. She had a teenage girl with her, with long plaits. There was also a tall, clean-shaven man, accompanied by a beautiful, heavily made-up lady and an elderly, wealthy-looking male foreigner, wearing large gold-rimmed glasses and a broad, lightly coloured coat and carrying a cane. Caesar made a dash from the semi-clothed man towards these new visitors and, with a melancholic expression in his old, dimmed eyes, began barking first at the lady's green umbrella, and then howled at the foreigner with such force that he turned pale, rocked on his heels and muttered something in an unknown language.

Unable to take any more, Iona gave Caesar such a thrashing that he stopped howling and disappeared with a whine.

"Wipe your feet on the mat," said Iona, his face adopting a severe and solemn expression, as it always did whenever he went into the palace. "Keep your eyes open, Dun," he whispered to Dunka, and opened the glass door from the terrace with a heavy key. The white gods on the balustrade looked welcomingly down at the visitors.

The visitors started to climb the white staircase covered with a crimson carpet, held in place by gold rods. The naked man appeared at the very front of the group, next to Iona. As he walked up the stairs, he pressed proudly down on the softly carpeted steps with the soles of his bare feet.

The evening light, filtering through the white blinds, trickled through the large glass panes behind the pillars. On the top landing, the visitors turned to look back at the plummeting staircase up which they had just come, the balustrade with its white statues, the white piers between the windows, hung with the dark canvases of portraits, and the cut-glass chandelier, threatening with its slender wire to crash down into the abyss below. High above them, pink Cupids twined and twirled as they flew into the distance.

"Look, Verochka, look," whispered the lady with the large stomach. "You see how princes used to live in normal times."

Iona stood to one side, his clean-shaven face quietly gleaming with pride in the evening light.

The naked man adjusted his pince-nez on his nose, looked around him and said:

"Built by Rastrelli.* No doubt about it. Eighteenth century."

"What do you mean, Rastrelli?" Iona rejoined, quietly clearing his throat. "It was built by Prince Anton Ioannovich, may God rest his soul, one hundred and fifty years ago. And that's a fact," he sighed. "The great-great-great grandfather of the present Prince."

Everyone turned to look at Iona.

"You clearly don't understand," the naked man replied. "It was built in Anton Ioannovich's time, it is true, but surely the architect was Rastrelli, wasn't it? Secondly, there's no such thing as a God or a soul, and the present Prince is no longer with us, thank God. And, anyway, why isn't the museum supervisor here?"

"The supervisor," Iona began to say, breathing heavily from anger towards the man, "is in bed with toothache, suffering badly at the moment, but she'll be better by the morning. And as for God and the soul, you're right: they don't exist for some people. You'll never get to heaven in those disgraceful shorts. I'm right, aren't I?"

All the young people immediately burst out laughing. The naked man blinked and puffed out his lips.

"But I must say your feelings of sympathy for God and the soul and for princes seem rather odd in such times... And I think..."

"Leave it, Comrade Antonov," said a girl's voice from the crowd in a conciliatory tone.

"Semyon Ivanovich, just let it go!" boomed a halting bass voice.

They went on farther. The last rays of the sunset were falling across the network of ivy, linking the glass door with the terrace and the vases. Six white pillars with carved foliage supported the choirs, in which at one time the musicians' trumpets had gleamed. The columns rose chastely and joyfully into the air, and a decorous row of light gilt chairs stood along the walls. Dark clusters of lights looked down from the walls, and the scorched white candles seemed as if they had been extinguished only the day before. The Cupids twirled and twined in garlands of flowers, and a naked woman frolicked around in ridiculous-looking clouds. Underfoot a slippery parquet floor reproducing the black-and-white squares of a draughts board spread out in all directions. The presence of this new crowd of people on this draughts board seemed strange, and the foreigner in his gold-rimmed glasses, who had separated himself from the rest of the group, appeared ponderous and gloomy. He stood behind a pillar and looked as if bewitched through the ivy into the distance.

The naked man's voice could be heard over the indistinct murmur of the others. Dragging his foot across the gleaming parquet floor, he asked Iona:

"Who made this parquet floor?"

"The serfs on the estate," Iona replied hostilely. "Our peasants."

The naked man smirked disapprovingly.

"They made a very good job of it, I have to say. They must have broken their backs, labouring away sawing out these pieces of parquet flooring, so that the idle rich could shuffle about on it later. Onegins*... cling... clang... They used to dance here throughout the night, no doubt. After all, there was nothing else for them to do, was there?"

"For God's sake! What an absolute plague this man is, pestering me," Iona sighed to himself. He shook his head and moved on.

The walls had disappeared behind huge dark canvases in faded gold frames. Covering an entire wall, Catherine the Great,* in ermine, with dyed eyebrows and a diadem on her fluffed-up white hair, looked down from under an enormous heavy crown. Her slender, sharply pointed fingers were lying along the arms of an armchair. The oil painting opposite featured a young snub-nosed man, with four-pointed stars on his chest, looking at his mother with an expression of loathing. Surrounding mother and son and reaching right up to the embellished ceiling, the princes and princesses of the Tugai-Beg-Ordynsky family looked down on the world.

Gleaming, darkly creviced, painted by the careful hand of an eighteenth-century artist according to unreliable traditions and legends, and sitting in the dark of a canvas that had long since faded, was the slant-eyed, dark-skinned and predatory figure of the sovereign founder of the Nogai Horde,* the Khan Tugai. He was wearing an Asian fur cap adorned with precious stones, and the hilt of his sabre was studded with semi-precious jewels.

The clan of the Tugai-Beg princes, a distinguished, spirited people`, a line stocked with princes, khans and emperors, had been looking down from the walls for five hundred years. These blotchy canvases told the clan's story, punctuated with tales now of military prowess, now of shame, love, hatred, vice and corruption…

On a pedestal stood a bronze bust, green with age, of an old mother in a bronze bonnet with bronze ribbons tied under her chin, with an imperial monogram on her breast, looking like a lifeless, oval mirror. The dry mouth had shrunk, the nose had become sharp. Inexhaustibly reflecting a depraved idea, and bearing throughout the whole of her life two outstanding quali-ties – that of a dazzling beauty and that of a hideous Messalina.* In the raw mist of a glorious and terrible northern city she had become inextricably associated with legend: in her declining years she had experienced love for the first time, a love bestowed on her by the very same general in the white elk fur whose portrait was hanging in the study next to that of Alexander I.* She had passed from his hands into the hands of Tugai-Beg's father and given birth to the present Prince, the last in the line. As a widow, she had become renowned for the fact that she used to swim naked in a pond on the end of a rope held by four handsome footmen…

Pushing through the crowd, the naked man tapped on the bronze bonnet with his fingernail and said:

"Here, comrades, we see a remarkable person. Someone from the first half of the nineteenth century famous for her depravity…"

The lady with the stomach went purple in the face, grabbed her little girl's hand and hastily took her to one side.

"God knows what all that was about… Look, Verochka, look at these portraits of all the ancestors…"

"The lover of Nikolai Palkin,"* the naked man continued, adjusting his pince-nez. "A number of bourgeois writers have even written novels about her. But what she got up to in this estate boggles the mind. Not a single handsome lad would have escaped her attentions… she used to organize Athenian nights…"

Iona's mouth twisted, his eyes filled with misty tears and his hands started to shake. He wanted to say something, but he kept quiet, merely taking a couple of deep breaths. Everyone began looking with curiosity first at the naked man, and then at the bronze old woman. The heavily made-up lady walked round the bust, and even the important foreigner, even though he did not understand a word of Russian, stood there for a long time shooting piercing glances at the naked man's back.

They walked on through the Prince's study, with its spears, broadswords and curved sabres, its imperial suits of armour, its Guards cavalry helmets, its portraits of the last emperors, with arquebuses, muskets, swords, daguerrotypes and yellowing photographs – depicting groups of cavalry guards officers in whose regiment the older members of the Tugai-Beg clan had served, and of the regular cavalry, in which the younger members had served – its photographs of galloping horses from the Tugai-Beg stables and its cupboards full of heavy ancient books.

They walked through smoking rooms, their floors covered wall to wall with Turkoman carpets, with hookahs, ottomans, collections of pipes on stands, and then on through small drawing rooms, their walls hung with pale-green tapestries and ancient oil lamps. They went on through the spinney where the branches of the palm trees had still not withered, through the green games room with its gleaming gold-and-light-blue Meissen porcelain, where Iona looked meaningfully across at Dunka. Here, in the games room, there was a portrait of a single handsome officer, dazzling in his white uniform and leaning on his sword handle. The lady with the stomach looked at the helmet with its six-cornered star, at the sleeves of his long gloves and at the black moustache curving upwards.

"And who is that?" she asked Iona.

"That is the last prince," Iona replied with a sigh. "Anton Ioannovich, in the uniform of a Guards cavalry officer. They all served in the Guards cavalry."

"And where is he now? Has he died?" asked the lady deferentially.

"What do you mean, 'died'? They're now abroad. They went abroad at the very beginning..." Iona said falteringly, angry at the thought that the naked man might intervene again and say something or other.

And indeed the naked man smirked and opened his mouth, but someone's voice from the crowd of young people interjected:

"Just leave it, Semyon... he's an old man."

And the naked man held his tongue.

"What? Still alive?" exclaimed the lady, astonished. "That's wonderful!... And does he have any children?"

"No, there are no children," Iona replied sadly. "They have not been blessed by the Lord... no, not been blessed. And his younger brother, Pavel Ioannovich, was killed in the war. Yes. Fighting the Germans... He served in the... in the mounted grenadiers. He wasn't from here; he had an estate in Samara Province..."

"There's an old man for you..." someone whispered admiringly.

"Should be put in a museum himself," the naked man muttered.

They went into the marquee. The pink silk rose up in the form of a star and flowed down the walls in waves, while all sounds were muffled by the pink carpet. A carved double bed stood in an alcove of pink tulle. It looked as if two people had been sleeping in it recently, just the night before. Everything seemed alive in the marquee: the mirror in its silver-leafed frame, the album on the little table in its ivory binding and the portrait of the last Princess on an easel – a young princess, dressed in pink. The lamp, the cut-glass bottles of scent, the photos in their frames, the discarded pillow – everything seemed to be alive... Iona must have shown visitors round the bedroom some thirty times, and each time he had experienced a sense of pain, outrage and a constriction in his heart at the thought of these alien feet treading these carpets, and alien eyes roaming all over the bed. Shameful. Yet this time he felt especially upset because of the presence of the naked man and also because of something else, something vague and beyond his comprehension... So he gave a sigh of relief when the tour of the palace came to an end. He took the visitors through the billiard room into the corridor, and then down the second east staircase, onto the side terrace and out of the palace.

The old man himself watched the visitors filing out through the heavy door and Dunka locking it up.

Evening and the sounds associated with evening set in. Somewhere in the vicinity of Oreshnyev, the shepherds started playing their pipes and, beyond the ponds, there was the thin tinkling of the bells of cows being driven home. There was the distant crackle of gunfire indicating the Red Army camps at shooting practice.

Iona traipsed along the gravel towards the palace, his keys jangling on his belt. Every time, when the visitors had gone, the old man would religiously return to the palace and go round it on his own, talking to himself and examining everything carefully. This was followed by a time of calm and relaxation, when he was able to sit in his little lodge, smoke and think various old man's thoughts.

It was a suitable evening for this, light and warm, but nevertheless Iona felt distinctly ill at ease – probably because he had been so upset and agitated by the naked man. Muttering to himself, he stepped onto the terrace, looked around gloomily, rattled his keys and went in. Treading softly on the carpet, he climbed the staircase.

On the landing, at the entrance to the ballroom, he stopped and turned pale.

There was the sound of footsteps in the palace. They could be heard coming from the direction of the billiard room, moving through the spinney and then stopping. The old man's heart stopped, and he felt he was about to die. Then his heart started beating rapidly, in time with the sound of the footsteps. There was no doubt about it: someone's firm footsteps were approaching him, and the parquet floor in the study was already squeaking.

"Thieves! Disaster!" flashed through Iona's head. "I knew it... I sensed something like this would happen... disaster." He gave a shuddering sigh, looking around him in horror, not knowing what to do, where he could run, what to shout. Disaster...

Iona caught a glimpse of a grey coat in the doorway to the ball-room, and the figure of the foreigner in the gold-rimmed glasses appeared. On seeing Iona, he started up in fear, and even took a step backwards, but he quickly recovered and merely pointed a finger at Iona in alarm.

"What are you doing here, sir?" mumbled the terrified Iona. His arms and legs were trembling. "You should not be here. Why didn't you leave with everyone else? My God..." Iona caught his breath and fell silent.

The foreigner looked Iona steadily in the eye and, drawing near to him, said quietly in Russian:

"Iona, calm down! Don't talk so much. Are you alone?"

"Yes, I'm alone," Iona said, taking a deep breath. "Why do you ask, for Heaven's sake?"

The foreigner looked around him anxiously, then looked past Iona's head up to the hallway. When he was convinced there was no one behind Iona, he took his right hand out of his back pocket, and spoke again, but this time loudly and with a burr.

"Didn't you recognize me, Iona? That's bad, very bad... If you don't know who I am, that's not good at all."

The sound of his voice so stunned Iona that his knees gave way, his hands grew cold and his bunch of keys crashed jangling onto the floor.

"Oh, my good Lord! Your Highness! Anton Ioannovich, sir! What is this? What are you doing here?"

The room became clouded with tears; the gold-rimmed glasses, the dental fillings, the familiar, bright slanting eyes – all started to leap around in the mist. Iona choked, his tearful sobs flooding the Prince's gloves and tie as he jabbed his trembling head into the Prince's rough beard.

"Calm down, Iona, calm down, for God's sake," muttered the Prince, his face puckered up in sympathetic alarm. "Somebody might hear."

"But sir," Iona whispered agitatedly, "how… how did you get here? There's nobody about, no one, apart from me…"

"That's wonderful. Pick up your keys, Iona, and come with me to the study."

The Prince turned and walked firmly through the gallery into the study. Dumbfounded and shaking all over, Iona picked up his keys and traipsed after him. The Prince looked round, took off his grey fur hat, threw it onto the table and said:

"Sit down, Iona, there, in that armchair."

Then, his cheek twitching, he tore off the sign saying "No sitting on the chairs" from another armchair with a portable stand, and sat down opposite Iona. The lamp on the table tinkled plaintively as his heavy body sank into the morocco-leather chair.

Iona's head was still in a total whirl, and his thoughts jumped about all over the place, like hares in a sack.

"Oh my goodness, Iona, you look so old… how you've aged!" exclaimed the Prince agitatedly. "But nonetheless I'm glad I've found you still alive. I must confess I thought I'd never see you again. I thought the people here would have done away with you already…"

Moved by the Prince's affectionate concern, Iona started sobbing quietly, rubbing his eyes.

"Really, really, please stop that…"

"But how… how on earth did you get here, sir?" asked Iona, his nose wrinkling. "And how on earth did I, silly old fool that I am, fail to recognize you? My eyesight is going… But how *did* you manage to return, sir? But your glasses, above all your glasses, and your beard… And how did you get back in, without me noticing?"

Tugai-Beg took a key out of his waistcoat pocket and showed it to Iona.

"I got in through the small veranda, from the park, my old friend! As for my glasses..." (as he said this, the Prince removed his glasses) "...I put them on at the border. They have ordinary glass in them."

"But the Princess... Lord, the Princess, is she with you?"

The Prince's face instantly aged.

"The Princess died, last year," he said, his mouth twitching. "She died in Paris from pneumonia. So she wasn't able to see her own home again, but it was constantly in her mind – it was such a strong memory. And she impressed on me the need to kiss you should I ever see you. She firmly believed we would see each other again. She prayed to God constantly. So you see, God has brought me here."

The Prince stood up, embraced Iona and kissed him on his tear-stained cheek. In floods of tears Iona made the sign of the cross to the book cupboard, to the portrait of Alexander I, and to the window, at the very bottom of which the sunset was melting away.

"May God rest her soul, may God rest her soul," he murmured in a trembling voice. "I will hold a memorial service for her in Oreshnyev."

The Prince looked around anxiously, thinking he had heard a squeak on the parquet flooring somewhere.

"Did I hear something?"

"No, it was nothing. Don't alarm yourself, sir. We are alone. And it couldn't be anybody else. After all, who would come here, apart from me?"

"Well, that's all right then. Listen, Iona, I haven't got much time. We need to talk."

Once again Iona's thoughts started to race. Talk about what, indeed? He was here, wasn't he? He had arrived. Alive! And now... the peasants, what about the peasants on the estate?... And the fields?

"So, Your Highness," he said, looking imploringly at the Prince, "what is going to happen now? What about the house? Perhaps they'll give it back to you?"

When he heard this, the Prince burst out laughing with such force that his teeth bared only on one side of his face – the right side.

"Give it back?! What an idea, my good man!"

The Prince opened a yellow cigarette case and lit a cigarette.

"No, Iona, my good fellow. Nobody's going to give me anything back... You've evidently forgotten what happened... No, that's not the point at all. You have to keep in mind that I've come here only for a moment, and in secret. You have absolutely nothing to worry about; nobody will know anything about this. You must not be alarmed on that score. I've come here," continued the Prince, glancing through the window at the rapidly disappearing woods. "I've come here first of all just to see what's going on. I knew one or two things already. People have written to me from Moscow saying that the palace remains untouched, and that it is being regarded as a national treasure... nat-io-nal..." (The teeth on the right side of the Prince's mouth disappeared, as those on his left side bared themselves.) "If it belongs to the nation, then so be it, damn it. I don't mind. Just so long as it remains intact. It's even better that way... But the point is that there are still some important documents of mine here. I need them extremely urgently. Concerning the Samara and Penza estates. And also concerning Pavel Ioannovich. Tell me, is my study still intact, or has it been dismantled?" The Prince looked anxiously in the direction of the doorway with the heavy curtains.

The rusty wheels in Iona's brain started to turn. In front of his eyes flashed the figure of Alexander Ertus, an educated man wearing exactly the same glasses as the Prince. An uncompromising, significant figure. Every Sunday the erudite Ertus would arrive at the palace from Moscow, walk around it in his squeaky red boots, take charge of everything as he ordered people to make sure that everything remained untouched, and sit for hours on end in the study, up to his neck in piles of books, manuscripts and letters. Iona would bring him glasses of weak tea, and he would eat ham sandwiches and scratch away with his pen. At times he would ask Iona about life in the old days and take notes, with a smile on his face.

"The study is just as it was, untouched," mumbled Iona. "But, Your Highness, sir, the trouble is that it's sealed. Sealed."

"Sealed by whom?"

"Alexander Abramovich Ertus, Party committee member..."

"Ertus?" Tugai-Beg asked, lisping. "Why was it Ertus exactly, and not someone else who sealed my study?"

"He's a committee member, sir," Iona replied guiltily, "from Moscow. He was entrusted with the oversight of the palace, you see. There's going to be a library here, down below. They'll be teaching there. So he's setting this library up."

"Ah, so that's it! A library," exclaimed the Prince, bristling. "What a nice idea! I hope my books will be enough for them? Such a pity I didn't know, otherwise I would have brought them some more from Paris. But there will be enough, won't there?"

"Yes, there will, Your Highness," Iona wheezed in confusion. "We've got a huge number of books." A shiver ran along Iona's spine as he saw the look on the Prince's face.

Tugai-Beg sat hunched in his armchair, scratching his chin with his fingernails. Then he cupped his chin in his fist, looking absurdly like the portrait of the slant-eyed figure in the tall fur cap.

"There'll be enough, you say? That's wonderful. This Ertus of yours, I can see, is an educated and talented man. Sets up libraries and sits in my study. Yes, indeed. Indeed... But do you know, Iona, what will happen once this Ertus has set up his library?"

All eyes now, Iona said nothing.

"I will hang this Ertus on that lime tree over there" – the Prince gestured out of the window with his pale hand – "that one by the gate." Iona obediently and forlornly looked where the Prince was pointing. "No, the one on the right, by the railings. And, moreover, the first day Ertus will hang there facing the road, so that the peasants will be able to feast their eyes on the person setting up the library for them, and the next day facing the palace, so that he himself will be able to feast his eyes on his own library. I swear to you, Iona, that I will do that, whatever it might cost me. The moment will come – you can be sure of that Iona – and perhaps that moment will be very soon. And I have enough connections to be able to get hold of Ertus. Have no fears on that score…"

Iona sighed convulsively.

"And you know who we'll string up next to him?" Tugai continued harshly. "That naked man, Antonov Semyon. Semyon Antonov." As he mentioned the name, he looked up to the sky. "Word of honour, I'll find Comrade Antonov at the bottom of the sea, if he hasn't pegged it by then or if he hasn't been hanged on Red Square with the rest of them. But even if he has already been hanged, I'll bring him here and hang him again for a day or two. Semyon Antonov has already once had the benefit of our Khanate Headquarters hospitality, and has walked around the place naked in his pince-nez." Tugai swallowed his saliva, causing his Tatar cheeks to bulge out. "Well, I'll welcome him here one more time, once again naked. If, that is to say, he falls into my hands alive, eh Iona!… I won't be congratulating Semyon Antonov. He'll hang not only without his trousers, but without his skin! Did you hear, Iona, what he said about the Princess, my mother? Did you hear?"

Iona sighed bitterly and looked away.

"You are a faithful servant and, for the rest of my life I will never forget how you responded to that naked man. You're no doubt wondering now why I didn't kill him there and then? Eh? After all, you have known me for many years, haven't you Iona?" Tugai-Beg reached for his coat pocket and pulled out a gleaming ribbed sword handle. White specks of foam appeared in the corners of his mouth, and his voice became weak and hoarse. "But I didn't kill him! I didn't kill him, Iona, because I stopped myself in time. But only I know what it cost me not to kill him. I couldn't do it, Iona. It would have been feeble and it would have failed, and I would have been arrested, and I would not have been able to achieve anything I had come here to do. But we will do it,

Iona, in a bigger and better way," the Prince muttered in conclusion and fell silent.

Iona sat there in confusion, a cold shiver running down his spine at the Prince's words, as if he had swallowed a mint.

He no longer had any coherent thoughts in his head, just scraps of thoughts. The twilight had crept imperceptibly into the room. Frowning, Tugai put his hand back into his pocket, stood up and glanced at the clock.

"Well, Iona, it's late. We must hurry. I'm leaving tonight. We'll sort everything out. First of all" – and here a wallet appeared in the Prince's hand – "take this, Iona, take it, my loyal friend! This is all I can give you – things are a bit tight for me too."

"I couldn't possibly accept that," wheezed Iona, waving the wallet away.

"Take it!" insisted Tugai and thrust the white notes into the old man's nautical jacket. "But just be careful not to exchange them here, otherwise they'll start pestering you, asking where you got hold of them. Please allow me, Iona, to stay in the palace until my train. I'm leaving for Moscow at 2 a.m. I'll be in my study, sorting out some documents."

"But the seal, sir…" Iona began to say plaintively.

Tugai went up to the door, pulled the heavy curtain back and, and with one tug, ripped off the cord with the sealing wax. Iona gasped.

"Lot of nonsense," Tugai said. "Above all, don't be afraid! Don't be afraid, my friend! I can guarantee to arrange things so that you won't appear responsible. You believe me, don't you? Well, then…"

It was approaching midnight. Iona was fast asleep in the lodge. The exhausted Tatyana Mikhailovna and Dunka were asleep in the wing. The palace lay white in the moonlight, blind and silent…

In the study, with the black blinds tightly drawn shut, a single kerosene lamp shone on the open desk, casting a gentle green light onto the pile of papers on the floor, the armchairs and the red cloth. Next door, in the larger study with the double blinds drawn shut, stearin candles glowed in their candelabras. The bindings on the books on the shelves sparkled softly. Bald-headed Alexander I had come to life and looked affectionately down from the wall.

A man in civilian clothes and wearing a helmet of the Cavalier Guards Regiment sat at his desk in the smaller study. An eagle soared majestically above the tarnished metal with the star. A thick oilskin notebook lay in front of the man, on the top of the pile of papers. At the head of the first page were the following words, in minute handwriting:

Alex. ERTUS
The History of the Khan Headquarters

And beneath:

1922–23

Leaning on the desk with his cheeks in his hands, Tugai sat reading, not taking his glazed eyes off the black lines of writing. Absolute silence reigned and Tugai could hear his own watch in his waistcoat as it inexorably ticked off the minutes. The Prince sat there perfectly still for twenty minutes and then for half an hour.

Suddenly, a mournful whine penetrated the blinds. The Prince awoke out of his reverie and stood up with a crash of armchairs.

"Oh, that blasted dog," he growled and went out into the front study. In the dim glass of the cupboard a vague outline of a Cavalier Guards officer with a shining head came towards him. Coming up to the glass, Tugai looked closely at it, turned pale and smiled a sickly grin.

"Poof," he whispered, "it's enough to make you go out of your mind."

He removed his helmet, wiped his temple, thought for a moment, looking into the glass, and then suddenly flung his helmet furiously onto the ground with such force that the crash resounded round the room, making the glass in the bookshelves jangle plaintively.

Then Tugai hunched up, kicked his helmet into the corner, walked across the carpet to the window and then back again. Alone, clearly beset by important and worrying thoughts, he became visibly weak and old, muttering to himself and biting his lips.

"It's not possible... no, no..."

The parquet flooring creaked, and the flames in the candles flickered and died down. Greying, blurred figures kept on appearing in the glass of the cupboards and then disappearing again. Turning sharply in his tracks, Tugai went up to a wall, and began to examine it carefully. On an oblong photograph a group of people, frozen in time and therefore for ever immortalized, sat or stood in a tight semicircle. They had eagles on their heads. Long gloves with white sleeves, the handles of broadswords. In the very centre of the enormous group sat an unprepossessing man with a beard and moustache, looking like a regimental doctor. But the heads of the cavalier guards sitting and standing around him were half turned, looking intently at the small man buried under his helmet.

The small man dominated the white, tense cavalier guardsmen, just as the photograph itself was dominated by its bronze inscription. Every word was written with a capital letter. Tugai stood there for a long time, looking at himself sitting two figures away from the small man.

"It cannot be," Tugai said out loud, and looked round the huge room, as if inviting numerous interlocutors as witnesses to what he was saying. "It's a dream." Once again he started muttering to himself, then continued incoherently: "It's one of two things: either he's dead, or he... that man... is alive... or... I... can't make head or tail..."

Tugai ran his hands through his hair, turned, saw himself approaching the glass bookshelf, and thought involuntarily: "I've aged." Then again he started muttering to himself:

"They've gone and trampled on me, on my living flesh, as if on a corpse. Perhaps I really am dead? Perhaps I'm just a shadow? But I'm alive, aren't I?" Tugai looked questioningly up at Alexander I.

"I can still sense and feel everything. I can distinctly feel pain, but above all I feel angry." Tugai seemed to catch a glimpse of the naked man in the dark room, and a cold wave of hatred swept through his veins. "I regret I didn't kill him. I regret that…" The fury began to well up inside him and his tongue turned dry.

Once again he turned and silently walked to the window and back again, each time stopping by the wall and studying the group of people in the photograph. This went on for about fifteen minutes. Then, suddenly, he stopped, ran his hands through his hair, clutched at his pocket and pressed down on the repeater of his watch. His watch softly and mysteriously struck twelve times; after a pause it struck another quarter, and then, after another pause, three minutes.

"Oh, my God," Tugai whispered and began to hurry. He looked round the room and, before doing anything else, took his glasses from the desk and put them on. But this time they made very little difference to the Prince's appearance. His eyes were slanting, like the Khan in the portrait, and there was only the faint gleam of some despairing thought, conceived a long time ago. Tugai put on his coat and hat, returned to his own little study, picked up the pile of parchment and sealed paper documents that he had laid out carefully on the armchair, folded it and squeezed it with difficulty into his coat pocket. Then he sat down at his desk and started looking through the pile of papers for the final time. His cheek twitched and, with a sideways glance, he set to work. Rolling up his wide coat sleeves, he first of all picked up Ertus's manuscript, rereading the first page. Then he bared his teeth, and tore at the manuscript, scraping at the paper with his nails so forcefully that one of them broke off.

"…A plague on it all!" he wheezed, rubbing his finger, and began again, this time more carefully. Ripping the sheets off one after the other, he gradually reduced the notebook to shreds. He scraped the piles of papers from the desk and the armchairs, and dragged them down from the cupboards. He ripped the small portrait of a lady from the time of Empress Elizabeth,* shattered the frame into tiny pieces with one blow of his foot, added the tiny fragments to the piles of paper on top of the desk, then moved it all to the corner under the small portrait. He removed the lamp and took it into the front study. Then he returned with the candelabra and neatly lit the whole heap in three places. Smoke began to circulate and to wreathe around in the heap and, in the flickering light, the study came unexpectedly and cheerily to life. Within five minutes the smoke had become choking.

Firmly closing the door and the curtains, Tugai set to work in the adjacent study. Flames crackled around the ripped open portrait of Alexander I, and the bald head smiled craftily through the smoke. The ancient volumes burnt upright where they stood on the table, and the cloth was smouldering. The prince sat some distance away in an armchair and watched. His eyes were now filled with tears from the smoke and from a kind of cheerful madness. Again he started muttering to himself:

"Nothing can be returned after this. It's all finished. There will be no point in lying any more. So, my dear Ertus, we'll be able to take all this away with us when we go."

As the prince moved slowly from room to room, the grey smoke followed him wherever he went, and sections of the main hall started to burst into flame. Fiery shadows played and darted about on the insides of the curtains.

In the pink marquee the Prince unscrewed the burner from the lamp and poured the kerosene over the bed; a drop of it spilt onto the carpet. Tugai hurled the burner onto the drop of kerosene. At first nothing happened: the flame diminished and then disappeared, but then it suddenly flared up again and spurted upwards with such force that Tugai nearly leapt back. Within a moment the bed curtains had caught alight and then, all of a sudden, every last speck of dust in the entire marquee was ablaze.

"That's done now, for sure," said Tugai and quickly left the room.

Making his way through the spinney and then the billiard room, he clattered out into a dark corridor and down a winding staircase into the gloomy lower floor. Then he darted like a shadow to the moonlit door that led onto the eastern terrace, opened the door and went out into the park. Not wishing to hear Iona's first shouts from the lodge or the howls of the dog, he sank his head into his shoulders and dived into the darkness, along familiar, secret paths...

# The Crimson Island

A NOVEL BY COMRADE JULES VERNE
TRANSLATED FROM THE FRENCH INTO AESOPIAN
BY MIKHAIL A. BULGAKOV

## Part I: The Fiery Mountain Erupts

### Chapter 1

#### HISTORY AND GEOGRAPHY

I N THE OCEAN LONG SINCE KNOWN as the Pacific Ocean because of its storms and disturbances, below the 45th parallel, can be found the most immense of uninhabited islands, peopled by glorious tribes – the red Ethiopians, the white Arabs and Arabs of an uncertain colouring, to whom seafarers have for some reason given the name double-dyed.

When the good ship *Hope* belonging to the famous Lord Glenarvan* first arrived at the island it discovered a number of unusual practices there. Despite the fact that the red Ethiopians outnumbered the white and the double-dyed Arabs both taken together by a factor of ten, the island was ruled exclusively by the Arabs. Adorned by fish bones and sardine tins, the leader Sizi-Buzi* sat on a throne in the shade of a palm tree. Next to him sat the high priest and commander-in-chief Rikki-Tikki-Tavi.*

73

For their part, the red Ethiopians were busy working in the maize fields, catching fish and gathering turtle eggs.

Lord Glenarvan began as he had always become accustomed to doing, wherever he was, by running up a flag and saying in English:

"This island... will be somewhat mine."

This led to some misunderstanding. The Ethiopians, unfamiliar with any language other than their own, made themselves a pair of trousers out of the flag. Whereupon His Lordship began to whip the Ethiopians under the palm trees. When he had finished whipping them all, he entered into negotiations with Sizi-Buzi, from whom he learnt that the island belonged to him, Sizi-Buzi, and that a flag was "unnecessary".

Apparently, the island had already been discovered twice. Firstly by the Germans, and then by some people or other who ate frogs. As proof, Sizi pointed to the sardine tins and smilingly intimated that the "firewater" was "very tasty, yes indeed..."

"They've got wind of something, the sons of bitches!" growled Lord Glenarvan in English and, slapping Sizi on the shoulder, graciously gave him permission to call the island his own in future.

Then an exchange of goods took place. From the *Hope* the sailors unloaded the following items onto the shore: glass beads, rotten sardines, saccharin and firewater. Shouting exultantly, the Ethiopians carried beaver skins, ivory, fish, eggs and pearls to the shore.

Sizi-Buzi kept the firewater for himself, together with the sardines and the beads, and gave the saccharin to the Ethiopians.

Orderly relations were established. Vessels began to call in at the bay, unloading precious English goods, and picking up Ethiopian trash. A correspondent from *The New York Times*, in white trousers and with a pipe, settled on the island and immediately went down with tropical gonorrhoea.

In geography textbooks the island became known as "Ethiopian Island" ("*L'Île Éthiopienne*").

# Chapter 2

## SIZI DRINKS FIREWATER

T HE ISLAND NOW ENTERED on a period of unprecedented prosperity. The high priest and commander-in-chief and Sizi-Buzi himself were literally swimming in firewater. Sizi's face finally became like varnished leather and smooth and round, without any wrinkles. The army of white Arabs, adorned with beads, stood by the tent, the forest of spears gleaming.

Passing vessels could often hear shouts of triumph echoing from the island:

"Long live our leader Sizi-Buzi, and our high priest! Hurrah! Hurrah!"

The Arabs shouted. Loudest of all shouted the double-dyed.

The Ethiopians remained deafening in their silence. Not having been given any firewater and worn out by back-breaking work, the aforesaid Ethiopians were in a state of apathy that bordered even on a vague discontent. And since the Ethiopians, like every people, have their troublemakers, so from time to time subversive thoughts arose:

"What about that then, eh lads? This ain't right at all. They've" (referring to the Arabs) "got vodka, they've got beads, and what have we got: saccharin and fuck-all else! And who does all the work? We do of course!"

This all ended very nastily – and, once again, unpleasantly for the Ethiopians. From the very beginning, as soon as minds started to boil over, Sizi-Buzi sent a punitive Arab expedition to attack the Ethiopian wigwams, reducing them in two shakes of a dog's tail to a single denominator.

Thrashed to within an inch of their lives, they bowed down to their waists and said:

"Our children will also obey."

And thus, in this manner, the good times were restored.

# Chapter 3

## CATASTROPHE

T HE WIGWAMS BELONGING to Sizi and the high priest were situated in the best part of the island, at the foot of a fire-breathing mountain that had last erupted three hundred years ago.

One night, totally unexpectedly, the mountain came to life and the seismographs in Pulkovo and Greenwich indicated an ominous absurdity. Smoke flew out of the top of the fire-breathing mountain, followed by flames, and then a rush of stones and then hot lava, like boiling water from a samovar.

By morning everything had been wiped clean. The Ethiopians realized they had been left without their leader Sizi-Buzi and without their high priest, and with just the army commander. In place of the royal wigwams was layer upon layer of lava.

# Chapter 4

## THE GENIUS KIRI-KUKI*

T HE VERY FIRST REACTION on the part of the Ethiopians was to be shattered by the shock, and there were even some tears amongst the mass of them, but this was immediately followed by the completely natural question that ran through the minds of the Ethiopians as well as of the surviving Arabs headed by their army commander: "What is going to happen now?"

The question gave rise to a murmur that was at first vague, but then loud and clear, and it is uncertain how this would have developed had not something astonishing happened.

First, above the crowd resembling a poppy field with the occasional white specks and blotches, someone's drink-ravaged face and unsteady eyes appeared. These were followed by the full figure of someone standing on a barrel – someone who was known to the entire island as the drunkard and good-for-nothing Kiri-Kuki.

The Ethiopians were thunderstruck for a second time. The cause of this was Kiri-Kuki's astonishing appearance. Everybody, big or small, had become accustomed to seeing him hanging about, now in the bay where the fiery delights were being unloaded, and now in the vicinity of Sizi's wigwam, and everyone knew perfectly well that Kiri was a hundred per cent double-dyed Arab. And now here he was appearing in front of the dumbfounded islanders adorned from head to toe in red Ethiopian war paint. Even the most practised eye would not have been able to distinguish the empty-headed scoundrel from a genuine Ethiopian.

Kiri swayed about on the barrel, first to the right and then to the left and then, opening his large mouth, roared the following astonishing words, which the delighted *New York Times* correspondent immediately jotted down in his little notebook:

"Since we have now become free Ethiopians, I would like to say thank you!"

Not a single one of these maritime Ethiopians had any idea why Kiri-Kuki was saying thank you, or what he was saying thank you for! And the whole huge assembly responded to him with a thunderous astonished shout:

"Hurrah!"

This shout raged throughout the island for several minutes, until it was cut through by a new yell from Kiri-Kuki:

"Now, brothers, you must all get down and swear an oath!"

And when the delighted Ethiopians yelled "Who to?" Kiri shouted "To me!!!"

This time it was the Arabs' turn to be stunned. But they were not paralysed for long. Shouting, "He's hit the nail on the head, the scoundrel," the army commander was the first to dash up and toss Kiri into the air in celebration.

All that night cheerful fires burnt on the island and the flames from the fires were reflected high up in the sky. Intoxicated with joy and from the bottles of firewater opened by the efficient Kiri, the Ethiopians danced round the fire.

Alarmed passing vessels bombarded the ether with radio messages, preparing to fire on the island to maintain order, but soon the entire civilized world was set at rest by the following telegram from the *Times* correspondent:

"Island idiots celebrating national festival stop scoundrel a genius."

# Chapter 5
## BOUNT*

AFTER THAT, EVENTS UNFOLDED with unnatural speed. On the very first day, to please the Ethiopians, Kiri named the island "Crimson Island", as a mark of the Ethiopians' basic colour. Rather than pleasing the Ethiopians, who were indifferent to fame, this angered the Arabs. On the very next day, in order to please the Arabs, he confirmed the Arab Rikki-Tikki as the army commander, but this failed to please the Arabs, because they all wanted to be made the commander, while at the same time angering the Ethiopians. On the third day, so as to please himself personally, he made himself an unkempt headdress from an empty sprat tin, extraordinarily similar to the crown of the late-lamented Sizi. This pleased nobody and angered everybody, for the Arabs supposed that each of them was worthy of such a tin, whereas the Ethiopians, made dissolute by all the firewater, were against such a tin on principle, since it reminded them of the very painful occasion when they had been reduced to a single denominator.

Kiri-Kuki's very last decision concerned firewater, and with this he finally came to grief. Kiri announced that firewater would be available to everyone equally, but he did not keep his word. It was very simple: if it were to be made available to everybody, then a lot of it would be needed. But where could you get it from? In exchange for the water, Kiri sold off a whole harvest of maize, but without obtaining much water. However, the stomachs of not only the Ethiopians but also of the Arabs suffered as a result, and there was much dissatisfaction.

One fine hot day, when Kiri was lying in his wigwam, incapable as usual of any useful activity, an Ethiopian with an expression on his face clearly reflecting that of a potential troublemaker, went to see the army commander Rikki-Tikki. At the moment of his appearance, Rikki was drinking firewater at the same time as crunching away at a roast piglet.

"What do you want, you Ethiopian pigface?" asked the morose commander drily.

The Ethiopian let the compliment slip past him and went straight to the point.

"What's this here?" he whined. "What's all this? Look at you with your vodka and your roast pig, eh? I see we've gone back to the old days, have we?"

"Aha! So you'd like some roast pig?" the warrior answered with some restraint.

"Well, what do you think? Ethiopians are human too, ain't they?" the visitor rejoined impertinently and insolently set aside one of the crackling pig's legs for himself.

Rikki took the pig's leg and, whirling it round, smacked the Ethiopian in the teeth with it with such force that juice splattered from the pig, while blood gushed from the Ethiopian's mouth, and tears accompanied by large green sparks from his eyes.

"Get out!!!" yelled Rikki, bringing any further discussion to an end.

It is not known what the Ethiopian did when he got back home but, whatever it was, it is a well-known fact that – by the end of the day – the whole island buzzed like a beehive. And that night the frigate *Chancellor*, which happened to be passing by the island, observed two glows emanating from fires in the southern Bay of Blue Peace, and alarmed the whole world with the following telegram:

"Island fires all signs point to Ethiopians donkeys celebrating again Hatteras."*

But the venerated captain had been mistaken. There were fires, it was true, but there was absolutely nothing festive about them. It was simply that, in that area of the bay, the Ethiopian wigwams were on fire, having been set alight by Rikki-Tikki's punitive expeditionary force.

By morning the pillars of flame had turned into smoke, indicating, moreover, not two, but now nine fires. And by night-time they had turned back again into (sixteen) palm-tree fires.

The world was disturbed by the newspaper headlines in Paris, London, Rome, New York, Berlin and other cities: "What is going on?"

And then came a telegram from the *Times* correspondent that greatly startled the world:

"Arab wigwams burning six days. Hordes of Ethiopians… (indistinct) crook Kiri ra… (indistinct)."

And then, the next day, the whole world was shattered by another telegram, this time not from the island, but from a European port:

"*Ephiop sacatil grandiosni bount. Ostrov gorit, povalnaya tschouma. Gori troupov. Avansom piatsot. Korrespondent.*"*

# Part II: The Island on Fire

## Chapter 6

### MYSTERIOUS DUGOUT CANOES

A T DAWN THE SENTRIES on the European shore shouted: "Ships ahoy!"

Lord Glenarvan appeared with his spyglass and studied the black specks for a long time.

"Me no understand," said the gentleman. "Look like primitive canoes to me."

"Thunder and lightning!" exclaimed Michel Ardan,* tossing the Zeiss to one side. "I'll wager a Washington dollar against a rotten rouble of '23 vintage if that's not Arabs."

"Absolutely," confirmed Paganel.*

Ardan and Paganel were right.

"What that mean?" His Lordship asked, astonished for the first time in his life.

Instead of replying, the Arabs merely sniggered. They were a positively terrible sight. When they had caught their breath somewhat, terrible things became clear: there were masses of Ethiopians. The damned troublemakers had burnt these idiots. The demand: to send the Arabs to hell. The scoundrel Kiri-Kuki had been the first to sneak off in a canoe. The remains of the punitive expedition headed by Rikki-Tikki were in the dugout canoes. They had only just made it to His Lordship.

"A hundred million curses!!" thundered Ardan. "They're planning to live in Europe, *comprenez-vous*?"*

"But who will feed you?" enquired Glenarvan in alarm. "No, you go back island…"

"But, Your Highness," wept the Arabs, "we can't so as much step onto the island now. The Ethiopians will simply kill us all. And, secondly, our wigwams have been burnt to the ground. But if you could send some military force to the island to subdue those bastards…"

"Thank you," His Lordship replied ironically, indicating the correspondent's telegram, "you have plague there. We not yet out of our minds. One of mine sailor more precious than all your flea-ridden island. Yes."

"Quite right, Your Excellency," agreed the Arabs. "Everyone knows how worthless we are. And with regard to the plague, Mr Correspondent tells the truth. Killing like flies, like flies. And people are starving again."

"So then," said His Lordship contemplatively, "…right. We look and see." Then he gave the order: "Quarantine them!"

## Chapter 7

### ARAB TORMENTS

IT IS IMPOSSIBLE TO SAY what the Arabs had to undergo at the hands of His Lordship. It began with them being washed with carbolic acid and then herded behind some fence like a group of donkeys. They were fed just enough to keep them alive. But since it is impossible by such a method to establish the precisely correct norm, a quarter of the Arabs gave their souls to the Lord in any case.

Finally, having left the Arabs to stew in their own juice in quarantine, His Lordship sent them off to work in the stone quarries. There were overseers at the quarries, and the overseers had oxhide whips…

# Chapter 8

## THE DEAD ISLAND

T HE SHIPS WERE GIVEN ORDERS to patrol the island so that it was always within gunshot range. This they did. At night feebly burning glows could be seen while, during the day, the island smouldered with black smoke. In addition there was a revolting, suffocating stench. The smell of dead bodies floated across the blue waves.

"That's kaput for the island," remarked the sailors, looking through their binoculars at the treacherous green strip of coast.

The Arabs, who had been transformed into pale shadows on the food provided for them by His Lordship, gloated.

"Serves them right, the bastards. Let them die, and go to the pigs. When they've all snuffed it, we'll go back and occupy the island. And as for that scoundrel Kiri-Kuki, we'll rip his intestines out with our own hands, wherever he's got to."

His Lordship maintained a calm silence.

# Chapter 9

## THE TAR-COVERED BOTTLE

I T HAD BEEN WASHED onto the European shore one day by a wave. When it had been disinfected with carbolic acid in the presence of His Lordship, it was opened, turning out to contain indecipherable scribbles in Ethiopian. An interpreter managed to work out what they said and presented the document to His Lordship:

"Dying from hunger. Small children (misspelt) dying. Plague still bad. We're people too, aren't we? Send bread. Your loving Ethiopians."

Rikki-Tikki turned blue and yelled:

"Your Excellency!... No, absolutely not... Let them die! To feed them, after the way they rebelled, and..."

"I'm not intending to..." His Lordship replied coldly, and lashed Rikki on the ear for importuning him with advice.

"That is essentially swinish behaviour," Michel Ardan muttered between his teeth. "We could send them a little maize."

"I am grateful to you for your advice, Monsieur," Glenarvan replied drily. "Who, I wonder, would pay for the maize? This Arab mob has gorged itself on goodness knows how much already. I don't need any idiotic advice from you."

"Is that right?" Ardan asked with a frown. "Be so kind as to let me know, sir, when we can fight. And I swear to you, my good sir, I shall be able to hit you from a distance of twenty paces as easily as if you were Notre Dame Cathedral."

"I will not congratulate you, Monsieur, if you should ever find yourself at a distance of twenty paces from me," rejoined His Lordship. "The weight of your body will be increased by the weight of the bullet that I will place in one of your eyes, whichever one you would like to choose."

His Lordship's second was Phileas Fogg;* Ardan's, Paganel. Ardan's weight remained the same, and Ardan's shot missed His Lordship. Instead it hit one of the Arabs sitting behind a bush to watch out of curiosity. The bullet entered the Arab between his eyes and left by the back of his head. The Arab died when the bullet had reached the halfway point – in the middle of his brain.

Ardan and Glenarvan shook hands and went their separate ways.

But the story of the bottle did not end here. During the night fifty Arabs escaped from the European shore on canoes, leaving behind the following insolent note for His Lordship:

"Thank you for the carbolic acid and the oxhide whips of the overseers. We look forward to the day when we are able to break their legs with them. We are going back to the island. We shall make peace with the Ethiopians. Better to die from the plague at home than from your rotten salted beef. Respectfully yours, the Arabs."

The escapees went off with a spyglass, an unserviceable machine gun, one hundred tins of condensed milk, six gleaming doorknobs, ten revolvers and two European women. His Lordship thrashed the remaining Arabs and recorded the value of what had been taken in his notebook.

# Part III: The Crimson Island

## Chapter 10

### AN ASTONISHING TELEGRAM

S IX YEARS WENT BY. People forgot about the isolated dead island. From time to time, sailors on their ships looked through binoculars at its luxuriant green shoreline, its cliffs and foaming surf. But that was all.

Seven years were set aside for the plague to run its course and for the island to be pronounced safe. The plan was that, at the end of the seventh year, there should be an expedition with the aim of resettling the Arabs back on the island. The Arabs, as emaciated as skeletons, were languishing in the stone quarries.

But then, at the beginning of the seventh year, the civilized world was shaken by some astonishing news. Radio stations in America, France and England received the following message:

"Plague over. Alive and well, thank God, just what we wanted. Respectfully yours, the Ethiopians."

That morning newspapers all over the world appeared with the following two-inch-high headlines:

ISLAND SPEAKS!!

MYSTERIOUS MESSAGE!!! ETHIOPIANS ALIVE?!

"By the flannel underpants of my grandmother," roared M. Ardan, "this is beyond belief! What is astonishing is not that they've survived, but that they're sending telegrams. Is it possible, perhaps, that the Devil has built them a radio station?!"

Lord Glenarvan received the news in pensive mood. As for the Arabs, they were totally shattered by it. Rikki-Tikki-Tavi smirked and asked His Lordship:

"Now, Your Holiness, there's only one thing to do: strike at them, send an expedition. After all, what is going on there, one has to ask?! The island is yours by right. How much longer do we have to languish in this place?"

"Us'll have to see," His Lordship answered.

## Chapter 11

### CAPTAIN HATTERAS AND
### THE MYSTERIOUS LAUNCH

ONE BEAUTIFUL DAY in May a wreath of smoke appeared in the ocean near the island, and soon a ship under the command of Captain Hatteras, subordinate to Lord Glenarvan, put in to shore. The sailors manned the shrouds and the ship's sides and looked with curiosity at the island. The following picture presented itself to their eyes: in the placid waters of the bay, among a whole group of evidently newly dugout canoes, a strange launch lay prominently at anchor right at the water's edge. The mystery of the telegram received an immediate explanation: in the distance, in the emerald tropical forest, they could see the mast of a hideously erected radio tower.

"A hundred devils!" shouted the captain. "Those blockheads have built that misshapen monstrosity themselves!"

The sailors guffawed as they looked at the lopsided result of the Ethiopians' labour.

One of the ship's boats approached the shore and disembarked the captain with a group of sailors.

The first thing that struck the intrepid voyagers was the unusual abundance of Ethiopians. Hatteras was surrounded not only by adults but also by large numbers of children. Plump little

Ethiopians were sitting in clusters at the very edge of the sea and fishing, their feet dangling in the blue water.

"The devil take me if this plague hasn't been of benefit to this people!" declared the astonished Hatteras. "Their faces look as if they've been fed with 'Hercules' porridge! Well, let's go on and look further…"

Further on, he was particularly struck by the ancient launch sheltering in the bay. It only took one experienced look for him to be convinced that it originated from a European shipyard.

"I don't like this," Hatteras muttered through his teeth. "If that moth-eaten wreck was not stolen, then who, one wonders, were the scoundrels who slipped through to the island during the quarantine? It looks very like a German craft to me!" And, turning to the Ethiopians, he asked: "Hey, you, you redskin devils! Where did you steal that boat from?"

The Ethiopians gave a sly smile, revealing their pearly-white teeth, but said nothing in reply.

"So you don't want to answer?" frowned the captain. "Very well, I'll make you more willing to talk."

As he said this he made his way towards the launch. But the Ethiopians barred his path and that of his sailors.

"Get out of our way!" barked the captain and reached for his back pocket with a practised gesture.

But the Ethiopians stayed where they were. In a second Hatteras and the sailors found themselves in a tight, compact circle. The captain's neck turned crimson. In the crowd he suddenly noticed one of the white Arabs who had escaped from the stone quarries.

"Aha! An old acquaintance!" exclaimed Hatteras. "Now I understand the source of the trouble! Come here, you wretch!"

But the wretch had no desire to approach the captain. Instead he announced:

"No, I won't!"

Captain Hatteras looked around him in fury, and his neck turned a violet colour, forming a wonderful contrast with the white brim of his helmet. The fact was that he could make out weapons in the hands of many Ethiopians, and that the weapons looked remarkably like German rifles, and that the Arab was holding the pistol he had stolen from Glenarvan. The normally cheerful faces of the sailors turned grey and serious. The captain looked up at the scorching blue sky, then out to sea, where his ship was rocking on the waves. The white specks of the sailors who had remained on board were clearly visible as they calmly observed events on shore.

Captain Hatteras knew how to control himself. His neck gradually returned to its normal colour, indicating that his paralysis had been overcome for now.

"Allow me to proceed back to my ship," he said hoarsely but politely.

The Ethiopians made way and Hatteras, escorted by his sailors, returned to his ship. An hour later and the anchor chains began to rattle. Within another hour, all that could be seen on the horizon of the sunlit ocean was a small wreath of smoke.

# Chapter 12

## AN INVINCIBLE ARMADA

IN THE BARRACKS OCCUPIED by the Arabs something indescribable was taking place. The Arabs were emitting shouts of victory and standing on their heads. That day they were given thick golden soup by the bucketful. They were no longer going about in rags. They had been given magnificent cotton trousers and as much paint as they needed for their warrior tattoos. Racks holding their new quick-firing rifles and machine guns stood by the barracks.

Most striking of all was Rikki-Tikki-Tavi. Rings gleamed in his nose, and he was adorned with gaily coloured feathers. His face shone like that of a fully blown church priest at Eastertide. He walked around like a madman, saying only one thing:

"Right, right, right. You'll be dancing to my tune now, my darlings. Give us time, and we'll make it across. We'll make it across all right."

As he said this, he made jabbing gestures with his fingers as if poking out some invisible person's eyes.

"Fall in! Attention! Hurrah!" he shouted and started darting about in front of the ranks of Arabs who were weighed down by all the soup they had eaten.

The Arab battalions started to board the three massive armoured troop ships in the harbour. And at this point something unexpected happened. A ragged threadbare figure with his head shaven in the form of a crew cut appeared in front of the assembled ranks, right in the middle. When the dumbfounded Arabs looked at the figure more closely, they saw that it was none other than Kiri-Kuki himself. All this time he had been wandering around the place – goodness knows where.

He was insolent enough to march out in front of the assembled ranks of Arabs and to address Rikki-Tikki with an ingratiating smile:

"You haven't forgotten me, have you, mates? I'm one of you, after all. I'm an Arab too. Take me to the island with you. I'll come in handy…"

He was not able to finish what he was saying. Rikki turned green and whipped a broad sharp knife out of his belt.

"Your Healthness," he said, turning to Lord Glenarvan, his lips quivering. "This is the man… he's the one… this is the Kiri-Kuki that was the spark that set the forest on fire. Permit me, Your Excellency, to cut his throat personally."

"Well, of course. Go ahead," His Lordship replied good-naturedly. "Only get on with it, don't hold up the embarkation."

Kiri-Kuki hardly had time to squeal before Rikki had sliced through his throat from ear to ear in one masterful stroke.

Then Lord Glenarvan and Michel Ardan paraded in front of the assembled ranks, and His Lordship pronounced a farewell speech:

"Go, kill Ethiopians. Me help, shoot from boat. After you get paid for this."

And, to the accompaniment of music, the Arab battalions embarked on the ships.

## Chapter 13
### AN UNEXPECTED FINALE

O N THIS DAZZLING DAY, the island appeared like a shining jewel. The troop ships approached the shore and the armed ranks of Arabs began to disembark. Rikki, bursting with fighting spirit, was the first to jump off onto the shore and, brandishing his sabre, shouted the command:

"Brave Arabs, follow me!"

And the Arabs streamed after him.

What happened next was this: an indescribably large Ethiopian force rose up out of the fertile earth of the island and faced their uninvited visitors. The Ethiopians started to move forward in the densest columns imaginable. There were so many of them that, in the twinkling of an eye, the green island turned red. They pressed forward in droves from all sides, and a dense bristling layer of spears and bayonets, like toothbrushes, lay over the red ocean. Interspersed amongst them every so often, in the form of detachment commanders, were those very same Arabs who had escaped from the stone quarries. These same Arabs were covered all over in Ethiopian markings and were brandishing revolvers. Their faces clearly expressed the fact that they had nothing to lose. They were all yelling one and the same thing, the military command to "fix bayonets!!"

To which the Ethiopians responded with a blood-curdling yell:

"Kill them, the sons of bitches!!!"

When the two opposing forces met, it became clear that Rikki's army was merely a white island in a raging crimson ocean. The ocean spilt over and surrounded the Arabs on each flank.

"By the horns of the devil," gasped M. Ardan on board the flagship, "I swear I have never seen anything like it!"

"Give them supporting fire!" commanded Lord Glenarvan, tearing himself away from his spyglass.

And Captain Hatteras gave them supporting fire. The fourteen-inch cannon barked, and the shell, falling short, exploded precisely at the juncture between the Arabs and the Ethiopians. Twenty-five Ethiopians and forty Arabs were blown to smithereens. The second shell met with even greater success: fifty Ethiopians and one hundred and thirty Arabs. There was no third shell, as Lord Glenarvan, who had been watching the results of the firing through his spyglass, seized Captain Hattteras by the throat and dragged him away from the cannon.

"Cease fire, damn you to hell!" he yelled. "You're firing on Arabs, damn you!!"

After Hatteras's first rounds of gunfire, the columns of Arabs shrieked and howled with unimaginable intensity, and they had started to buckle.

Even Rikki-Tikki, who had found himself in the middle of an irate maelstrom, had shrieked. Suddenly the contorted face of one of the rank-and-file Arabs emerged from out of the maelstrom. He leapt up to his shell-shocked leader and shouted hoarsely, foaming at the mouth as he spoke:

"What's this? It's not enough that you drove us to the stone quarries and left us to stew for seven years!! And now this!! You have intentionally put us in the firing line! Ethiopians in front, and a shell on the head from behind?!! Aaaargh!"

In a flash the Arab grabbed a knife and plunged it triumphantly into Rikki-Tikki, gauging the exact spot between the fifth and sixth ribs on his left side with unerring accuracy.

"Help... me," gasped the leader, who was by the end of the phrase already in that other world, before the throne of the Almighty.

"Hurrah!!!" roared the Ethiopians.

"We surrender!! Hurrah! Let us make peace, lads!!" yelled the confused Arabs, tossed around in the raging waters of the immense Ethiopian army.

"Hurrah!!" cheered the Ethiopians in response.

And everything on the island became engulfed in boundless chaos.

"Seven hundred fevers and a Siberian ulcer!!" shouted M. Ardan, his eyes glued to his Zeiss. "May I be hanged if those blockheads haven't gone and made peace!! Look, sir!! They're fraternizing!"

"So I can see," His Lordship replied in sepulchral tones. "But I would very much like to know now who is going to recompense us for all our costs of feeding that rabble in the stone quarries."

"Abandon that idea, my dear sir," said M. Ardan, in a suddenly heartfelt tone. "You'll get nothing here but tropical malaria. And, in general, I would advise you to weigh anchor immediately. Look out!!!" he shouted suddenly and crouched down. And, instinctively, His Lordship crouched down next to him. And not before time. A gleaming cloud of Ethiopian arrows and Arab bullets flew over their heads like a gust of wind.

"Let them have it!!" roared Lord Glenarvan.

Hatteras fired, but without success. The shell burst high in the air. The combined Arab and Ethiopian force replied with another salvo. This time, moreover, their aim was lower and, with his own eyes, His Lordship saw seven of his sailors turn crimson and fall onto the deck, writhing in pain.

"To hell with this expedition!!" roared the far-sighted Ardan. "Full speed ahead, sir! Their arrows are poisoned. We must get out of here fast, if you don't want to bring the plague with you to Europe."

"Give them a farewell shot," said His Lordship hoarsely.

And that famous cobbler and artilleryman Hatteras fired a farewell shot somewhat off course and to one side, and the ships weighed anchor. A third volley of arrows fell harmlessly into the water.

Within half an hour, the smoke from the huge troop ships could be seen on the horizon as they cut through the smooth surface of the ocean. The seven bodies of the poisoned sailors who had been thrown overboard bobbed up and down in the foaming wake. The island became wreathed in haze, and its emerald sunlit shoreline disappeared.

# Chapter 14

## THE FINAL SIGNAL

THAT NIGHT THE TROPICAL SKY over Crimson Island was infused with a fiery glow, and the ships sent the following message crashing out to all radio stations:

"On island festival of extraordinary size stop the devils are drinking coconut vodka!!"

At which the Eiffel Tower received green electric flashes forming the following message of unprecedented insolence:

To Glenarvan and Ardan!

As part of united celebration we are sending you to (indecipherable) and to your (indecipherable).

Respectfully yours, Ethiopians and Arabs.

"Shut down the receivers," roared Ardan

The Tower immediately shut down. The electric messages ceased, and what happened after that nobody knows.

# A Week of Enlightenment

O NE EVENING OUR COMPANY COMMANDER comes and says to me:

"Sidorov!"

And I reply:

"That's me!"

He gives me a piercing look and asks:

"What are you?" he says.

"I'm not anything," I say.

"You're not educated, are you?" he asks.

And of course I reply:

"You're quite right, comrade commander, I'm not."

Then he looks at me again and says:

"Well, then, since you're not educated, I shall send you to see a performance of *La traviata** this evening."

"But what's the point of that, may I ask?" I say. "It's not our fault I'm not educated. We weren't taught anything before the Revolution."

But he replies:

"Idiot! What are you afraid of? It's not meant as a punishment, but for your benefit. You'll learn something there, you'll see a performance of something which you'll enjoy."

That particular evening, however, Panteleyev and I had planned to go to the circus.

So I said:

"But, comrade commander, can't I get a pass to go the circus rather than to the theatre?"

"Circus?" he said, with a frown. "What's the point of that?"

"Well," I said, "it's so exciting... There'll be a clever elephant performing, and there'll be clowns and wrestling..."

He waved a finger at me.

"I'll give you elephant!" he said. "You backward ignoramus! Clowns... I ask you... clowns! You're a rustic bumpkin clown yourself! Elephants... now they're clever, but you, good grief, are just hopeless. What on earth is the point of a circus? Eh? But at the theatre you'll be able to learn something... It's wonderful, it's good... Anyway, in short, I can't waste any more time talking to you like this... Get your ticket, and be off with you!"

There was nothing for it but to pick up my ticket. Panteleyev – he hadn't been educated either – picked up his ticket, and we set off. We bought ourselves three cups of sunflower seeds, and arrived at the "First Soviet Theatre".

At the entrance barrier we can see a veritable tower of Babel. People are streaming into the theatre. And amongst us illiterates there are literate people, for the most part young women. One of these young women goes up to the person who is checking the tickets and shows him hers, but he asks:

"Excuse me, comrade madam, but are you educated?"

She, the idiot, takes umbrage at this.

"What a strange question! Of course I'm educated: I went to high school."

"Aha," says the man at the barrier, "high school. Very nice too. In that case allow me to wish you goodbye!"

And he takes her ticket away from her.

"Why did you do that?" she shouts.

"That," he says, "is very simple: we are only admitting uneducated people."

"But I want to go to the opera or a concert as well."

"Well, then," he says, "if that is what you want to do, then please go to the Caucasian Union. They've brought all the educated people together there: doctors, physicians, professors. They sit and drink tea with syrup, because they're not given any sugar, and Comrade Kulikovsky sings romances to them."

So the young woman goes away.

Anyway, Panteleyev and I were admitted without any problem and were taken directly to the stalls and seated in the second row.

We took our seats.

The performance had not yet begun, and so, out of boredom, we munched a little cup of sunflower seeds each. We sat there like that for about an hour and a half before, eventually, the theatre went dark.

As I watch, someone comes out and takes the most important seat, behind a little railing. Wearing a coat and sealskin hat. Moustache, greying beard and looking so strict. He climbed up, took his seat and straight away put on a pair of pince-nez.

I ask Panteleyev (he might be illiterate, but he knows everything):

"And who might that be?"

And he answers:

"That," he says, "that is the con... dactor. He's the head man around here. Important person!"

"So," I ask, "why has he been put on show, sitting there, behind the railing?"

"He's there," he replies, "because he's the most educated person in the opera. They put him there, in other words, as an example to us all."

"But why have they put him so that he's sitting with his back to us?"

"Well," he said, "that way it's easier for him to condact the orchestra..."

Then this director opened some book in front of him, looked at it and started waving his white stick about. Immediately violins started playing under the floor. Softly and so plaintively that it made one want to cry.

And, indeed, this director seemed far from being the least educated person in the place, because he was doing two things at once: reading his book and waving his stick about. And the orchestra began to get more heated. The more it played the more heated it became! After the violins, the pipes and, after them, the drum. The entire theatre was filled with a crash of thunder. And then there was a great blast from the right-hand side. I looked down at the orchestra and shouted:

"Panteleyev, blow me, if that isn't Lombard, the chap from our regiment."

He had a look too, and then said:

"Yes, you're right, it is! There's no one who plays the trombone quite like him!"

This made me so happy that I shouted:

"Bravo, Lombard, encore!"

But immediately a policeman appeared out of nowhere.

"Please do not disturb the peace, comrade!" he said to me.

So we fell silent.

Meanwhile the curtain had opened and we saw that all hell had broken loose on the stage! Gentlemen in jackets and ladies in dresses dancing and singing. Naturally there was drinking and card-playing going on as well.

Just like before the Revolution, in other words.

And now here he was among all the other Alfredos. Eating and drinking Tozka's health.

And it turned out, brother of mine, that he was in love with that very same Traviata. It's simply that he doesn't say so in words, but always in song. And she answers him in song as well.

And it seems he won't be able to avoid marrying her, except that he, this very same Alfredo, has a father called Lyubchenko. And suddenly, in the second act, this man appears on the stage, as if from nowhere.

Not very tall, but imposing to look at, grey hair and a strong, resonant voice – a baritone.

And he immediately starts singing to Alfredo:

"So you, you such and such, have gone too far, haven't you?"

Anyway, he sang and sang, and sent all this Alfredo's scheming to the devil. In the third act Alfredo drank himself into the ground from grief, and really launched into this Traviata of his in the most scandalous way, my brothers.

He swore at her with all his force, in front of everybody.

He sang:

"You," he said, "are such and such, and in general," he said, "I don't want to have anything more to do with you."

She, of course, was in floods of tears, yelling, such a scandal!

And she goes and falls ill with consumption from grief in the fourth act. They send for the doctor of course.

The doctor arrives.

Although he's wearing a waistcoat, I can see that this doctor fellow shows all the signs that he's one of us, a proletarian. Long hair, and a wonderful voice, as if he's singing in a barrel.

He goes up to Traviata and sings:

"Keep calm," he says, "but you are seriously ill, and will certainly die."

And he doesn't even write out any prescription, but simply says goodbye and leaves.

Well, Traviata sees that there's nothing for it – she has to die.

But then Alfredo and Lyubchenko come in and beg her not to die. Lyubchenko now gives his consent to their wedding. But all to no avail.

"I'm sorry," says Traviata, "I cannot. I must die."

And indeed, the three of them sing together and Traviata dies.

Then the conductor closes his book, takes off his pince-nez and leaves. And everybody else leaves too. That's it.

Well, I think: thank God for that, we've been educated, and it's all over as far as we're concerned! So boring!

And I say to Panteleyev:

"Right, Panteleyev, off to the circus tomorrow!"

I went to bed and dreamt the whole time about Traviata singing and Lombard blasting away on his trombone.

Anyway, the next day I go to see the company commander and say:

"Permission, comrade commander, to go to the circus this evening."

But he snaps at me:

"So you've still got elephants on the brain," he says. "No circuses! No, my friend, this evening you're going to a concert at the Trade Union Hall. Your comrade Bloch will be there," he says, "with his orchestra. He'll be playing the second Rhapsody."*

And I sit down, thinking: "There go your elephants!"

"So does that mean," I ask, "Lombard will be there blasting away on his trombone?"

"Absolutely," he says.

That's lucky, God forgive me. I'll be going to the same place where he'll be going with his trombone!

I look at him and ask:

"How about tomorrow? Can I go then?"

"Tomorrow," he says, "will not be possible. Tomorrow I'm sending you all to the theatre."

"What about the day after tomorrow?"

"The day after tomorrow you're off to the opera again."

And in general, he adds, your days of sloping off to the circus are over. This was now the week of enlightenment.

This makes me furious! This could be the end of me, I think. So I ask:

"So you'll be forcing everyone in the company to do this, will you?"

"Why everyone?" he asks. "Not the educated. Your educated soldier can manage even without the second Rhapsody! No, it's just you uneducated lot, damn you. The educated can go wherever they want!"

I went out and put my thinking cap on. I could see that things were in a bad way! If you were uneducated that meant you'd never get any pleasure out of anything.

So I thought and thought until I arrived at an idea.

I went to the company commander and said:

"Permission to put in a request!"

"Permission granted!"

"Permission to go to school to be educated," I said.

At this the commander smiled and said:

"Good man!" and enrolled me in the school.

Well, anyway, I went to school and, what do you think? They educated me!

And now, as an educated person, I'm on the side of the angels!

# The Unusual Adventures
# of a Doctor

M Y FRIEND, DOCTOR N., has gone missing. Some people
say he's been killed, others that he drowned during the
landing at Novorossiisk,* and others again say that he's still alive
and well and living in Buenos Aires.

Be that as it may, a suitcase containing three night shirts, a
shaving brush, Dr Rabov's pocket prescription guide (1916 edi-
tion), two pairs of socks, a photograph of Professor Mechnikov,
a stale French roll, a copy of the novel *Marya Luseva Abroad*,*
six piramidon pills, strength 0.3, and the doctor's notebook has
come into the hands of his sister.

His sister has sent this notebook on to me by post, together
with a letter beginning with the following words: "You are a
writer and his friend. Publish this, because it is interesting." (This
was followed by female deliberations on "the value of reading",
spattered with tears.)

I don't find it to be particularly interesting – some of it is completely indecipherable (Doctor N. has atrocious handwriting).
Nevertheless I am reproducing here the incoherent notes from the
doctor's notebook without any alterations, apart from dividing
them into chapters and giving them a new title.

It goes without saying that I'll send any payment to Doctor N.
in Buenos Aires as soon as I receive absolute confirmation that
he really is there.

# Chapter 1

## NO TITLE — JUST A HOWL

F ATE, WHY ARE YOU PURSUING ME like this? Why wasn't I born a hundred years ago? Or even better: in a hundred years' time? Or better still, if I hadn't been born at all. One chap said to me today: "Never mind: you'll have something to tell your grandchildren!" What a blockhead! As if I only had one dream, and that was to be able, when I was an old man, to tell my grandchildren all kinds of rubbish about how I came to be hanging on a fence!...

And in any case, not only will I not have any grandchildren, I won't even have children, since, if things carry on like this, I will undoubtedly be killed almost immediately...

..................................................................................
..................................................................................

To hell with grandchildren. My specialism is bacteriology. My love is my study with its green lamp and its books. Ever since I was a child I have hated Fenimore Cooper, Sherlock Holmes, tigers and gunshots, Napoleon, wars and all the wonderfully daring exploits of Koshka the sailor.*

I am not drawn towards any of this. I am drawn towards bacteriology.

But in the meantime...

My green lamp has gone out. *The Chemotherapy of Spirillosis* lies sprawling on the floor. There's the sound of shooting in the alleyway. By my reckoning this is the fifth government that has mobilized me.

# Chapter 2

## IODINE SAVES LIFE

*Evening... of December*

T HE FIFTH GOVERNMENT has been booted out, and I very nearly lost my life... By five o'clock in the afternoon everything became very confused. Machine guns have been firing on the eastern outskirts. That's "their" machine guns; the machine guns on the western outskirts are "ours". Some people are running along with rifles. Generally it's all nonsense. Cabs go by. I can hear people saying that there's now a "new lot in power here".

"Your unit" (what do they mean "my" unit, damn it!) is on Vladimirskaya Street. I run along Vladimirskaya Street, not understanding a thing. Total confusion. I ask everyone where I can find "my" unit, but everyone dashes by without answering. And then suddenly I can see some people with red tassels on their caps crossing the street and shouting:

"Stop him! Stop him!"

I look round. Who are they talking about?

It turns out they're talking about me!

It was only then that I realized what I should have done: simply run home! And so I dashed off. Fortunately I had the good sense to nip down an alleyway. But there was a garden at the end with a fence. I started climbing the fence.

They all shouted, "Stop!"

But however inexperienced I might be in all these wars, I instinctively understood that I shouldn't stop on any account. I clambered over the fence. Behind me the "Crack! Crack!" of rifle fire. And then I was attacked by an enraged, shaggy white dog which appeared from nowhere. It grabbed my army coat and ripped it to shreds. I hung from the fence, clinging to it with one hand, and holding on to a little bottle of iodine (200 grams) with the other. First-class German iodine. There was no time to think. Behind me the stamp of feet. The dog would destroy me. With a sweep of my arm I hit the dog on the head with the bottle. The dog was instantly covered in a gingery-red colour. With a howl it disappeared. Across the garden. Alleyway. Peace and quiet. Home…

…I still haven't got my breath back!

…At night there was cannon fire somewhere in the south, but I have no idea who was firing. Insanely regret having lost the iodine.

# Chapter 3

## THE NIGHT OF THE 2ND TO THE 3RD

S OMETHING INDESCRIBABLE is taking place… Now this new government has been chucked out. It must have been the worst government on this earth. Thank God. Thank God. Thank…

I was mobilized yesterday. No, the day before yesterday. I spent whole days and nights on a bridge covered in ice. Fifteen degrees below zero (Réaumur), plus wind. All night the wind whistled through the gaps in the bridge. On the far side of the river the city was alight. As was Slobodka on this side. We were in the middle. Then everybody started to run into the city. I have never seen such congestion. Cavalry. Infantry. And cannon, and field kitchens – all on the move. There was a nurse with one of the field kitchens. I was told I would be taken to Galicia. Only then did I have the wit to start running myself. All shutters were closed, all entrances barricaded off. As I ran by a church with plump white pillars people shot at me from behind, but they missed. I hid in a courtyard under a projecting roof, and sat there for two hours, emerging only when the moon had disappeared. I ran home through deserted streets, without meeting a single soul. As I ran along I pondered my fate. It was laughing at me. I was a doctor, working on a dissertation, and yet there I was lurking like a rat in some strange courtyard in the middle of the night! At times I was sorry I was not a writer. But anyway who would believe me? I am convinced that, were these notes to fall into anybody's hands, they would think I'd made everything up.

Cannon fire towards morning.

# Chapter 4

## THE ITALIAN ACCORDION

*15th February*

A CAVALRY REGIMENT arrived today and occupied the entire block. In the evening someone from the second squadron came to my surgery (emphysema). While he was sitting in the queue in the waiting room waiting his turn, he played on his large Italian accordion. This emphysema patient played wonderfully well ('The Hills of Manchuria'), but the other patients were extremely put out by it, and it was totally impossible to carry on listening. I saw him out of turn. He liked my apartment very much. He wanted to move in, together with his platoon commander. He asked me if I had a gramophone.

The pharmacist got his emphysema medicine ready in twenty minutes, and without any charge. That's astonishing, take my word for it!

*17th February*

Managed to sleep tonight. The gramophone downstairs is broken.

Got documents with eighteen stamps saying that it was impossible to billet anyone else in my apartment. Stuck one on the front door, another on the study door and a third in the dining room.

*21st Feb.*

More people were billeted in my apartment...

*22nd Feb.*

...and I was mobilized.

*...March*

The cavalry regiment has gone off to fight with some ataman or other.* At the back of the column there was a cart carrying a gramophone that played 'You Ask for Songs'. What a nice invention!

Cannon fire towards morning...

## Chapter 5

..................................................................................
..................................................................................

## Chapter 6

### ARTILLERY BARRAGE AND BOOTS

..................................................................................
..................................................................................

## Chapter 7

They're taking me with them of course.
..................................................................................
..................................................................................
...cannon fire
...and...

# Chapter 8

## KHANKAL GORGE*

*September*

A T TIMES IT SEEMS that this is all a dream. The mountains rear up as if at the behest of an angry god. Mists drift around in the gorges. Thunderclouds roll between the mountains. And the streams roar down over the rocks.

> ...the turbid stream.
> The angry Chechen clambers up
> And sharpens his dagger...*

Uzun-Khadzhi is in Chechen-Aul.* The aul is stretched out over the plain against the background of the bluish haze of the mountains. Bullock carts and two-wheeled carts move along the tracks of the flat Khankal Gorge in a cloud of dust. The Cossacks from the Kizlyar Mountains have taken up their positions on the left flank, the hussars on the right. The artillery batteries are on the flattened fields of maize. They're firing shrapnel at Uzun. The Chechens are fighting the "white devils" like maniacs. A red-cross flag flutters on a two-wheeled cart standing by a stream. The swollen body of a horse sprawls on the bank. This is where they're bringing me Cossacks covered in blood, and they're dying in my hands.

The thundercloud has gone behind the mountains. The sun is pouring down its scorching heat, and I take eager gulps of the foul water from my mess tin. Two nurses bustle about, raising heads lolling on the straw of the two-wheeled carts, dressing the wounded with white bandages and giving them water to drink.

A whole clutch of machine guns are rattling affably away.

The Chechens are rushing out of the aul, fighting desperately. But it won't be any use; the aul will be taken and burnt to the ground. How on earth can they expect, with their lousy three-inch guns, to prevail against the three batteries of the Kuban infantry?...

Their dashing cavalry regiment raced across the flattened and scorched fields of maize with guttural yells, striking at the flank of the Terek Cossacks.

The Cossacks almost gave way, but the Kuban infantrymen poured up in support, the machine guns rattled away once more and drove the cavalrymen away from the fields of maize and onto the plateau, where the doomed mountain huts were visible through binoculars.

*Night*

Everything is quieter. The shooting has died down. The gloom has become thicker, the shadows more mysterious. Then night's velvety curtain and the infinite ocean of stars. The stream gushes angrily. The horses snort and bonfires twinkle in the dark, among the Kuban battalions on the right flank. The blacker it gets, the greater the feeling of trepidation and melancholy. Our bonfire crackles away, the smoke blowing now into my eyes, now away from me. Cossack faces shift and change oddly in the flickering light, emerging suddenly out of the darkness and then plunging back into the abyss once more. And the night appears limitless, black, unstable. It plays with you, frightening you. The gorge stretches away into the distance. There is a mysterious quality in the velvety night. There is nothing behind us in support. And it begins to seem as if, somewhere behind us, there's an oak wood coming to life. Shadowy figures in Circassian dress could well be creeping up on us, hugging the dewy grass. Creeping up, creeping up... And before you have had time to blink, these irate shadows will be dashing out, ablaze with hatred, screaming and yelling and... amen!

Poof, damn it to hell!

"There's no guarantee" – that's my philosophical response to my dilettante musings concerning the unreliability and capriciousness of this night as I sit by the bonfire of the Third Terek Cossack Cavalry Regiment – they won't leap out at us from the flank... Such things have been known to happen.

Oh, just stop it, will you! "From the flank"! Good God! What is all this? The horses are chewing at the manure, rifle barrels glisten in the light of the bonfire. "There's no guarantee"! The mists drift around in the dark. Uzun-Khadzhi is in the doomed aul...

So, who do I think I am? Lermontov, perhaps?! He'd be in his element here, wouldn't he! So what am I doing here then?

I collapse onto the tarpaulin, wrap myself in my greatcoat and gaze up at the velvety dome sprinkled with specks of diamonds overhead. And immediately the dim, white bird of depression hovers over me. I can see my green lamp in front of me, the circle of light falling on my gleaming sheets of paper, the walls of my study... Then everything turned upside down and went to the devil! Hundreds of miles and I'm back to that terrible night, on the tarpaulin. In the Khankal Gorge...

Nevertheless, I start to dream. But about what? First my lamp with its shade, then the night turns into a gigantic black lamp-shade studded with the dancing flames of the bonfire. Now the quiet scratching of a pen, now the crackle of maize stalks on fire. Suddenly you are drowning in the murky mists of your dream, but then you leap up with a shudder. Swishing swords, guttural yells, gleaming daggers, silver-headed cartridges... Oh, my God!... We're under attack!

...No, it's all right! I'm just imagining it all... Everything's calm. The horses are snorting, the rows of exhausted Cossacks are asleep under their black cloaks. The coals are covered in ash, and the night air is cold. In the distance the glimmer of a pale dawn.

Unimaginable tiredness. To hell with the Chechens. It would take a whole eternity to get me up – like lead. The dying bonfire fades from sight... They'll leap on me from the flank, cut my throat like a chicken. Well, let them. What does it matter?...

What a repellent person that Lermontov is. I could never stand him. Khadzhi. Uzun. In one volume, in a red binding. On the binding there is a golden officer with unseeing eyes and winged epaulettes. "Now I am a free child of the ether."\* A flask full of ether has exploded in the sunlight. Softer, softer, deeper, darker. Sleep.

# Chapter 9

## SMOKE AND FLUFF

*Morning*

IT'S ALL OVER. Clumps of black smoke rose up from the plateau. The Terek Cossacks raced across the fields of maize. A machine gun started whining once again, but very soon fell silent.

Chechen-Aul has been taken.

And here we are on the plateau. Pillars of flame rise up to the sky. The little white houses are on fire, the fences and trees crackle. A whirlwind of flame hurtles through the street, small clumps of smoke merge into one huge cloud and quietly recede into the background, as in a setting for the opera *The Demon*.\*

The ground and air are full of fluff. The intrepid mountain Cossacks race like a whirlwind into the aul and then back again. Packaged behind their saddles, chickens and geese scream in horror.

Since morning, at the spot where we've pitched camp, there has been a veritable feast of Lucullus.\* Fifteen chickens have been thrown into the cauldron. The golden, fatty soup is delicious. Shugayev carves up the chicken, as Herod did the first-born.

But over there, in the mysterious gap between the massive mountains on whose edges thinning clumps of mist are rolling, somewhere over there the mysterious Uzun and his horsemen are riding away, burning for vengeance.

I'll bet my life that all this will end very badly. And serves us right – you shouldn't set fire to auls.

And it won't end at all well for me either. But I have already become reconciled to that idea. I try to convince myself that this is all a dream. A long, appalling nightmare.

I have always said that my medical assistant Golendryuk is a clever man. Tonight he's gone missing without trace. But although he hasn't told us where he was going, I think I know where he is: he is making his way to where he wants to go; that is, he is on his way to the railway, at the end of which stands a little town. A little town where his family is. My commanders have ordered me to "conduct an investigation". With pleasure. I sit on the medicine box and conduct an investigation. My conclusion: medical assistant Golendryuk has disappeared without trace. During the night of such-and-such a date. Stop.

# Chapter 10

## WE GET THROUGH TO THE CHECHENS

*A hot September day*

S CANDAL! I have lost my unit. How could this possibly have happened? Stupid question – anything could happen in a place like this. Anything you like. But, in short, no unit.

A baking sun overhead, scorched grass all around. A remote track. By the side of the track a two-wheeled cart, in the cart there's me, my medical orderly Shugayev and a pair of binoculars. But the main thing is there's not a soul to be seen. Not a soul on the plateau. However carefully you look through the Zeiss there is absolutely nothing. Everyone has disappeared into the ground – the ten-thousand-strong detachment with their cannon, as well as the Chechens. If it weren't for the smoke rising from the smouldering fire at Chechen-Aul, you could believe there'd never been anybody here.

Drawing himself up to his full height, Shugayev stood on the cart. He looked to his left, turned right round and looked to his right, then behind him, then in front, then up to the sky and climbed down, saying:

"What a lousy situation!"

I couldn't have put it better myself. It's not difficult to predict what will happen in the event of meeting the Chechens. For this you don't need to be a prophet.

...............................................................................

...Well, anyway, I am going to record everything down in my little notebook, everything to the last detail. It's interesting.

We set off in no particular direction.

...A raven soaring high into the sky. Another swooping down. And over there, there's a third. Why are they whirling around like that? We drive up in our cart. A Chechen lies on the edge of an abandoned field. His arms spread out like a cross. His head flung back. A ragged black Circassian cloak. Bare legs. No dagger. No bullets in his ammunition pouch. The Cossacks are a thrifty nation, just like Gogol's Osip.*

"Even a little piece of string will come in useful."*

Under his left cheekbone there is a black hole, from which a bloodstain, congealed in the sun, trickles down his chest like a ceremonial sash. Emerald flies swarm around, plastering the wound. The angry ravens circle close overhead croaking...

On, on!...

...The Zeiss is hallucinating! A hill, and on the very top of the hill, a bentwood chair! Absolute desert all around! Who has dragged a chair to the top of the hill? What for?...

...We drive cautiously round the hill. Nobody. We continue on our way, with the chair still lying there.

It's hot. I'm glad I've brought a full mess tin of water with me.

*Late afternoon*

It's over. They've attacked. There they are, the mountains, a stone's throw away. There is the gorge. And people are riding out of the gorge. Horses, horses! Silver swords gleaming... I wonder who will be getting my notebook? So nobody will read it! Shugayev has a greenish tinge to his face. As do I probably. Instinctively I finger the Browning in my pocket. Idiotic! What good will that do? Shugayev makes a sudden movement. Wants to spur the horses on and then freezes.

Idiotic. Their horses are a pleasant sight. How far would you get with two carthorses? You wouldn't get anywhere at all. Any one of them could throw up his rifle, take aim, and the game will be over.

"Oh, oh, oh," is all Shugayev could say.

They have spotted us. They race towards us, raising a cloud of dust. They gallop up to us, white teeth and silver gleaming. I glance up at the sun. Farewell, sun.

And, miracle of miracles!... They gallop up and circle round us, the horses dancing. They don't seize us, but they start making a racket:

"Ta-la-ha-ha!"

God knows what they want. I thrust my hand into my pocket, grasp the handle of the Browning and turn off the safety catch. If they grab me, I'll put the barrel in my mouth. Better that way. That's what I've been taught.

But they carry on with their infernal racket, beating themselves on the chest, baring their teeth and pointing into the distance.

"Allah-ma-mya... Bolgatoe-e!"

"Shali-Aul! Ga-go-gyr-gyr."

Shugayev has seen a thing or two in his life. Experienced chap. Suddenly his face flushed, the red overlaying the green. Then he waved his arms about and started talking in some astonishing language:

"Shali, you say? Right, right. Our Shali-Aul has gone, you say? Right, right. Bolgatoe. But where are all our forces? Over there?"

They break out into smiles. Amazing teeth. They wave their arms about and nod their heads.

Finally Shugaev's face takes on its normal colouring.

"They come in peace, doctor, sir! In peace! They've made peace. They say that our forces have gone to Shali-Aul via Bolgatoe. They want to go with us! Those are our troops over there! Would you believe it, our troops!"

When I look, I can see the dust at the foot of the slope. The end of the column leaving. Shugayev can see better than the Zeiss.

The Chechens have an admiring expression. They can't take their eyes off the Zeiss.

"They like the binoculars," giggled Shugayev.

"Oh yes, I can see that for myself. Yes, indeed. Let's catch up with the column straight away!"

Shugayev sways around on his seat, reading my thoughts. Then he says comfortingly:

"Don't get alarmed. They won't touch us here. Our forces are only over there! Only over there! If they'd been a mile or so farther away, then…" He merely made a gesture.

And everywhere around: "Gyr… gyr!"

If only I could just understand a single word of what they were saying! But Shugayev can understand and carries on talking to them. With his hands as well as with his tongue. They gallop alongside us, their swords jingling. Never travelled with an escort like that in my life…

# Chapter 11

## BY THE BONFIRE

T HE AUL'S ON FIRE. They're pursuing Uzun. Cold night. We huddle up to the bonfire, the flames playing on the sword hilts. They sit with their legs tucked under them and look with curiosity at the red cross on my sleeve. These are people who have made peace, submissive. Our allies. Shugayev is telling them with his hands and his tongue that I am the chief and most important doctor. They nod, with a respectful expression, their eyes shining. But if our forces had been a mile or so farther away...

# Chapter 12

..........................................................................................

# Chapter 13

*December*

THE COLUMN IS READY to move off. Everyone is drunk: the commander, the Cossacks, the group of train conductors and, worst of all, the engine driver. Eighteen degrees of frost. The carriages are like ice. Not a single stove. We leave at dead of night, the carriage doors firmly closed. We've wrapped ourselves up in anything that comes to hand. I give all the orderlies raw alcohol to drink. After all, you can't leave people to die, can you! The carriage sways, the wheels banging and screeching beneath us. We've set off.

I can't remember going to sleep or how I managed to leap out. But then I do clearly remember rolling down a slope covered with powdery snow and watching the carriages crashing and splintering, like matchboxes. They have smashed into each other. In the dim light of dawn people are pouring out of the carriages. Groaning and yelling. The engine driver has gone too fast, ignoring a red light and crashing into an oncoming train...

I'm sorry for Shugayev. His leg is broken.

Spend the rest of the night in the room at the station until morning, dressing the wounded and examining the dead...

When I have dressed my last patient, I go out onto the railway track, piled high with fragments of broken carriages. I look up at the pale sky. I look around me...

I see the shade of my medical assistant Golendryuk in front of me. But so what, damn it! I'm a member of the intelligentsia.

# Chapter 14

## THE GREAT FAILURE

*February*

C HAOS. The station is on fire. Then I speed off in a train. The end carriage is being flung about... Some lunacy or other. And now the wave has reached as far as here......

..................................................................

Today, at last, I've finally understood. Oh, immortal Golendryuk! That's enough idiocy and insanity. In the course of a single year I have managed to witness ten volumes' worth of Mayne Reid! But I'm not Mayne Reid, nor am I Louis Boussenard.* I am fed up to the back teeth, and bitten all over by lice. To be a member of the intelligentsia does not mean at all you have to be an idiot...
Enough!
The sea is getting closer and closer! The sea! The sea!

..................................................................

A curse on all wars, now and for ever more!

# Psalm

A T FIRST IT SOUNDS like a rat scratching at the door. But then I hear a very polite human voice:

"Can I come in?"

"Please, do."

The door hinges sing.

"Come in and sit down on the sofa."

(From the doorway): "But what about the floor?"

"Just walk quietly, and pick up your feet. Well, what's new?"

"Nuffing."

"Then who, may I ask, was that howling in the corridor this morning?"

(Long, heavy pause.) "Me."

"Why?"

"Mum was beating me."

"What for?"

(Extremely tense pause.) "I bit Thurka on the ear."

"Well, then."

"Mum thays Thurka's a good-for-nuffing. He teathes me, he'th taken money from me."

"All the same, there's no law which says you have to bite someone's ear for the sake of a few copecks. It means you're a stupid little boy."

(Offended.) "I don't want to be friendth with you any more."

"Well, don't then."

(Pause.) "When Dad getth back, I'll tell him." (Pause.) "He'll thoot you."

"Oh, he will, will he? Well, then, I'm not going to make any tea. What would be the point? If I'm going to be shot?"

"No, you mutht make the tea."

"Will you have some with me?"

"With thweets, too?"

"Of course."

"Then I'll have thome."

Two human bodies squatting down, one small, the other big. The kettle is singing away, boiling, and a cone of warm light shines on a page of Jerome K. Jerome.*

"I suppose you've forgotten the poem, have you?"

"No, I haven't."

"Well, go on then, let's hear it."

"I'll b... buy mythelf some thoos..."

"To match the dress coat."

"To match the dreth coat and at night I thall thing..."

"A psalm."

"A thalm... And I'll get mythelf a dog..."

"Noth..."

"No... no... thing..."

"And we'll start to live..."

"...thtart ... to live."

"Exactly. The tea will boil, we'll have a drink, we'll start to live." (Deep sigh.) "We'll thtart... to live."

Singing kettle. Jerome. Steam. Cone of light. Gleaming parquet.

"You're lonely."

Jerome falls on the parquet flooring. The page fades.

(Pause.) "And who told you that?"

(Innocent clarity.) "Mum."

"When?"

"When she thewed on a button for you. Thewed. Thews and thews and thays to Natathka..."

"I see. Wait, wait, keep still, otherwise I'll scald you... Ow!"

"Ow, itth hot!"

"Take a sweet, whichever one you want."

"I want that large one."

"Blow on it, blow on it, and stop swinging your legs."

(Woman's voice from the wings.) "Slavka!"

There's a knock on the door. The hinges sing pleasantly.

"Here he is, with you again. Slavka, come back home!"

"No, no we're having some tea."

"But he's only just had some."

(Quietly honest.) "I... didn't have any."

"Vera Ivanovna, come and have some tea."

"Thank you, I've just..."

"Come on, I won't let you..."

"My hands are wet... I'm hanging up the washing."

(Unsolicited intercession.) "Don't you dare tug at my mum."

"All right, I won't tug at her... Vera Ivanovna, please sit down."

"Wait a moment, I'll hang up the washing, and then I'll come."

"Wonderful. I'll keep the kerosene stove on."

"And you, Slavka, have some tea, and then go home. Have a sleep. You're being a nuisance."

"I'm not being a nuithanthe. I'm not being naughty."

The door hinges creak unpleasantly. Cones of light fall in various directions. The kettle is silent.

"How about having a sleep?"

"No, don't want to. Tell me a thtory."

"But your eyes are shutting."

"No, they're not. Tell me a thtory."

"Well, all right, come here. Rest your head. Like that. Story, you say? What story would you like, eh?"

"The one about the little boy, the little boy who..."

"About the little boy? That's a difficult story. Well, if that's what you want..."

"...So, then. Once upon a time there was this little boy. About four. In Moscow. With his mum. And this boy was called Slavka."

"Aha... Like me?"

"... Quite a good-looking little boy but, very unfortunately, he loved to pick a fight. And he used to fight by any means he could – with his fists, with his feet, and even with his galoshes. And one day, on the staircase, there was a little girl from no. 8, a wonderful little girl, quiet, very pretty, and he hit her on the face with a book."

"She fightth too."

"Hold on. I'm not talking about you."

"A different Thlavka?"

"Totally different. Where did I get to? Ah, yes... Well of course, they used to beat this Slavka every day – after all, you can't have fighting going on. But Slavka, nonetheless, didn't calm down. And matters got to the point where, one fine day, Slavka quarrelled with this other boy, Shurka, and, without too much thought, clenched his teeth on his ear and bit half of it off. There was such an almighty row. Shurka yelled. Slavka was whipped, and he yelled as well... Somehow or other they managed to reconnect Shurka's ear with some sort of glue. Slavka of course was made to stand in the corner... And then suddenly there's a ring on the doorbell. And a total stranger appears – some man with a huge ginger beard and wearing blue-framed glasses. 'May I ask, which one of you is Slavka?' he asks in a bass voice. Slavka answers: 'I'm Slavka.' 'Well, Slavka,' he says, 'I am the supervisor, the person responsible for all boys who love to fight, and I have to remove you from Moscow, my dear Slavka, and take you to Turkestan.' Slavka realizes that things aren't looking good, and says he's sincerely sorry for what he's done. 'I confess,' he says, 'that I have fought on the staircase, that I have played pitch penny, and that I lied to my mum, when I told her I hadn't played... But I will never do that again, because I am beginning a new life.' 'Well,' says his supervisor, 'that's another matter. In that case you deserve to be rewarded for such genuine remorse.' And immediately he takes Slavka to the warehouse where they keep all the rewards for handing out to people. And Slavka sees that the warehouse contains an immense quantity of all sorts of things. Balloons, and cars, and airplanes, and striped balls, and bicycles, and drums. And the supervisor says: 'Choose whatever you fancy.' But what Slavka chooses for himself, I've forgotten…"

(Low, deliciously sleepy voice.) "Bithycle."

"Yes, that's right, I remember now – a bicycle. And immediately Slavka gets on his bicycle and rides straight onto Kuznetsky Bridge, ringing his bell, while everyone stands on the pavement looking on in astonishment. 'What an amazing person this Slavka is. How does he manage not to be hit by a car?' But Slavka sounds his horn and shouts at the cabbies to 'keep to the right!' Cabs and cars race along, Slavka is becoming more and more excited, and the soldiers march along playing a march so loudly that it rings in your ears…"

"Already?"

The hinges sing. Corridor. Door. White arms, bare to the elbow.

"My God. Give him to me; I'll undress him."

"But come back. I'm waiting."

"It's late…"

"No, no… I won't hear of it."

"Well, all right."

Cones of light. There's a humming noise. Turn the wick up. Jerome not needed now – lies on the floor. A small, joyful hell burns away behind the blurred glass of the kerosene lamp. I will sing the psalm in the night. We'll manage to get through somehow or other. Yes, I am lonely. It's a sad psalm. I don't know how to live. Worst of all in life are buttons. They drop off, as if they've become rotten. One popped off my waistcoat yesterday. And today one came off my jacket and another off the back of my trousers. I'm no good with buttons, but I see everything and can understand everything. He won't come, and he won't shoot me. That time in the corridor she said to Natashka: "My husband will be back soon, and then we'll go to St Petersburg." But that's wrong: he won't come back. He won't come back, believe you me. He has been away for seven months, and I have happened to see her weeping on three occasions. You can't hide tears, you know. But he has lost so much, by abandoning those warm, white arms. That's his business, but I don't understand how he could have forgotten Slavka…

How happily the hinges sang.

No cones. A black mist in the blurred glass of the lamp. The kettle has long since fallen silent.

The light from the lamp peers out through the blurred glass with thousands of little eyes.

"You have wonderful fingers. You should have been a pianist…"

"When I get to St Petersburg, I'll start playing again…"

"You won't go to St Petersburg. Slavka has got just the same curls on the back of his head as you have. But I am not happy. It's boring being like this, extraordinarily boring. It's impossible to live like this. Buttons everywhere, buttons, butt…"

"Don't kiss me… don't kiss me. I must go. It's late…"

"You won't go: you'll just start crying. You have this habit."

"That's not true. I don't cry. Who told you I did?"

"I know: I've seen you myself. You will cry and I am so sad, so sad…"

"What am I doing… what are you doing?…"

No cones of light. No lamplight glowing through the blurred glass. Mist. Mist.

I have no buttons. I shall buy Slavka a bicycle. I will not buy any shoes to match a dress coat, I will not sing a psalm at night. Never mind; we'll start to live somehow.

# Moonshine Lake

A T TEN O'CLOCK on the eve of Easter Sunday our wretched corridor fell silent. In the blessed silence I was struck by the electrifying thought that my dream had come true and that old woman Pavlovna, the cigarette seller, had died. I came to this conclusion because I could no longer hear the yells of her son Shurka, whom she regularly used to abuse.

I gave a voluptuous smile, sat down in my tattered armchair and opened a volume of Mark Twain. Oh, what a blessed moment, what a radiant hour!...

...And at ten o'clock, in the corridor, the cock crowed thrice.

The fact of the cock's existence wasn't particularly unusual. After all, Pavlovna had kept a piglet in her room for some six months. And, in general, Moscow isn't Berlin – that's in the first place. And, in the second, if you've lived for eighteen months in corridor no. 50, you've ceased to be astonished by anything. It wasn't the fact of the unexpected appearance of the cock that frightened me, but the fact that it was crowing at ten o'clock in the evening. Cockerels are not nightingales – before the war they used to crow at dawn.

"Surely those devils haven't given the cock something to drink, have they?" I asked my long-suffering wife, tearing myself away from my Mark Twain.

But she didn't have any time to reply. The cock's introductory fanfare was followed by an uninterrupted screech. Then the sound of a man's voice bellowing. But what a bellow! It was an uninterrupted deep bellow in the key of C sharp, a deep howl of spiritual pain and despair, the sort of sound that precedes death.

There was the sound of every door banging and footsteps thundering along the corridor. I threw Mark Twain down and dashed out into the corridor.

In the corridor, under a light, surrounded by a tight ring of astonished residents of the famous corridor, stood a man who was totally unknown to me. His legs were spread wide apart in the form of an upside-down letter Y and he was swaying unsteadily. Without closing his mouth he was emitting the same frenzied bellow that had so alarmed me. There, in the corridor, I heard the long non-articulated note (*fermato*) change into a recitative.

"So, I see," the stranger was shouting hoarsely, choking the whole time and in floods of tears, "Christ is risen! That's a fine way to behave! I won't let anyone else have it! Aaargh!!"

And as he said this, he grabbed clumps of feathers from the cock's tail as it struggled in his hands.

One glance was sufficient to be convinced that the cock was completely sober. But its eyes expressed unearthly torment. They were popping out of their sockets, as it flapped its wings and struggled to free itself from the stranger's tight grasp.

Pavlovna, Shurka, the driver, Annushka, Annushka's Misha, Duska's husband and both Duskas were standing round in a ring in total silence and completely still, as if they had been nailed to the ground. On this particular occasion I can't blame them. Even they had been deprived of the gift of speech. For the first time in their lives, they were, like me, witnessing the plucking of a live cock.

With a lopsided and despairing grin on his face the owner of no. 50, Vasily Ivanovich, was clutching at the cock first by an elusive wing, then by its legs, in an attempt to tear it away from the stranger.

"Ivan Gavrilovich! For the love of God!" he shouted, growing soberer in front of my eyes. "Nobody's going to take your cockerel, may it be thrice cursed! Stop torturing the bird so close to Holy Easter Sunday! Ivan Gavrilovich, get hold of yourself!"

I was the first to come to my senses and, in an inspired lightning flash, I knocked the bird out of the man's hands. The cock rose into the air, crashed heavily into the light, then came down to the ground and disappeared round the corner towards Pavlovna's pantry. And at once the man fell silent.

As an incident it was whatever you wish, but it was extraordinary only in that there was a happy outcome in so far as I was concerned. The owner of no. 50 did not say to me that, if I didn't like my apartment, I could go and find myself a detached house. Pavlovna didn't say that I sat up with my light on until five a.m. doing "goodness knows what", or that there had been no point at all in intruding into her room. Or that she had the right to thrash Shurka, because he was her Shurka. Or that I should raise my "own Shurkas" and eat them with my porridge. Telling Pavlovna that if she "hit Shurka on the head just once more", I would take her to court and she would go to prison for abusing a young child, didn't help the situation. She threatened to complain to the management and have me evicted. "If someone doesn't like it, let him go to where there are educated people."

No, in a word, none of that happened on this occasion. All the residents of the most famous block of apartments in Moscow dispersed in sepulchral silence. The owner of no. 50 and Katerina Ivanovna took the stranger by the arm and led him to the staircase. He walked along without saying a word, crimson-faced, trembling and swaying unsteadily, the light going from his baleful swivelling eyes. He looked like someone who had been poisoned by belladonna (*atropa belladonna*).

Pavlovna and Shurka caught the enfeebled cockerel under a tub and took it away as well.

On her return, Katerina Ivanovna said:

"That son of a bitch" (by that she meant the owner of the block, Katerina Ivanovna's husband) "goes off to the shop if you please and buys three litres of vodka from Sidorovna. Then he invites Gavrilych. 'Come on,' he says, 'let's try some of this.' Typical men: they get blind drunk, may God forgive me my sins, before the priest rings the church bell. I can't imagine what got into Gavrilych. They drink and drink, and my old man says to him: 'No need to hold on to the cockerel when you go to the toilet, Gavrilych. Here, let me take it.' But Gavrilych completely loses his temper and says, 'So you want to requisition my cockerel, do you?' And he starts to howl. God knows what was going through his head!…"

At two a.m. the owner of the apartment, beside himself with rage, smashed all the window panes, thrashed his wife, justifying his action by telling her that she had poisoned his life. At that moment my wife and I were at matins, and the scandal carried on without any involvement on my part. All the apartment's residents shuddered and summoned the chairman of the management committee. He appeared straight away. With shining eyes and with a face like a red flag, he took one look at the black-and-blue Katerina Ivanovna and said:

"I'm astonished at you, Vasil Ivanych. You're the head of this apartment block and you can't even control your wife."

This was the first time ever in the life of our chairman when he was less than overjoyed with his own words. He personally, together with the driver and Duska's husband, had to take the knife away from Vasil Ivanych, in the course of which he cut his hand (after hearing what the chairman had had to say, Vasil Ivanych had armed himself with a kitchen knife, intending to use it on Katerina Ivanovna: "I'll show her!").

When the chairman had locked Katerina Ivanovna in Pavlovna's pantry, he set about persuading Ivanych that Katerina Ivanovna had run away, and Vasil Ivanych fell asleep with the words:

"Right. I'll stab her tomorrow. She won't get away from me."

The chairman left saying:

"Well, that's Sidorovna's moonshine for you. It's fiendish, that stuff."

Ivan Sidorych appeared at three a.m. I hereby proclaim to the whole world, that if I were a man and not such a wet blanket I would have thrown Ivan Sidorych out of his room. But I am afraid of him. After the chairman, he is the strongest character

on the board of management. Maybe I will not succeed in sling-
ing him out (or maybe I will, who the hell knows?), but he is able
to poison my existence without the least difficulty. And, for me,
that is the most terrible thing. If my existence is poisoned then I
cannot write feuilletons, and if I can't write any feuilletons then
I shall be financially ruined.

"Greet... citizen journalist," said Ivan Sidorych, swaying like a
blade of grass in the wind. "I've come to see you."

"That's nice."

"I've come about the Esperanto..."

"?"

"I'd like to write something... article... I'd like to start a
society... so write this down: Ivan Sidorych, Esperanto scholar,
wishes..."

And Sidorych suddenly started speaking Esperanto (an astonishingly revolting language by the way).

Whatever it was the Esperanto scholar stood there in front of
me reading, I only know that he suddenly hunched up and started
to spout strange words without any endings, a kind of mixture of
Latin and Russian, and then went on to something more mutually
comprehensible.

"However, I apologi... Come again tomorrow."

"You'll be most welcome," I said graciously, leading Ivan
Sidorych to the door (for some reason he had wanted to leave the
room through the wall).

"Can't you sling him out?" asked my wife when he had gone.

"No, my love, I can't."

At nine o'clock the following morning, the celebrations opened
with a sailors' dance from Holland, performed by Vasily Ivanovich
on the accordion and danced by Katerina Ivanovna. And then
there was an incoherent and inebriated speech from Annushka's
Misha in which he paid his respects to me on behalf of himself
and on behalf of a number of other citizens, all unknown to me.

At ten o'clock the junior janitor turned up (slightly the worse
for drink), and then, at twenty past ten, the senior janitor arrived

(completely sozzled). And then, at twenty-five minutes past ten, the boiler man appeared (in a terrible condition, said nothing and, still saying nothing, left immediately, losing the five million I gave him, right there, in the corridor).

At midday, Sidorovna cheekily poured out three fingers' worth less vodka than Vasily Ivanovich was due. At which he went to the appropriate authorities with the evidence and announced:

"People are selling moonshine. I want you to make an arrest."

"Are you sure you've got that right?" he was asked by the appropriate authorities. "According to our information, there is no moonshine in your block."

"Really?" said Vasily Ivanovich with a twisted smile. "I find your words totally astonishing."

"No, we're right: there isn't any. And, anyway, how is it that you've turned up sober, if you've got moonshine with you? Why don't you go home and sleep it off? Come back tomorrow and tell us whose moonshine it is."

"Right… I understand," Vasily Ivanovich said, with a dumbfounded smile. "So, there's no way of stopping them then? Let them sell us short. But as for whether I'm sober or not, have a sniff at this vodka."

The three litres of vodka clearly turned out to smell of "fuel oil".

"Bring her here!" they said to Vasily Ivanovich. So he brought her.

When Vasily Ivanovich woke up, he said to Katerina Ivanovna:

"Run to Sidorovna and get three litres of vodka."

"Get a grip, you bloody old fool," replied Katerina Ivanovna. "Sidorovna's been closed down."

"What? How did they sniff her out?"

I was in seventh heaven. But not for long. Within half an hour, Katerina had appeared with a full three litres. It turned out that a fresh source had been found at Makeich's, two doors away from Sidorovna. At seven that evening I tore Natasha away from her husband, the baker Volodya ("Don't you dare hit her!", "She's my wife!", etc., etc.)

At eight o'clock that evening, with the high-spirited sailors' dance still crashing away and with Annushka just starting to dance, my wife got up from the sofa and said:

"I can't stand it any longer. I don't mind what you do, but we must get out of here."

"But my love," I answered in despair, "what can I do? I can't get a room; it would cost twenty billion, and I only get four. Until I've finished the novel, we've no hope of getting anything. Be patient."

"I'm not asking for myself," my wife replied, "but you will never be able to finish your novel. Never. It's hopeless. I shall take morphine."

When she said this I felt myself turning to iron.

When I replied, my voice was full of metal:

"No, you won't take morphine, because I won't allow you to. But I will finish the novel, and I venture to say that it will be of such quality that it will set the sky on fire."

Then I helped my wife to get dressed, locked and bolted the door, asked Dusya No. 1 (she drank nothing except port) to make sure that nobody broke the lock and took my wife to my sister on Nikitskaya Street for the three days of the festival.

## Conclusion

I HAVE A PLAN. My plan is that, within two months, I shall have turned Moscow into a city of teetotallers, if not fully, then at least by ninety percent.

On the following conditions: I will be the head of the project. I myself will pick the workforce, from students. Their salary will have to be set at a very high level (about 400 gold roubles – justified by the project's importance). One hundred people. For me personally, a three-roomed apartment with a kitchen and, at the same time, one thousand gold roubles. A pension for my wife in the event that someone murders me.

Unlimited powers. People to be arrested immediately on my order. The judicial process to take place within twenty-four hours, and no fines in lieu of imprisonment.

I shall destroy the lives of all Sidorovnas and Makeiches, together with the destruction of all "Little Hideyholes", "Flowers of Georgia", "Tamara's Castles" and similar places.

Moscow will become like the Sahara, in which the oases will be lit up by electric signs saying "Open Until Midnight", and selling only light-red and white wines.

# Makar Devushkin's Story*

W E MAY NOT LIVE AS PEOPLE DO in the capital, but nonetheless it's an interesting, complicated existence, and there
are an unbelievable number of things going on here, each more
astonishing than the next.

## Trousers and Elections

Look, for example, what happened in the following case: our local
Party secretary Fitilyov bought himself a pair of striped cheviot
cloth trousers. In a world-class city, such as Moscow for example,
there would be nothing surprising in this – everyone goes around
in striped trousers there – but in our part of the world it's quite
a novelty!

Everybody wanted to see Fitilyov's trousers of course. But the
trouble was that Fitilyov was a very organized person, and he did
not want people to show the world his trousers until the time was
right. And then, completely unexpectedly, a notice was posted
up announcing the legendary general meeting of all the station's
Party members. The agenda included such items as a report by
the Chairman of the local Education Trade Union Committee, a
report from the Railway Workers' Management Committee and,
as a finale, a report from the local Party Committee, together with
the holding of re-elections – the main point of the proceedings.

In addition, the general word went around that our secretary, the celebrated Fitilyov, would be speaking at this splendid

gathering, and that he would be wearing his new acquisition. As a result, the hall became so packed full of people that it became unbearably stuffy. And, indeed, Fitilyov appeared in a pair of trousers with such creases and so magnificently tailored that they resembled those on the metal statue of Pushkin in Moscow.

So then, all very excellent. At exactly six o'clock the chairman stood up and declared the meeting open, and our magnificent Education Trade Union chairman appeared, coughed and barked out his speech to the gathering. He began with a report on the railwaymen's congress, a report which lasted from six o'clock to nine o'clock, or, as we say nowadays, twenty-one hundred hours, and during which he drank a total of half a decanter of first-class water. I cannot describe the reaction in the hall, except for the fact that the entire first row fell asleep, followed by the second row, just as on a battlefield. The chairman rang his bell, asking people to remain alert, but to no purpose. How can someone be alert when he is asleep?

But a thunderstorm in the form of repairman Vasya Danilov broke out, disturbing the usual flow of a professional meeting. Vasya stood up from the ranks and burst into tears as if he had lost his life's companion, his wife. Then, addressing his remarks to the speaker in a thunderous voice, he said:

"If you don't shut your trap, I'll top myself! After an eight-hour shift there's no way I'm going to go on sitting here listening to your facts."

At this there was much excitement among the packed rows of people, who only calmed down when Vasya was excluded from the meeting.

As Vasya left the room, sobbing all the way to the door, he made the following remark that many found enticing:

"I'm off to the pub, comrades. I won't be able to stand another speech unless I've had some beer."

And a number of other people left the room with him. Worried that there might not be sufficient people to form a quorum, the chairman dismissed the first speaker, replacing him with a second speaker who spoke about the work of the management committee until twenty-three hundred hours, with an extra two hours on some figures or other. No trousers were of any help here, and even Fitilyov himself started looking down at his white hands and fell asleep while pretending to be listening. The young women who had been looking admiringly at the handsome figure of Fitilyov all left the room – they couldn't stay any longer, even though he was a bachelor.

And then finally, after midnight, Fitlilyov came to life at the end of the speech and excelled himself by killing the meeting stone dead on the spot. He stood up on the platform, screwed up his eyes and declaimed:

"In the name of the All-Russian Communist Party of Bolsheviks..."

The entire assembly woke up, because everybody thought he would be making a radio announcement of international significance, but he went on:

"...of the local Party cell here at the station, and in the name of the Area Party Committee, I present the list of candidates for the local Party Committee. And since, comrades, I have been entrusted to oversee this process, I will permit no candidate to be rejected or replaced."

Accompanied by his colleagues, Vasya Danilov had returned to the hall, cheerfully looking forward to the re-elections, preparing to launch into a healthy critique of the candidates, and he even opened his mouth to do so.

"So there's a pretty kettle of fish!" he shouted, and raised his hand in agreement, without criticizing anybody.

And everybody followed suit.

But when they had all dispersed, some worm wriggled away inside me so that I could hold out no longer. I asked our Party representative, Nazar Nazarych, a cultivated fellow:

"Is it true – all that stuff about 'in the name of the All-Russian Communist Party', and that no one should dare utter a word?"

And he said:

"Nothing of the sort!... It's a pity I was ill in bed, otherwise I would have sorted it out. Absolute scandal! Khlestakov in striped trousers.* It's not real life, but disgusting red tape!"

And he went on and on.

So that's the kind of original meeting we have in our primitive neck of the woods.

# A Scurvy Character

IF YOU ARE TO BELIEVE the statistics that have been compiled recently by a certain citizen (I have read them myself) proclaiming that, for every thousand people, there are two geniuses and two idiots, one has to acknowledge that the metalworker Puzyryov was undoubtedly one of the two geniuses. This genius Puzyryov came home one day and said to his wife:

"So, Marya, I have no money left at all."

"That's because you spend it all on drink, you useless fool," Marya replied. "So what are we going to eat now?"

"Don't worry, my dear," Puzyryov answered solemnly. "We'll be able to eat!"

As he said this, Puzyryov bit his lower lip with his upper teeth so fiercely that it started to spurt blood. Then the brilliant bloodsucker began to lick at this blood and swallow it, until he had sucked it all up like a tick.

Then the metalworker put on his cap, licked his lip and went to the hospital, to Dr Poroshkov's surgery.

"What's the matter, my good chap?" Poroshkov asked Puzyryov.

"I'm dying, citizen doctor," Puzyryov answered, and clutched at the door post.

"What do you mean?" said the doctor in astonishment. "You're looking wonderful."

"Won... der... ful? May God punish you for saying such a thing," Puzyryov replied, his voice fading, and he began to lean over to one side like a blade of grass.

"So tell me what you're feeling then."

"This mor...ning I began to bleed... Right, I thought, that's it, goodbye... Puzyryov. Until we meet again in the next world. You will be in paradise, Puzyryov... Goodbye Marya, my wife, I say... Think well of me, your Puzyryov!"

"Bleed?" asked the doctor sceptically, feeling Puzyryov's stomach. "Bleed? Bleed, you say? Does it hurt?"

"Ow!" Puzyryov exclaimed, his eyes rolling. "Will I have time to write my will?"

"Comrade Fenatsetinov," Poroshkov shouted to his assistant, "stomach examination, and we'll do a blood test."

"What the devil!" muttered the incredulous Poroshkov, as he looked at the glass container. "Your blood! My God, your blood! Never seen anything like it. And someone who on the face of it is in such wonderful shape..."

"Farewell, world," said Puzyryov, as he lay on the couch. "Never again will I stand by my lathe, never again participate in meetings, never again put forward any resolutions..."

"Don't be down-hearted, there's a good fellow," Poroshkov said sympathetically, trying to console him.

"What's wrong with me? Something serious?" Puzyryov asked, wilting away.

"You've got a large stomach ulcer. But that's all right, we can make it better. Firstly, you need to rest in bed, and then I will give you some pills."

"But will it be worth it, doctor?" said Puzyryov. "You don't need to waste your precious medicines on a dying metalworker. They'll be more use for the living... don't worry at all about Puzyryov: he's already half in his grave..."

"Poor chap, he's in such a state!" thought the soft-hearted Poroshkov, and gave Puzyryov some valerian drops.

For his large stomach ulcer Puzyryov was given eighteen roubles seventy-nine copecks, time off work and some pills. Puzyryov tossed the pills down the toilet, and used the eighteen roubles seventy-nine copecks in the following way: he gave the seventy-nine copecks to Marya for the housekeeping, and spent the eighteen roubles on drink...

"We have no money again, dear Marya," said Puzyryov, "pour a drop or two of sweet-grass vodka in my eyes."

That very same day Puzyryov went to see Dr Kaplin with his eyes bandaged. Two medical orderlies led him by the arm, as if he were an archbishop. He said, sobbing:

"Farewell, farewell, world! I've ruined my eyes working at my lathe..."

"What the devil's this!" said Dr Kaplin. "I've never seen such a nasty inflammation in my life before. How did you get it?"

"It's probably something I've inherited, my dear doctor," Puzyryov said with a sob.

For the eye inflammation Puzyryov received a clear twenty-two roubles and a pair of glasses in a tortoiseshell frame.

Puzyryov sold the tortoiseshell frame at the market and divided the twenty-two roubles as follows: he gave two roubles to Marya, then he took one and a half roubles back, saying he would give them to her that evening, and then he spent this one and a half plus the remaining twenty on drink.

Then this genius Puzyryov filched five caffeine tablets from somewhere or other and gulped down all five at once, so that his heart began leaping around like a frog. He was carried on a stretcher to Dr Miksturina, who gasped when she saw him.

"Your heart has such a defect," said Dr Miksturina, who had only just graduated, "that you should immediately be taken to the clinic in Moscow, where students would explore every part of your body. It will be such a pity to let a defect like that go to waste!"

The diseased Puzyryov received forty-eight roubles and went on a trip to Kislovodsk for two weeks. He divided the forty-eight roubles as follows: he gave eight roubles to Marya, while he spent the remaining forty by striking up an acquaintance with an unknown blonde woman he met on the train near Mineral Waters.

"I have no idea what I am going to fall ill with now," he said to himself, "except that I'll have to develop the most massive boil on my leg."

For the boil Puzyryov received thirty copecks. He went to the chemist's and, with these thirty copecks, bought some turps. Then, from an accountant friend, he borrowed a syringe for injecting arsenic, and used the syringe to inject the turps into his leg. It was so painful that Puzyryov howled.

"Well, now we'll get about fifty roubles from those idiot doctors for this boil," he thought as he hobbled to the hospital.

But then disaster struck.

At the hospital there was a medical board in session, headed by a morose, unfriendly man in gold-rimmed glasses.

"Hmm," said the unfriendly man and gave Puzyryov a piercing look through the golden hoops of his glasses, "a boil, you say? Right... off with your trousers!"

Puzyryov took off his trousers and before he had had time to look round the boil had been lanced.

"Hmm..." the unfriendly man said, "So, it looks as if you have turps in your boil. Can you explain to me, comrade metalworker, how it managed to get there?"

"I have no idea," Puzyryov answered, feeling an abyss yawning beneath him.

"Well, I have," said the hostile gold-rimmed glasses.

"Don't ruin me, citizen doctor," Puzyryov said and burst into tears, this time perfectly genuine and without any inflammation.

But they did ruin him, all the same.

And serves him right too.

# The Murderer

D R YASHVIN GAVE a strange, crooked smile and asked: "Can I tear off the page from the calendar? It's now exactly midnight – that means it's now the 2nd."

"Please, go ahead," I answered.

With his pale, slender fingers Yashvin took hold of one corner of the calendar and carefully removed the top sheet, revealing a page of rather cheap paper with the number "2" and the word "Tuesday". But Yashvin's attention had been caught by something extraordinarily interesting on the grey page. He frowned as he examined it more closely, and then he looked up and into the distance – he could obviously see something that was visible only to him, something mysterious lying somewhere beyond the wall of my room, and perhaps, even, far beyond night-time Moscow and the menacing haze of a February frost.

"What's caught his attention there?" I wondered, with a sidelong glance at the doctor. I had always found him interesting. Somehow his outward appearance did not seem to go with his profession. People who did not know him always assumed he was an actor. Although he had dark hair he was at the same time extremely fair-skinned, and this lent him a particular charm that singled him out from many others. He was very clean-shaven, always neatly dressed, and he simply loved going to the theatre. Whenever he spoke about the theatre, it was always with great taste and erudition. What distinguished him from all our other house surgeons – and, on this occasion, as one of my guests – was above all his footwear. There were five of us in the room. Four were wearing cheap-looking box-calf boots with rather crude rounded toes, whereas Dr Yashvin was wearing sharply pointed patent-leather shoes and yellow gaiters. I should add, moreover, that Yashvin's foppishness never made a particularly unpleasant impression on people and, to give him his due, he was a very good doctor. Bold, successful and, most importantly, finding the time to read, despite his frequent visits to performances of *Die Walküre* and *The Barber of Seville*.*

It was not a question of his shoes, of course, but of something else. He had one unusual quality which interested me: although he was generally a taciturn and secretive person, he could at times become an astonishing storyteller. He spoke very calmly, without embellishment or any mannerisms such as overemphasizing his words or irrelevant bleating noises, and always on very interesting topics. The normally restrained, foppish doctor seemed to burst into life, only occasionally making short-lived flowing gestures with his pale right hand, as if marking the existence of significant moments in his narrative. When recounting something amusing, he would never smile, but his figures of speech were so apposite and eloquent that every time I listened to him just one wistful thought came into my head. "You're a very good doctor, but you've taken the wrong road; you should have been nothing else but a writer..."

And that was the thought that was going through my head now – even though on this particular occasion Yashvin was not saying anything, but peering at the figure "2" and into the unknown distance.

"What's caught his attention? Some picture or other, perhaps?" I glanced over my shoulder and saw the most uninteresting picture possible, depicting an incongruous-looking horse with a powerful chest standing next to an engine. Underneath there were the words: "Comparative size of a horse (one horsepower) with an engine (five hundred horsepower)".

"That's all nonsense, comrades," I said, continuing our conversation. "Common-or-garden gossip. People, damn them, heap blame on doctors as if they were no longer alive, and in particular they blame us, the surgeons. Think about it: someone will remove an appendix a hundred times, but then, the hundred and first time, the patient goes and dies on the operating table. He's murdered the patient, I suppose, has he?"

"Yes, that's what they always say: he's murdered the patient," Dr Hintz replied.

"And if it's someone's wife, then the husband will come to the clinic and hurl a chair at you," agreed Dr Plonsky fervently and even smiled. We smiled with him, although essentially there's not much to smile about when it comes to hurling chairs about in a clinic.

"I cannot stand it," I continued, "when people start falsely apologizing, saying things like 'I killed him, goodness I murdered him!' None of us murder anybody, and if we do kill one of our patients, then it's the result of an unfortunate coincidence. It's really funny, isn't it! Our profession is not compatible with the idea of murder, damn it!... I define murder as the premeditated and intentional destruction of someone and, in the worst case, with the desire to kill him. A surgeon with a pistol in his hand – that I can understand. But I have never come across a surgeon like that in my life, and am very unlikely to do so."

Dr Yashvin suddenly turned his head towards me, and I noticed the intense expression in his eyes.

"I am at your service," he said.

As he said that he jabbed his finger into his tie and once again gave a crooked smile, but this time with the corner of his mouth rather than with his eyes.

We looked at him in astonishment.

"What do you mean?" I asked.

"I have killed someone," he said.

"When?" I asked absurdly.

Yashvin pointed to the figure "2" and answered:

"Just imagine, what a coincidence. As soon as you started talking about death, I looked at the calendar and saw that the date was the second. And, actually, I always remember that particular night when the date comes round every year. You see, it's exactly seven years, to the night, and possibly…" Yashvin took out his black watch and looked at it. "Yes, that's right, almost to the hour, on the night of the first to the second of February I killed him."

"A patient?" asked Hins.

"Yes, a patient."

"But not deliberately?" I asked.

"Yes, deliberately."

"Well," remarked the sceptic Plonsky through his teeth, "he must have had cancer. He was dying in agony, and so you gave him ten times the prescribed dose of morphine…"

"No, morphine's got nothing at all to do with it," Yashvin replied. "And he certainly didn't have cancer. I can remember it perfectly well: there was about fifteen degrees of frost, and the stars… Oh, what stars there are in the Ukraine! Here I am, I have been living in Moscow for almost seven years, and yet I still have this yearning to go back to my motherland. My heart misses a beat, as I am tormented by the longing to get on a train and return. To see the snow-covered precipices once again… the Dnieper… There's no more beautiful city in the world than Kiev."

Yashvin tucked the page from the calendar in his wallet, settled down in an armchair and continued:

"Redoubtable city, threatening times… I've seen terrible things which you Muscovites have never seen. It was 1919, the first of February exactly. It was already dusk, about six o'clock in the evening. At that moment I was busy doing something very strange. The lamp on my table was lit, it was warm and cosy in my room, and I was sitting on the floor stuffing various bits and pieces into a small suitcase and whispering one word to myself:

"'Run, run…'

"I would put a shirt into the case and then take it out again… the damned thing wouldn't fit in. It was only hand luggage, a tiny little suitcase; my underpants took up so much space, then the hundreds of cigarettes, my stethoscope. The suitcase was bulging. I chucked the shirt down and began to listen. The window panes had been sealed with putty for the winter, but I could hear something... the sound was muffled, but I could definitely hear something... way, way in the distance there was the dull boom-boom of heavy artillery. A burst of gunfire followed by silence. I looked out of the window – I lived on a steep slope at the top of St Alexei's Hill, I could see the whole of Podol.* Night was rolling in from the Dnieper, shrouding the houses, and row upon row of lights were gradually being turned on... Then another burst of gunfire. And every time I could hear the gunfire on the far bank of the Dnieper, I would whisper to myself:

"'Come on, again, again!'

"The fact was that, at that time, everyone in the city knew that Petlyura* was on the point of abandoning it. If not on that particular night then on the next. The Bolsheviks were advancing from the other side of the Dnieper, masses of them if people were to be believed, and it has to be said that the entire city was waiting for them not merely with impatience but, I would even say, with delight. Why? Because the way Petlyura's forces had behaved in Kiev during the final month of their occupation of the city was beyond imagination. Pogroms flaring up constantly, people being murdered every day, with of course Jews being singled out in particular. Requisitions all the time, with cars racing around the city carrying people with red braided tassels on their fur hats, with distant gunfire that recently had not let up even for an hour. Day and night. Everybody was in a state of anxiety, with sharp, alarmed eyes. And, lying in the snow under my window, were two bodies. They had been there for half a day, since the night before – no more. One was wearing a grey greatcoat, the other in a black army blouse, and neither of them had boots on. And the people would now dart away to one side, now gather together in groups to watch, and bareheaded old women would suddenly appear from gateways and shout, shaking their fists at the sky:

"'Just you wait! The Bolsheviks are coming, they're coming.'

"Those two people, who had been killed for some unknown reason, were a pitiable and disgusting sight. So much so that, in the end, I started waiting for the Bolsheviks as well. And the Bolsheviks were getting closer and closer. The distance began to melt away, and the distant cannon now began roaring, as if from the bowels of the earth.

"Anyway...

"Anyway... there I was alone in my room in the comforting but also slightly threatening glow of the lamp, my books lying all over the place (the point was that, in the midst of all this confusion, I was nurturing the lunatic idea of studying for a higher degree), and me standing over my small suitcase.

"I have to say that events erupted into my room, taking me by the scruff of my neck. Everything began to develop in nightmarish fashion. On the evening in question I had returned home from the suburbs, from the hospital where I worked as a house doctor in the gynaecological department and there, tucked into a crack of the door, I had found a nasty-looking official packet. I ripped it open there and then on the landing, read what was written on the sheet of paper and sat down right there on the staircase.

"The following words had been typewritten in blue:

"'This hereby notifies you...'

"In short, to translate into Russian:

"'On receipt of this, you are to report within two hours to the medical authorities and await further instructions.'

"The position, in other words, was this: here we had this very same brilliant army leaving dead bodies on the streets, old man Petlyura, the pogroms, and I was part of it all with a red cross on my sleeve... I sat there on the staircase, thinking about it for no more than a minute. I leapt up as if on springs, went into my apartment, and there was the suitcase taking centre stage. My plan quickly ripened. Get out of the apartment with a few clean clothes and go to a medical orderly friend of mine in the suburbs, a gloomy-looking man with clear leanings towards the Bolsheviks.

I would sit it out in his place until Petlyura had been kicked out. But what if he weren't kicked out? Perhaps these long-awaited Bolsheviks were simply a myth. Where were the guns now? They had fallen silent. No, there was the roar once more…

"I angrily tossed my shirt to one side, clicked the suitcase shut, put my Browning and a spare cartridge case in my pocket, put on my greatcoat with its red-cross armband, took a final melancholy look around the apartment, switched off the lamp and groped my way through the twilight shadows out into the hall, switched on the light, took my hood and opened the door onto the landing.

"And, immediately, two figures with short cavalry carbines slung over their shoulders stepped into the hall, coughing.

"One of them was wearing spurs, the other was without spurs, but both were in fur hats with blue tassels dangling jauntily on their cheeks.

"My heart missed a beat.

"'Are you Dr Yashvin?' asked the first cavalryman in Ukrainian.

"'Yes,' I replied glumly.

"'You are to come with us,' the first one said.

"'What is the meaning of this?' I asked, coming to my senses a little.

"'Sabotage, that's what,' he answered, his spurs crashing, as he gave me a sly, cheery look. 'Doctors don't want to be mobilized and are therefore answerable to the law.'

"The hall went dark, the door clicked, staircase… street.

"'But where are you taking me?' I asked, fingering the soft cold ribbed handle in my trousers pocket.

"'To the First Cavalry Regiment,' answered the one with the spurs.

"'What for?'

"'What do you mean "what for"?' the other one asked in astonishment. 'You have been appointed to us as a doctor.'

"'Who is the regimental commander?'

"'Colonel Leshchenko,' the first one answered with some pride, as his spurs jangled rhythmically against my left side.

"'What a stupid son of a bitch I was,' I thought, 'dreaming over my suitcase. Because of some underpants… What would it have cost me to have left five minutes earlier?…'

"The black frosty sky was already hanging over the city and the stars were out as we came to a detached house. Electric lights flickered in the window panes, patterned with frost. With a crash of spurs I was led into a dusty empty room, dazzlingly lit by an electric light hanging under a broken opal-glass lampshade. In one corner there was the protruding nose of a machine gun and, in the same corner, I was struck by the sight of rust-red streaks next to the machine gun, where there was an expensive tapestry hanging down in tatters.

"'That must be blood surely,' I thought, and my heart lurched unpleasantly.

"'Colonel, sir,' the one with the spurs said quietly, 'we've brought you a doctor.'

"'A Yid?' someone exclaimed suddenly from somewhere in a dry, hoarse voice.

"The door hung with a tapestry depicting shepherds was flung open silently and someone ran into the room.

"He was wearing a magnificent greatcoat and spurred boots. There was a tight Caucasian belt with silver buckles round his waist, and a Caucasian sword on his thigh glittered in the reflected electric light. He was wearing a lambskin cap with a crimson top and crossed by a golden galloon. His slanting eyes had a malicious, wary, somewhat strange expression, as if they contained little black balls leaping around inside. His face was covered in pockmarks and his black trimmed moustache twitched nervously.

"'No, he's not a Yid,' the cavalry man answered.

"Then the man came right up to me and looked in my eyes.

"'You're not a Yid,' he said with a strong Ukrainian accent, speaking incorrectly in a mixture of Russian and Ukrainian, 'but you're no better than one. And when the war is over I'll hand you over to a military tribunal. You'll be shot for sabotage. Don't let him out of your sight!' he ordered the cavalry man. 'And give the doctor a horse.'

"I stood there in silence with, it has to be assumed, a pale face. After that everything started to proceed as if in a blurred dream. Someone in the corner said plaintively:

"'Please, colonel, sir…'

"I vaguely made out a quivering little beard and a ragged army greatcoat. All around I could glimpse the faces of cavalry men.

"'So, a deserter?' sang a familiar voice hoarsely. 'You bastard, you!'

"I saw the colonel, his mouth twitching, remove an elegant and ominous-looking pistol from his holster and strike the man with the ragged coat in his face with the butt. The man threw himself to one side, beginning to choke in his own blood. He fell to his knees, the tears pouring from his eyes.

"And then the white frost-covered city disappeared from sight. The tree-lined road stretched along the banks of the stony black and mysterious River Dnieper. Strung out like a snake, the First Cavalry Regiment was moving along the road.

"At the back of the column two-wheeled carts bounced and occasionally rumbled along. The black lances swayed and the pointed hoods, covered in hoar frost, were sharply prominent. I was sitting on a cold saddle, shifting my sometimes painfully numb toes around in my boots, breathing through the opening in my hood, fringed by a layer of hardened frost, and feeling my little suitcase attached to the pommel of my saddle pressing against my left thigh. My ever-present escort rode along silently next to me. Just like my feet, everything inside me seemed to have become frozen. From time to time I looked up at the large stars in the sky, and I could hear the occasional yell of the deserter ringing in my ears and then fading away, as if it had dried up. Colonel Leshchenko had ordered him to be beaten with rods, with the beating taking place in the detached house.

"The black distances had fallen silent, and I was overcome with sorrow at the thought that the Bolsheviks had probably been repulsed. My fate seemed hopeless. We were advancing into Slobodka, where we were to take up positions and guard the bridge across the Dnieper. If the fighting were to quieten down and if I were no longer needed immediately, then Colonel Leshchenko would put me on trial. At the thought of this something went dead inside me and I wistfully and lovingly looked up at the stars. In view of my unwillingness to make myself available within a two-hour period at such a difficult time, it was not difficult to guess what the outcome of any military tribunal might be. An outrageous fate for someone with a diploma.

"Two hours later, however, everything had changed once more, as if in a kaleidoscope. The black road had now disappeared, and I found myself in a whitewashed room. A lamp stood on the wooden table, and there were some breadcrumbs and a broken medical bag. My feet had recovered and I had warmed up – there was a bright-red fire blazing in the black metal stove. From time to time cavalrymen would appear for treatment. Mostly for frostbite. They took off their boots, unwound their leggings and squatted by the fire. There was a sour smell of sweat, cheap tobacco and iodine in the room. At times my escort would leave me and I would find myself on my own. 'Run!' I would half-open the door, look out and see a staircase lit by a guttering stearin candle, faces and rifles. The entire house was packed with people, and it would have been difficult to escape. I was right in the heart of their headquarters. From the door I would return to the table and sit down in exhaustion, placing my head in my hands and listening attentively. Looking at the clock, I noticed that every five minutes a scream would emanate from downstairs underneath me. I already knew exactly what was going on – people were being beaten with rods. Sometimes the screaming turned into something like the resonant roar of a lion, and at other times into gentle – or so it seemed through the floor – entreaties and groans, as if two people were having an intimate conversation with a friend, but then sometimes breaking off abruptly, as if cut with a knife.

"'Why are you doing that to them?' I asked one of Petlyura's men, as he stretched out his trembling hands in front of the fire. He had rested his bare foot on a stool, and I was smearing the black-and-blue ulcer next to his frostbitten big toe with ointment.

"'There's an underground group located in Slobodka,' he replied. 'Communists and Yids. The colonel's interrogating them.'

"I said nothing. When he had gone, I wrapped my head in my hood so as to muffle the sounds. I sat there like that for about a quarter of an hour, my head full of images of a pockmarked face under gold galloons. Then I was woken out of my reverie by the voice of my escort.

"'The Colonel is asking for you.'

"I stood up and, removing my hood in front of my escort's astonished gaze, I followed him out of the room. We went downstairs to the lower floor and I went into a white room, where I saw Colonel Leshchenko in the lamplight.

"He was naked to the waist and writhing around on a stool, clutching a bloodstained piece of gauze to his chest. A confused-looking young lad stood next to him, stamping his feet, his spurs jangling.

"'The bastard,' said the colonel through grated teeth. Then he turned to me and said: 'Well, doctor, bandage me up. Leave us,' he ordered the young lad, who made his way to the door, his spurs crashing. The house had gone quiet. And, at that moment, the window pane shook. The colonel glanced at the dark window, as did I. 'Artillery,' I thought. I gave a trembling sigh and asked:

"'How did you get this?'

"'With a penknife,' the colonel replied morosely.

"'Who did it?'

"'It's none of your business,' he replied angrily and scornfully. 'So, doctor, things don't look too good for you.'

"It suddenly struck me what had happened: 'Somebody must have been unable to stand his torture, threw himself on him and stabbed him. That must have been it…'

"'Take the gauze off,' I said, bending down to his chest covered in black hair. But before he had time to remove the bloody rag, there was the sound of hurried footsteps behind the door and a voice shouted coarsely:

"'Stop, stop, damn it... where...'

"The door crashed open and an unkempt woman burst into the room. There was no sign of tears on her face, and she even seemed cheerful. It was only later, a long time afterwards, that it occurred to me that a state of extreme fury can express itself in very strange ways. Someone's grey hand tried to catch hold of the woman's headscarf, but she tore herself free.

"'Go away, lad, go away,' the colonel ordered and the hand disappeared.

"The woman looked at the semi-clothed colonel and said drily, without any tears:

"'Why did you shoot my husband?'

"'He was shot, as he deserved to be,' the colonel replied and winced in pain. The scrap of gauze under his fingers was growing redder and redder.

"She smiled in such a way that I could not tear myself away from the expression in her eyes. I had never seen eyes like that. And then she turned to me and said:

"'And you a doctor!'

"She jabbed her finger at the red cross on my sleeve and shook her head.

"With her eyes blazing, she made disapproving noises and said: 'You, you bastard... you've got a university degree, and yet here you are with this riff-raff... On their side, bandaging up their wounds! He carries on hitting people in the face until they go out of their minds... And you bandage up his wound?...'

"Everything went blurry in front of my eyes. So much so that I began to feel sick, and I felt that the most terrible and unexpected moments in my ill-fated career as a doctor had just started to unfold.

"'Are you talking to me?' I asked, feeling myself trembling. 'To me?... But you know...'

"But she did not want to listen to me. She turned to the colonel and spat in his face. He leapt up and shouted:

"'Lads!'

"When they burst into the room, he said angrily:

"'Twenty-five lashes with the rod.'

"She said nothing, and they dragged her away. The colonel closed the door and put it on the latch. Then he lowered himself onto the stool and threw the piece of gauze away. Blood was seeping out of the small wound. The colonel wiped away the spittle from the moustache on the right side of his face.

"'A woman?' I asked in a totally hostile voice.

"His eyes flared with anger.

"'Aha…' he said, giving me a threatening look. 'Now I can see exactly what type of person I've been given instead of a doctor…'"

............................................................................

"I must evidently have fired one bullet into his mouth, because I can remember him swaying on the stool and the blood gushing out of his mouth. Then bloodstains appeared on his chest and stomach, the light in his eyes faded, turning from black to the colour of milk, and he crashed to the floor. As I shot at him I can remember wanting not to lose count and to fire the seventh and final bullet. "That one's for me," I thought. The smoke from the Browning had a very pleasant smell. The door was just beginning to creak open as I kicked out the window pane and threw myself out. Luck was on my side: I jumped out onto an empty courtyard, ran past stacks of logs and out onto a dark street. I would certainly have been caught, but by chance I dashed into a very narrow gap between two walls. I sat on a broken brick in this small cave-like passage for several hours. I could hear the cavalry men racing by. The little passageway led to the Dnieper, and the troopers spent ages scouring the river bank looking for me. In my crevice I could see a single star above me; I thought it was Mars for some reason. Then it seemed to explode. That was the first shell bursting, veiling the star. And then the entire night crashed around Slobodka, as I sat in my brick cave, saying nothing and thinking of my higher degree, wondering whether the woman had died under the lashes. And when everything had gone quiet and it was just beginning to get light, I left the passageway, unable to stand the pain any longer – my feet were frostbitten. Slobodka had gone quite silent, everything was peaceful, and the stars had turned pale. When I came to the bridge, it was as if Colonel Leshchenko and the cavalry regiment no longer existed... Just horse droppings on the trampled road surface...

"And I walked the whole way to Kiev on my own, entering the city in broad daylight. I came across a strange-looking patrol, wearing some sort of caps with ear flaps.

"They stopped me and asked me for my documents.

"'I am Doctor Yashvin,' I said. 'I'm running from Petlyura's men. Where are they?'

"'They left last night,' they said. 'Kiev is now under a revolutionary committee.'

"And I saw one of the patrol looking me straight in the eyes. Then he gave a sympathetic wave of his hand and said:

"'Go home, doctor.'

"And so I went home."

After a moment's silence I asked Yashvin:

"Did he die? Did you kill him, or was he only wounded?"

Yashvin answered, smiling his strange smile:

"Oh, you need have no fears on that score. I killed him. You can trust me: I'm a surgeon."

# The Cockroach

Moscow! What a remarkable city! Such a famous city! And such famous boots!

These famous boots were being carried under Vasily Rogov's arm. Vasily Rogov himself was at one end of Novinsky Boulevard, where it emerges from Smolensk market. It was a grey day, with the sky the colour of putty, and it was even drizzling very slightly. But, however grey the day, nothing can put a stop to a Smolensk Sunday! Marquees stretched the entire way along from the Arbat to Novinsky Boulevard. Behind Vasily Rogov there were eight accordions playing various different pieces, imbuing people with a feeling of happy nostalgia. People stood in three rows reaching from the Arbat to the first withered trees, trading every possible item: from the bald and barefoot Leo Tolstoy, boot polish, apples and striped trousers, to kvass, the defence of Sevastopol, blackcurrants and carpets.

Anyone who has money will be like a fish in the sea at Smolensk market. Vasily Rogov had swum in the ocean with a pair of boots and a Finnish dagger. The boots you can understand – he had long wanted to buy a pair. But what was the point of a Finnish dagger? It had somehow bought itself.

When Rogov had counted out his twenty roubles for the boots in the tent, a one-eyed man appeared as if from nowhere, wearing a general's greatcoat for some reason.

"You've bought some boots, granddad!" the one-eyed man remarked with a nasal twang. "Excellent boots. But have you ever seen a Finnish dagger like this one?"

There was a flash of lethal steel in front of Rogov's eyes…

"I don't want it," said Rogov, tucking the boots more firmly under his arms.

"Costs six roubles," the man said, "but I'll let you have it for four, and that's only because the stall's closed down now."

"You haven't got any stall," Rogov replied scornfully. "My God!" he thought. "There are so many of these crooks at the Smolensk market!"

"You could kill anybody you want with a knife like this," the man leered, running his finger along the treacherous blade, "if you stick it to them under the ribs."

"You want to watch out; there are policemen about," Rogov replied, making his way through the forest of backs.

"You can have it, mate, for three and a half," the man said in his nasal voice, and Vasily Rogov, who had for some reason been given the offensive nickname of Cockroach at the bakery, felt the man's breath on the back of his long neck. "Just name your price, mate! It's not done to say nothing at the Smolensk market."

At that moment one of the accordions struck up with a march and the entire market was filled with a sense of rumbustious nostalgia.

"A rouble!" Cockroach said with a snicker, feeling happy because of his boots.

"It's yours!" shouted the little man, tucking the knife into the top of one of Cockroach's new boots.

And not knowing why he did so, Cockroach fished out his purse from under his clothes and, with his left hand firmly clutching on to five chervontsy* – you get all sorts of things going on at Smolensk market! – plucked out a yellow rouble.

This was how Cockroach acquired a Finnish knife. There was evidently trouble lying in store for Cockroach.

Cockroach was upset as a consequence of acquiring a useless object. "So what am I going to do with it then? Cut people's throats?" As a result, he had to go into a pub. After drinking two bottles of beer, Cockroach began to feel that perhaps the knife wasn't so unnecessary after all. "It's a wonderful thing, a Finnish knife," the baker thought and went out onto Novinsky Boulevard.

And what a lively street it was! Against a background of a screen depicting the Kremlin above the dense, blue waters of the River Moscow, a photographer was taking a picture of a young girl with a rose in her hair. Somebody suffering from trachoma was singing a disturbingly melancholic song. A Chinese man was twirling a rattle, and people were walking to and fro. And then Cockroach heard an unusual voice, announcing loudly and clearly to everybody:

"I've got a cartload of money – my uncle brought it from Japan."

But then the voice said:

"I don't turn or spin the top myself – I just pay out the money."

And indeed he was right: he didn't spin the top. The wooden eight-sided top was spun by the person placing the bet. And you could place a bet on any one of the eight sides. The number was on a board, and the board was on an ordinary box, and around the box stood a group of men in a semicircle.

"It's a game," the voice observed, "without any trickery or without bias. Any one of you could win to buy your wife a piece of liver, or yourself some vodka. Or your kids a little milk."

He sounded just like one of the family. Just like at home. A perspiring young man in a cloth cap kept on betting three copecks on number 8 and kept on losing. And then suddenly it won, and the voice gave the cloth cap a fifteen-copeck piece. The cloth cap staked a five-copeck piece with a sweaty hand and – again – number 8! Twenty-five copecks. Cloth Cap ten copecks – number 8! One miracle after another. Fifty copecks. Nothing seemed to affect the voice. He seemed quite unperturbed – he just kept on paying out. Cloth Cap bet once more on the 8, only this time it didn't win. After all, it couldn't have gone on for ever, could it!

Somebody else bet on the 2. But the top fell on 3.

"You should have bet on the next number!" someone said.

"You can't know for sure."

By this time Cockroach was standing by the box. He removed the Finnish knife from the top of his boot and tucked it in his clothes by his purse, just to be sure – all kinds of things had happened on Novinsky Boulevard!

Cloth Cap bet ten copecks on number 7 and it won. Fifty copecks again.

"For ten copecks I will give you fifty, and for twenty copecks, a rouble!" the voice informed everyone impassively.

Fortified by the beer, Cockroach smiled broadly and, just for a laugh, bet three copecks on number 3, but it fell on number 5.

"The more you play, the more fun it is!" the voice said.

Cockroach bet a five-copeck piece on number 4 and guessed correctly. The voice gave him twenty-five copecks.

"Look at that!" the whisper went round the semicircle.

Cockroach was rather astonished and, confused, he bet ten copecks on number 8. His heart started to knock as the top swayed and tottered on the board. And it fell badly. Instead of number 8 it fell on number 1. For some reason he felt sorry for the ten copecks. "Damn it, I shouldn't have bet anything. I should have taken the twenty-five copecks and left."

Within a quarter of an hour, the semicircle had grown, turning into two rows. And everyone drew back, intimidated by Cockroach's enthusiasm. By now Cockroach could see only flat eyeless disks rather than faces all around him. But the voice's face could see everything perfectly, a face that seemed to have been anointed with oil, a clean-shaven face with a pimple on one cheekbone, and extremely cold eyes, like agate. The voice was as calm and as cold as ice. But Cockroach started to sag. His own mother wouldn't have recognized him. He had aged, the corners of his lips drooped, the skin on his face had turned a dirty grey colour, and his watery eyes had turned up towards the sky.

Cockroach started to bet with his fifth, and final, chervonets. A grey chervonets, which had been resting against his stomach. He took it out and the box's owner exchanged it as follows: for a torn rouble note, a new rouble note, a green three-rouble note and a five-copeck piece which had seen something of the world and which was as thin as a cigarette paper. Cockroach bet one rouble, then a second, but neither won. "What am I doing – one rouble after another?" he suddenly thought, and he felt he was toppling into an abyss. The three-rouble note! But that was no good. Then Cockroach plonked his five-copeck piece down, and everything on Novinsky Boulevard started swimming around, as the voice's claw, like a crow's, swept the coin off the board. Nobody around him stirred an inch. The entire world was indifferent to Cockroach's malevolent fate. As for the box's owner, he suddenly picked up his board and put it under one arm. Then he placed his box under his other arm and went off to one side.

"Wait!" Cockroach said hoarsely, grabbing the voice by the sleeve. "Just wait a moment!"

"Why should I wait?" the voice replied. "No more bets. It's time to go home."

"I'll play again," Cockroach said in a strange voice. He took out his boots and immediately, in the mist, located a possible buyer.

"Buy these boots," he said, and saw that he was offering his boots to the man in the cloth cap, the man who had started the betting. Cloth Cap pouted derisively, and Cockroach was at once struck by the fact that his face was as oily as the voice's.

"How much?" Cloth Cap asked, tapping on the sole of the boot with a broken fingernail.

"Twenty!" Cockroach said.

"Twelve," said Cloth Cap with reluctance, and turned to walk away.

"Give me the money! Give me the money!" pleaded Cockroach in desperation.

Whistling through his lips, Cloth Cap extremely languidly took out a ten-rouble note and two roubles from the pocket of his steel-blue army jacket and gave them to Cockroach. The box returned to its place and Cockroach began to feel a little calmer. He lost a rouble five times in a row. He placed the next rouble on his lucky number 3 and got five in return. Then Cockroach's heart was assailed by the worm of doubt. "When on earth am I going to get it all back?" he thought and placed the five roubles on number 6.

"The man's sweating!" someone observed a little way away.

A minute later and the space in front of Cockroach was empty. The box had gone, the board had gone, and everyone had dispersed. The boulevard continued its normal existence, indifferent to Cockroach, the Chinese man twirled his rattle and, in the distance, whistles rang out, announcing that the market was closing.

Cockroach swept the boulevard with his inflamed eyes, and then, with darting, wolf-like steps, caught up with Cloth Cap, who was walking away carrying the boots. When he came up alongside, Cloth Cap glanced across at him and made immediately as if to turn off the boulevard.

"No, you can't get away from me like that!" Cockroach said, not recognizing his own voice. "How dare you?"

"What do you want?" Cloth Cap asked, his eyes swivelling anxiously.

"What kind of chervonets was that you gave me? Eh? Come on, answer me!"

Then Cockroach's head was suddenly struck by a lightning bolt of despair, as everything became clear. The chervonets had had an ink stain which Cockroach recognized. He had been given this stained note yesterday as his salary at the bakery. He had lost this chervonets to the voice, then it had got into Cloth Cap's hands, and Cockroach realized that this Cloth Cap person was in cahoots with the voice. So the voice must have given it to Cloth Cap, then? No doubt about it.

"Get away from me. You're drunk!" Cloth Cap said sternly.

"I'm drunk?!" exclaimed Cockroach, in a high thin voice. "I'm not drunk. But you are in league with each other, you crooks!" he shouted.

The passers-by scattered in all directions.

"I don't know who you are," Cloth Cap replied, and Cockroach realized he was looking to see if he could find a way out onto the grass area.

Cockroach suddenly burst out sobbing.

"You've ruined me," he said, quivering. "You've killed someone. It's trade-union money... I should put it in the bank. I'll be taken to court." The whole world became flooded with tears, and Cloth Cap relented.

"What is this, my dear man?" he said sympathetically. "I myself, my dear fellow, have lost money. I myself have lost everything. You go and sleep it off."

"I'm not worried about the boots," said Cockroach in torment. "But the fifty is not mine. I had it on trust. You have ruined an orphan. Crooks!" Cockroach suddenly shouted shrilly. Cloth Cap frowned.

"You can go to hell!" he shouted, his face enraged, but his eyes were still shifting about. "I've never seen you before in my life."

"Get that man with the box back here!" muttered Cockroach, beside himself, turning on Cloth Cap. "Get him back here at once! Or I'll hand you in to the authorities! Where are the police anyway?" the horrified Cockroach asked of an old woman's face peering out inquisitively from under a shawl.

The face made the sign of the cross and in a flash disappeared on to the grass. Small boys whistled at her, like nightingales, as she disappeared.

"Give him what he wants," someone advised unpleasantly. "Why go on and on!"

Cloth Cap's eyes now started swivelling and leaping around like mice.

"Get away from me, you scum!" he hissed through his teeth. "I don't know anything about any box."

"You're lying, you scoundrel! I can see right through you!" exclaimed Cockroach, sobbing. "You bought my boots with *my* chervonets!"

"What, it had your stamp on it, did it?" Cloth Cap asked, moving away to one side at an angle. "I bought them from someone else altogether, a tall man, with a cataract, and you're a small man, you cockroach you! He's mistaken me for someone else, citizen!"

Cloth Cap added unctuously, smiling at interested onlookers with his oily cheeks alone. "And now he's pulling the wool over my eyes. Get away from me, you pest!" he suddenly hissed like a cat and, like a cat, he quietly padded away, his bell-bottomed trousers bobbing above the blunt soles of his shoes.

"Stop, I say, stop… or else!" Cockroach muttered quietly, clutching at his sleeve. "I'll hand you over to the authorities! Good people…"

"Goodness, you're boring!" Cloth Cap shouted, his eyes blazing, and he struck Cockroach in the chest with his elbow.

Cockroach found it difficult to breathe. "I've had it, poor me, poor unhappy delegate," he thought. "The crook's getting away…"

"Are you going to stop or not?" Cockroach whispered through white lips, as he despairingly saw the cat-like expression in Cloth Cap's eyes. Cloth Cap's eyes expressed self-assurance and decisiveness. Cloth Cap was not afraid of this brown little cockroach. In a moment they would be at the little revolving turnstile, and he would be able to slip away from Novinsky Boulevard!

"Stop! Stop, thief!" hissed Cockroach, clutching at the slippery sleeve with two fingers of his left hand. Without saying a word, Cloth Cap was making a dash for the turnstile. "Where are the police, for goodness sake," Cockroach whispered, gasping for breath.

Cockroach saw red. He took out his Finnish knife and, in an impulsive fit of rage, stuck it into Cloth Cap's left side. The boots fell from Cloth Cap's hands onto the grass. Cloth Cap turned to his side and Cockroach could see his face. There was no sign of any oil now. The face had instantly become dry, rather more pleasant-looking, and the mouse-like eyes had turned into huge black plums. He started foaming at the mouth. Wheezing, Cloth Cap raised his arms and staggered towards Cockroach.

"You want a fight?" Cockroach asked, seeing perfectly well that Cloth Cap was in no fit state to fight, or to worry about his boots, or anything! "You want to fight?... You've robbed me, and you now want to fight?" Cockroach swung the knife and stabbed Cloth Cap in the throat, and pink bubbles started appearing on his pale lips. Cockroach was overcome by a sense of intoxicated ecstasy. He slashed at Cloth Cap's face and, as Cloth Cap was falling onto the ground, slashed once again – this time at his stomach. Cloth Cap lay down on the green Novinsky grass, spattering it with drops of blood. "Wonderful Finnish knife... human blood is just like chicken's blood," thought Cockroach.

The boulevard erupted in whistles and roars and thousands of people, it seemed, were leaping about yelling at Cockroach.

"I'm a dead man, a pathetic little delegate," Cockroach thought. "I'm finished. Who on earth was that devil who sold me the knife, and what for?"

He hurled the knife down on the grass and listened to Cloth Cap, covered in a foam of bloody bubbles, choking and dying. Cockroach began to feel sorry for Cloth Cap and even, for some reason, for the crook with the box... "You can understand it: he was simply earning himself a crust of bread... true, he was a crook... but everyone has to spin around like a top, don't they?..."

"Don't hit me, citizens," the doomed Cockroach requested quietly. He felt no pain from the blows, but the fact that everything had gone dark made him dimly aware he was being struck in the face. "Don't hit me, comrades. I am the local party representative of bakery no. 13... Hey, don't hit me. I have lost trade-union money, and ruined my life. Tie me up, but don't hit me," Cockroach pleaded, covering his head with his hands.

Piercing whistles rang out over Cockroach's head.

"Goodness, how many policemen... an extraordinary number of them..." thought Cockroach, giving himself into the hands of strangers. "They should have been here earlier. But it doesn't matter now..."

"Let them hit me, comrade policeman," Cockroach said indifferently, swallowing the blood pouring from his shattered nose and aware of only one thing: he was being dragged along past stomachs, with people stamping on him. But at least they weren't hitting him on the head any more. "I don't care. I stabbed someone out of the blue, because I had bought a Finnish knife."

"Chaos, like in hell," Cockroach thought, "but there's someone's capable voice…"

The threatening capable voice, so loud it could be heard as far away as Kudrinsky Square, roared:

"Cab! I'll show you where to go, drive off! You bastard… off to the police station with you!!!"

# A Dissolute Man

T HE SIGNALMAN COUGHED and went into his boss's room. His boss was at his desk.

"Hello, Adolf Ferapontovich," said the signalman politely.

"What can I do for you?" replied his boss, no less politely.

"The point is… I… I'm in a virtual marriage," the signalman said, giving a guilty smile for some reason.

The boss gave the signalman a disdainful look.

"I've always thought you were a dissolute person," he observed. "You have a sensual mouth."

The signalman froze to the spot. For a moment neither of them said anything.

"You're free to go," the boss continued. "What are you standing by my desk for? If you've come to share the sordid secrets of your life, then I'm not interested."

"You see… I… I've come for a pass…"

"What pass?"

"A free pass for my wife."

"Your wife? But surely you're not married, are you?"

"That's what I've come to say… I'm in a virtual marriage."

"Tee-hee… You're quite a joker, I can see. What church did you get married in?"

"I didn't get married in any church."

"Where are you registered, my dear fellow?" the boss enquired in an exaggeratedly dry manner.

"Well… I… I'm not regist… As I was saying: I'm in a virt—"

"Well, then, my friend, you don't have a wife, but a mistress."

"What do you mean?"

"It's very simple. You have latched on to some ballerina, you rogue, and now you're tearing about all over the place. Give me a free pass, he says! What a clever man! Today it's a free pass, but tomorrow she'll be demanding a car or a motor boat. Or a rail trip abroad. She's not going to start going around in some pigsty, whatever happens. Then it will be a hat! Followed by lisle Persian stockings. You've had it, signalman; you're heading for the gutter. She'll cost you about three hundred gold roubles a month. And that's in a best-case scenario, if you generally economize. Otherwise it will be four hundred."

"But that's awful!" the signalman exclaimed, his voice rising to a slight whine. "I earn forty gold roubles!"

"So much the worse for you. You'll get into debt, you'll start writing promissory notes. The dressmaker's bill for one hundred and eighty gold roubles will have you gasping. Your eyes will stand out on stalks. You'll dither and dither, and you'll wave a promissory note about. The deadline to pay up will come, and of course you won't have any money to settle the account. First you'll lose your own money, then about five thousand of the state's money, then your French spanner, then your horn, then your little red and green flags, then your lamp, and finally your trousers. And you'll sit on the tracks with your dancer woman, wearing nothing except what you were born in. And then, of course, they'll take you to court in a sensational trial. And, taking everything into account, they'll put you into strict isolation, and you won't get away with less than five years. No, my good signalman, give her up. She's French, I suppose, this coquette of yours?"

"What do you mean, 'French'?" the signalman shouted. Everything in his head had turned topsy-turvy. "Are you laughing at me? We're talking about Marya. A hat?... What are you talking about – a hat! She wouldn't know what to do with a hat. She makes me vegetable soup!"

"Well I could make you vegetable soup, but that doesn't mean I'm your wife."

"But we live together in the same room, for goodness sake!"

"You and I could live together in one room, but that wouldn't be any proof."

"But you're a man!"

"I already know that, without you telling me," the boss said.

The signalman started seeing green.

He dived into his pocket and pulled out a newspaper.

"Be so good as to look at this, a copy of *The Hooter*,"* he said.

"What hooter?" his boss asked.

"A newspaper."

"I don't have any time to read newspapers at the moment, my friend. I usually read newspapers in the evening," his boss said. "Just tell me briefly, my young Lothario, what it is you want."

"It says here in *The Hooter* that virtual, so to speak, wives, who live with a husband at his expense, are given free passes... which... just like—"

"My friend," his boss interrupted gently, "you are mistaken. Maybe you think that *The Hooter* represents the law in so far as I'm concerned. *The Hooter*, my dear fellow, is not the law; it's a newspaper that people read, nothing more. And the law has nothing to say about ballerinas."

"So, in other words, I'm not going to get a pass?" asked the signalman.

"No, my dear fellow, you're not," his boss replied.

There was a moment's silence.

"Goodbye," the signalman said.

"Farewell, and repent of your behaviour!" the boss shouted after him as he left the room.

# Note on the Text

The text for these translations is taken from *Mikhail Bulgakov, Sobranie sochinenii* (Ann Arbor, MI: Ardis 1982–85) vols. 1 and 2, and from *Mikhail Bulgakov, Sobach'e serdtse, D'iavoliada, Rokovye iaitsa* (St Petersburg: Azbuka, 2011).

# Notes

p. v, *I have just… should imagine*: Mikhail Bulgakov, *Diaries and Selected Letters* (London: Alma Classics, 2013), p. 4.

p. v, *'Diaboliad'… The Fatal Eggs and A Dog's Heart*: All three stories have been published by Alma Classics in English translation (in 2010, 2014 and 2011 respectively). *The Fatal Eggs* was the last prose work to be published in Soviet Russia during Bulgakov's lifetime, although he was to have greater success as a playwright, notably *The Days of the Turbins* (first staged in 1926), a version of his novel *The White Guard*.

p. VII, *'The Crimson Island'*: Bulgakov turned the story into a play, with the stage version far more successful than the original in the opinion of many commentators. *The Crimson Island* was first performed in Moscow in 1928, but it was banned the following year.

p. IX, *only one future – its past*: Yevgeny Zamyatin, 'I am Afraid', *House of Arts*, Petrograd, 1921, p. 53.

p. 3, *The Russian Word*: A newspaper founded in 1895 but closed by the Bolsheviks in 1917 for its "slanderous activities".

p. 3, *Tiflis is some forty miles away*: Tiflis: the former name of Tbilisi, the capital of Georgia.

p. 3, *like Dickens's Jingle*: A reference to the character in Dickens's *The Posthumous Papers of the Pickwick Club* (1837).

p. 4, *Credito italiano... Finita la commedia*: "Italian credit [the name of an Italian bank]... The comedy is over!" (Italian).

p. 5, *Melnikov-Pechersky*: Pavel Ivanovich Melnikov (alias Andrei Pechersky) (1818–83), Russian writer, author of *In the Forests* (1871–74) and *On the Hills* (1875–81).

p. 5, *Peter the Great*: Peter I, Emperor of Russia from 1689 until his death in 1725.

p. 6, *To Thee, oh Warrior triumphant*: The opening words of the hymn of praise to the Virgin Mary.

p. 6, *straight out of Vasnetsov*: Viktor Mikhailovich Vasnetsov (1848–1926), artist.

p. 6, *Sashki, my kanashki*: Nonsense proverb.

p. 7, *The writer Yury Slyozkin*: Yury Lvovich Slyozkin (1885–1947).

p. 8, *Not the Ingush, but the Ossetians*: Caucasians peoples.

p. 9, *Izo. Lito. Photo. Theo*: Abbreviations given to the various different cultural sub-sections: Izo, fine arts; Lito, literature; Photo, photography; and Theo, theatre.

p. 12, *Chamber Cadet Pushkin*: Alexander Sergeyevich Pushkin (1799–1837), writer. "Chamber Cadet" (*Kamer-Junker*) was one of the lowest ranks in the order of nobility.

p. 13, *the river Terek*: Caucasian river, flowing from its source in Georgia to the Caspian Sea.

p. 13, *Gogol and Dostoyevsky*: Nikolai Vasilyevich Gogol (1809–52), writer; Fyodor Mikhailovich Dostoyevsky (1821–81), writer.

p. 13, *false wisdom gutters and shimmers... mind*: Quotation from Pushkin's poem 'The Song of Bacchus' (1825).

p. 14, *I shall accept the insult with indifference*: Quotation from Pushkin's poem 'I have erected a monument to myself, not built by hands' (1836).

p. 15, *Modes et Robes*: "Fashions and Dresses" (French).

p. 15, *Golden Horn*: The primary inlet of the Bosphorus, in Istanbul.

p. 16, *Yevreinov's arrived*: Nikolai Nikolayevich Yevreinov (1879–1953), writer and literary historian.

p. 16, *Writers, my brothers, in your fate…*: An incomplete quotation from a poem 'In the Hospital' (1855) by Nikolai Alexeyevich Nekrasov (1821–78).

p. 17, *An unkempt Osip*: Osip, servant to Khlestakov, the hero of Gogol's comedy *The Government Inspector* (1836).

p. 17, *Yesterday Rurik Ivnev left*: Rurik Ivnev, real name Mikhail Alexandrovich Kovalyov (1891–1981), writer.

p. 17, *Osip Mandelstam*: Osip Emilyevich Mandelstam (1891–1938), poet and prose writer.

p. 18, *The writer Pilnyak*: Boris Andreyevich Pilnyak (1894–1938). Born Vogau.

p. 18, *Serafimovich – arrived from the north*: Born Alexander Serafimovich Popov (1863–1949), writer.

p. 18, *Remember that in Tolstoy*: Lev Nikolayevich Tolstoy (1828–1910).

p. 18, *Anton Pavlovich Chekhov*: Anton Pavlovich Chekhov (1860–1904), dramatist and prose writer.

p. 19, *Chekhov's Surgery… story about a clerk's sneeze*: The references are to two stories by Chekhov: 'Surgery' (1884) and 'Death of a Civil Servant' (1883).

p. 19, *Nozdryov*: A character from Gogol's novel *Dead Souls* (1842).

p. 21, *the scene in which Salieri poisons Mozart*: A reference to one of Pushkin's little tragedies 'Mozart and Salieri' (1830).

p. 22, *Lumen cœli. Sancta rosa*: "Light of the sky. Sacred rose" (Latin).

p. 22, *And his threat is like thunder*: A quotation from Pushkin's poem 'There lived on this earth a poor knight' (1829).

p. 22, *Knut Hamsun*: Knut Hamsun (1859–1952), Norwegian writer.

p. 24, *Kuprin, Bunin or Gorky*: Alexander Ivanovich Kuprin (1870–1938), Ivan Alexeyevich Bunin (1870–1953), Maxim Gorky (1868–1936), born Alexei Maximovich Peshkov, all writers.

p. 25, *Woe from Wit or The Government Inspector*: *Woe from Wit* (1825): play by Alexander Sergeyevich Griboyedov (1795–1829); *The Government Inspector*: see first note to p. 17.

p. 27, *C'est la... L'internationa-a-ale*: "This is the final struggle... The Internationale" (French), the first and third lines of the chorus to 'The Internationale'.

p. 29, *Vladimir Mayakovsky*: Vladimir Vladimirovich Mayakovsky (1893–1930), poet and playwright.

p. 29, *his favourite opera Eugene Onegin*: The opera by Tchaikovsky, first performed in 1879, based on Pushkin's novel in verse (1825–32).

p. 30, *Meyerhold*: Vsevolod Emilyevich Meyerhold (1874–1940), theatre director and producer.

p. 31, *The Lower Depths. Mother*: *The Lower Depths* (1902), a play by Gorky; *Mother* (1907), a novel, also by Gorky.

p. 31, *Bryusov and Bely*: Valerii Yakovlevich Bryusov (1873–1924), poet and prose writer; Andrei Bely (1880–1934), poet and prose writer, born Boris Nikolayevich Bugayev.

p. 32, *Tout*: "Everything" (French).

p. 32, *Émile Zola*: French writer (1849–1902).

p. 34, *The Three Musketeers... incomparable Dumas*: Alexandre Dumas, *père*, French writer (1802–70). *The Three Musketeers* was first serialized in 1844.

p. 36, *"Shtorn"*: Real name Georgii Petrovich Shtorm (1898–1978), writer.

p. 37, *Veresayev, Shmelyov, Zaytsev*: Vikenty Vikentevich Veresayev (1867–1945), writer; Ivan Sergeyevich Shmelyov

(1873–1950), writer; Pyotr Nikanorovich Zaytsev (1889–1970), journalist.

p. 40, *A proper Kanatchikov's dacha*: Ironic name for the psychiatric hospital at Kanatchikovo, near Moscow.

p. 40, *1836. ON THE TWENTY-FIFTH OF MARCH... THE BARBER IVAN YAKOVLEVICH*: The opening lines of Gogol's short story *The Nose* (1836).

p. 41, *Razumikhin*: The close friend of the hero Rodion Raskolnikov in Dostoyevsky's novel *Crime and Punishment* (1866).

p. 42, *SUCH COMPLETE NONSENSE... AS IF NOTHING HAD HAPPENED*: A quotation from the conclusion to Gogol's *The Nose*, (see second note to p. 40).

p. 44, *Nekrasov and the reformed alcoholics*: For Nekrasov see second note to p. 16. The "reformed alcoholics" is a reference to a play by V. Grigorovsky, *The Reformed Alcoholic*.

p. 47, *Lev Tolstoy at Yasnaya Polyana*: Yasnaya Polyana was the family home of the Tolstoys, in Tula Province.

p. 47, *some Dukhobor*: A member of a Russian religious sect.

p. 49, *the Famine collections*: A reference to two literary anthologies on peasant themes.

p. 55, *Built by Rastrelli*: Francesco Bartolomeo Rastrelli (1700–71), French-born Russian-Italian architect, responsible for the design of many palaces and other court buildings in St Petersburg during the reigns of the Empresses Anna (1730–40) and Elizabeth (1741–62).

p. 56, *Onegins*: A sarcastic reference to the lifestyle of the upper classes as portrayed in Pushkin's *Eugene Onegin* (see second note to p. 29).

p. 56, *Catherine the Great*: Empress of Russia from 1762 to 1796.

p. 57, *the Nogai Horde*: Confederation of a number of Turkic and Mongol tribes inhabiting the area between the Caspian and Black Seas from the fifteenth to the eighteenth centuries.

p. 57, *a hideous Messalina*: Messalina was the third wife of the Emperor Claudius (10 BC to 54 AD), renowned for her dissolute character.

p. 57, *Alexander I*: Tsar of Russia from 1801 to 1825.

p. 58, *Nikolai Palkin*: "Nikolai the Cudgeller", a nickname given to Tsar Nicholas I (Emperor of Russia, 1825–55).

p. 70, *from the time of Empress Elizabeth*: See note to p. 55.

p. 73, *the famous Lord Glenarvan*: Fictional character from the novel *In Search of the Castaways* (*The Children of Captain Grant*) (1867–68) by Jules Verne (1828–1905).

p. 73, *Sizi-Buzi*: Bulgakov intended *The Crimson Island* as an allegorical retelling of the two 1917 Russian revolutions and the civil war that followed. Here Sizi-Buzi is Nicholas II, the last Tsar of Russia from 1894 to 1918.

p. 73, *Rikki-Tikki-Tavi*: Name given to the mongoose depicted in *The Jungle Book* (1894) by Rudyard Kipling (1865–1936).

p. 76, *Kiri-Kuki*: Alexander Fyodorovich Kerensky (1881–1970), prime minister in the Russian Provisional Government between the February and October revolutions of 1917.

p. 78, *Bount*: Unusual transliteration of the Russian word "bunt", "mutiny".

p. 79, *Hatteras*: Character from Jules Verne's novel *The Adventures of Captain Hatteras* (1864–65).

p. 80, *Ephiop… Korrespondent*: "Ethiopian started huge mutiny. Island on fire, plague everywhere. Mountains of corpses. Advance of 500. Correspondent."

p. 81, *Michel Ardan*: Character from the novels by Jules Verne *From the Earth to the Moon* (1865) and *Around the Moon* (1870).

p. 81, *Paganel*: Character from Jules Verne's novel *In Search of the Castaways* (see first note to p. 73).

p. 81, *comprenez-vous*: "Do you understand?" (French).

p. 84, *Phileas Fogg*: Character from Jules Verne's novel *Around the World in Eighty Days* (1873).

p. 95, *La traviata*: *La traviata* (1853), opera by Giuseppe Verdi (1813–1901).

p. 100, *the second Rhapsody*: Bulgakov almost certainly had in mind the second Hungarian Rhapsody (1847) by Franz Liszt (1811–86), one of his favourite compositions.

p. 103, *during the landing at Novorossiisk*: Novorossiisk, port on the Black Sea. The scene of a particularly bitter engagement during the Russian civil war.

p. 103, *the novel Marya Luseva Abroad*: Popular novel (1912) by Alexander Valentinovich Amfiteatrov (1862–1938).

p. 104, *Fenimore Cooper... Koshka the sailor*: James Fenimore Cooper (1789–1851), American novelist (in actual fact one of Bulgakov's favourite authors); Pyotr Markovich Koshka (1828–82), sailor of the Black Sea Fleet, renowned for his heroism during the defence of Sevastopol (1854–55).

p. 108, *some ataman or other*: Ataman is the title given to Cossack leaders of various kinds.

p. 109, *Khankal Gorge*: A geographical feature close to Grozny, the capital of Chechnya. The scene of fierce fighting in the Caucasian and Russian civil wars.

p. 109, *the turbid stream... his dagger*: From the poem 'Cossack Lullaby' (1838) by Mikhail Yurevich Lermontov (1814–41).

p. 109, *Uzun-Khadzhi is in Chechen-Aul*: Uzun Khadzhi Khan (?–1920), Emir of the so-called North Caucasian Emirate. An aul is a Caucasian mountain village.

p. 112, *Now I am a free child of the ether*: From the poem by Lermontov *The Demon* (1829–39).

p. 112, *the opera The Demon*: An 1871 opera by Anton Rubinstein (1829–94), based on Lermontov's poem.

p. 112, *a veritable feast of Lucullus*: Lucius Lucullus (*c*.117–56 BC), Roman general, renowned for his feasts.

p. 114, *just like Gogol's Osip*: See first note to p. 17.

p. 114, *Even a little piece of string will come in useful*: Phrase used by Osip in Act IV of Gogol's *The Government Inspector* (see first note to p. 17).

p. 118, *But I am not Mayne Reid, neither am I Louis Boussenard*: Thomas Mayne Reid (1818–83), American writer; Louis Henri

Boussenard (1847–1910), French writer, famous for his novels of adventure.

p. 120, *Jerome K. Jerome*: Jerome K. Jerome (1859–1927), the author of *Three Men in a Boat* (1889).

p. 133, *Makar Devushkin's Story*: Makar Devushkin was the hero of Dostoyevsky's first novel, *Poor Folk* (1846).

p. 136, *Khlestakov in striped trousers*: See first note to p. 17.

p. 142, *Die Walküre and the Barber of Seville*: *Die Walküre* (1870), the second opera in the Ring cycle by Richard Wagner (1813–83); *The Barber of Seville* (1816), opera by Gioacchino Rossini (1792–1868).

p. 145, *I lived on a steep slope... the whole of Podol*: There is no such street as St Alexei's Hill in Kiev, although there is a St Andrew's Hill, on which Bulgakov himself lived, at no. 13. Podol was a historic area of Kiev, by the River Dnieper.

p. 145, *Petlyura*: Semyon Vasilyevich Petlyura (in Ukrainian, Symon Vasylyovych Petlyura) (1879–1926), head of the Ukrainian state for two years from December 1918.

p. 156, *chervontsy*: The chervonets was a unit of currency introduced by the Soviet government in 1922, alongside the rouble. It was fully convertible and backed by the gold standard.

p. 167, *The Hooter*: Official organ of the Railway Workers' Union.

Extra Material

on

Mikhail Bulgakov's

*Notes on a Cuff
and Other Stories*

# Mikhail Bulgakov's Life

Mikhail Afanasyevich Bulgakov was born in Kiev – then in the Russian Empire, now the capital of independent Ukraine – on 15th May 1891. He was the eldest of seven children – four sisters and three brothers – and, although born in Ukraine, his family were Russians, and were all members of the educated classes – mainly from the medical, teaching and ecclesiastical professions. His grandfathers were both Russian Orthodox priests, while his father lectured at Kiev Theological Academy. Although a believer, he was never fanatical, and he encouraged his children to read as widely as they wished, and to make up their own minds on everything. His mother was a teacher and several of his uncles were doctors.

*Birth, Family Background and Education*

In 1906 his father became ill with sclerosis of the kidneys. The Theological Academy immediately awarded him a full pension, even though he had not completed the full term of service, and allowed him to retire on health grounds. However, he died almost immediately afterwards.

Every member of the Bulgakov family played a musical instrument, and Mikhail became a competent pianist. There was an excellent repertory company and opera house in Kiev, which he visited regularly. He was already starting to write plays which were performed by the family in their drawing room. He was a conservative and a monarchist in his school days, but never belonged to any of the extreme right-wing organizations of the time. Like many of his contemporaries, he favoured the idea of a constitutional monarchy as against Russian Tsarist autocracy.

A few years after her first husband's death, Mikhail's mother married an uncompromising atheist. She gave the children supplementary lessons in her spare time from her own teaching job and, as soon as they reached adolescence, she encouraged them to take on younger pupils to increase the family's meagre income. Mikhail's first job, undertaken when he was still at school, was as a part-time guard and ticket inspector on the local railway, and he continued such part-time employment when he entered medical school in Kiev in 1911.

He failed the exams at the end of his first year, but passed the resits a few months later. However, he then had to repeat his entire second year; this lack of dedication to his studies was possibly due to the fact that he was already beginning to write articles for various student journals and to direct student theatricals. Furthermore, he was at this time courting Tatyana Lappa, whom he married in 1913. She came from the distant Saratov region, but had relatives in Kiev, through whom she became acquainted with Bulgakov. He had already begun by this time to write short stories and plays. Because of these distractions, Bulgakov took seven years to complete what was normally a five-year course, but he finally graduated as a doctor in 1916 with distinction.

*War*     In 1914 the First World War had broken out, and Bulgakov enlisted immediately after graduation as a Red Cross volunteer, working in military hospitals at the front, which involved carrying out operations. In March 1916 he was called up to the army, but was in the end sent to work in a major Kiev hospital to replace experienced doctors who had been mobilized earlier. His wife, having done a basic nursing course by this time, frequently worked alongside her husband.

In March 1917 the Tsar abdicated, and the Russian monarchy collapsed. Two forces then began to contend for power – the Bolsheviks and the Ukrainian Nationalists. Although not completely in control of Ukraine, the latter declared independence from the former Tsarist Empire in February 1918, and concluded a separate peace deal with Germany. The Germans engineered a coup, placed their own supporters at the helm in Ukraine and supported this puppet regime against the Bolsheviks, the now deposed Nationalists and various other splinter groups fighting for their own causes. The Government set up its own German-supported army, the White Guard, which provided the background for Bulgakov's novel of the same name. The Bolsheviks ("The Reds"), the White Guard ("The Whites") and the Ukrainian Nationalists regularly took and retook the country and Kiev from each other: there were eighteen changes of government between the beginning of 1918 and late 1919.

Early in this period Bulgakov had been transferred to medical service in the countryside around the remote town of Vyazma, which provided him with material for his series of short stories

*A Young Doctor's Notebook*. Possibly to blunt the distress caused to him by the suffering he witnessed there, and to cure fevers he caught from the peasants he was tending, he dosed himself heavily on his own drugs, and rapidly became addicted to morphine. When his own supplies had run out, he sent his wife to numerous pharmacies to pick up new stocks for imaginary patients. When she finally refused to acquiesce in this any further, he became abusive and violent, and even threatened her with a gun. No more mention is made at any later date of his addiction, so it is uncertain whether he obtained professional help for the problem or weaned himself off his drug habit by his own will-power.

He returned to Kiev in February 1918 and set up in private practice. Some of the early stories written in this period show that he was wrestling with problems of direction and conscience: a doctor could be pressed into service by whichever faction was in power at that moment; after witnessing murders, torture and pogroms, Bulgakov was overwhelmed with horror at the contemporary situation. He was press-ganged mainly by the right-wing Whites, who were notoriously anti-Semitic and carried out most of the pogroms.

Perhaps as a result of the suffering he had seen during his enforced military service, he suffered a "spiritual crisis" – as an acquaintance of his termed it – in February 1920, when he gave up medicine at the age of twenty-nine to devote himself to literature. But things were changing in the literary world: Bulgakov's style and motifs were not in tune with the new proletarian values which the Communists, in the areas where they had been victorious, were already beginning to inculcate. The poet Anna Akhmatova talked of his "magnificent contempt" for their ethos, in which everything had to be subordinated to the creation of a new, optimistic mentality which believed that science, medicine and Communism would lead to a paradise on earth for all, with humanity reaching its utmost point of development.

*Turning to Literature*

He continued to be pressed into service against his will. Although not an ardent right-winger, he had more sympathy for the Whites than for the Reds, and when the former, who had forced him into service at the time, suffered a huge defeat at the hands of the Communists, evidence suggests that Bulgakov would rather have retreated with the right-wing faction, and maybe even gone into emigration, than have to work for the victorious Communists. However, he was prevented from doing this as just at this time he became seriously ill with typhus, and so remained behind when the Whites fled. Incidentally, both his brothers had fled abroad, and were by this time living in Paris.

From 1920 to 1921 Bulgakov briefly worked in a hospital in the Caucasus, where he had been deployed by the Whites, who finally retreated from there in 1922. Bulgakov, living in the town of Vladikavkaz, produced a series of journalistic sketches, later collected and published as *Notes on a Cuff*, detailing his own experiences at the time, and later in Moscow. He avowedly took as his model classic writers such as Molière, Gogol and particularly Pushkin, and his writings at this time attracted criticism from anti-White critics, because of what was seen as his old-fashioned style and material, which was still that of the cultured European intellectuals of an earlier age, rather than being in keeping with the fresh aspirations of the new progressive proletarian era inaugurated by the Communists. The authorities championed literature and works of art which depicted the life of the masses and assisted in the development of the new Communist ethos. At the time, this tendency was still only on the level of advice and encouragement from the Government, rather than being a categorical demand. It only began to crystallize around the mid-1920s into an obligatory uncompromising line, ultimately leading to the repression, under Stalin, of any kind of even mildly dissident work, and to an increasingly oppressive state surveillance.

In fact, although never a supporter of Bolshevism as such, Bulgakov's articles of the early 1920s display not approval of the Red rule, but simply relief that at last there seemed to be stable government in Russia, which had re-established law and order and was gradually rebuilding the country's infrastructure. However, this relief at the new stability did not prevent him producing stories satirizing the new social order; for instance, around this time he published an experimental satirical novella entitled *Crimson Island*, purporting to be a novella by "Comrade Jules Verne" translated from the French. It portrayed the Whites as stereotypical monsters and was written in the coarse, cliché-ridden agitprop style of the time – a blatant lampoon of the genre.

But by 1921, when he was approaching the age of thirty, Bulgakov was becoming worried that he still had no solid body of work behind him. Life had always been a struggle for him and his wife Tatyana, but he had now begun to receive some money from his writing and to mix in Russian artistic circles. After his medical service in Vladikavkaz he moved to Moscow, where he earned a precarious living over the next few years, contributing sketches to newspapers and magazines, and lecturing on literature. In January 1924 he met the sophisticated, multilingual Lyubov Belozerskaya, who was the wife of a journalist. In comparison with her, Tatyana seemed provincial and uncultured. They started a relationship, divorced their respective partners, and were entered in the local registers as married in late spring 1924, though the exact date of their marriage is unclear.

Between 1925 and 1926 Bulgakov produced three anthologies of his stories, the major one of which received the overall title *Diaboliad*. This collection received reasonably favourable reviews. One compared his stories in *Diaboliad* to those of Gogol, and this was in fact the only major volume of his fiction to be published in the USSR during his lifetime. According to a typist he employed at this time, he would dictate to her for two or three hours every day, from notebooks and loose sheets of paper, though not apparently from any completely composed manuscript.

But in a review in the newspaper *Izvestiya* of *Diaboliad* and some of Bulgakov's other writings in September 1925, the Marxist writer and critic Lev Averbakh, who was to become head of RAPP (the Russian Association of Proletarian Writers) had already declared that the stories contained only one theme: the uselessness and chaos arising from the Communists' attempts to create a new society. The critic then warned that, although Soviet satire was permissible and indeed requisite for the purposes of stimulating the restructuring of society, totally destructive lampoons such as Bulgakov's were irrelevant, and even inimical to the new ethos.

The Government's newly established body for overseeing literature subsequently ordered *Diaboliad* to be withdrawn, although it allowed a reissue in early 1926. By April 1925, Bulgakov was reading his long story *A Dog's Heart* at literary gatherings, but finding it very difficult to get this work, or anything else, published. In May 1926, Bulgakov's flat was searched by agents of OGPU, the precursor of the KGB. The typescript of *A Dog's Heart* and Bulgakov's most recent diaries were confiscated; the story was only published in full in Russian in 1968 (in Germany), and in the USSR only in 1987, in a literary journal. In 1926

Bulgakov had written a stage adaptation of the story, but again it was only produced for the first time in June 1987, after which it became extremely popular throughout the USSR.

*The White Guard*

Between 1922 and 1924 Bulgakov was engaged in writing his first novel, ultimately to be known as *The White Guard*. The publishing history of this volume – which was originally planned to be the first part of a trilogy portraying the whole sweep of the Russian Revolution and Civil War – is extremely complex, and there were several different redactions. The whole project was very important to him, and was written at a period of great material hardship. By 1925 he was reading large sections at literary gatherings. Most of the chapters were published as they were produced, in literary magazines, with the exception of the ending, which was banned by the censors; pirated editions, with concocted endings, were published abroad. The novel appeared finally, substantially rewritten and complete, in 1929 in Paris, in a version approved by the author. Contrary to all other Soviet publications of this period, which saw the events of these years from the point of view of the victorious Bolsheviks, Bulgakov described that time from the perspective of one of the enemy factions, portraying them not as vile and sadistic monsters, as was now the custom, but as ordinary human beings with their own problems, fears and ideals.

It had a mixed reception; one review found it inferior to his short stories, while another compared it to the novelistic debut of Dostoevsky. It made almost no stir, and it's interesting to note that, in spite of the fact that the atmosphere was becoming more and more repressive as to the kind of artistic works which would be permitted, the party newspaper *Pravda* in 1927 could write neutrally of its "interesting point of view from a White-Guard perspective".

*First Plays*

Representatives of the Moscow Arts Theatre (MAT) had heard Bulgakov reading extracts from his novel-in-progress at literary events, realized its dramatic potential, and asked him to adapt the novel for the stage. The possibility had dawned on him even before this, and it seems he was making drafts for such a play from early 1925. This play – now known as *The Days of the Turbins* – had an extremely complicated history. At rehearsals, Bulgakov was interrogated by OGPU. The MAT forwarded the original final version to Anatoly Lunacharsky, the People's Commissar for Education, to verify whether it was sufficiently innocuous politically for them to be able to stage it. He wrote back declaring it was rubbish from an artistic point of view, but as far as subject matter went there was no problem. The theatre seems to have agreed with him as to the literary merit of the piece, since they encouraged the author to embark on an extensive revision, which would ultimately produce a radically different version.

During rehearsals as late as August 1926, representatives of OGPU and the censors were coming to the theatre to hold lengthy negotiations with the author and director, and to suggest alterations. The play was finally passed for performance, but only at the MAT – no productions were to be permitted anywhere else. It was only allowed to be staged elsewhere, oddly enough, from 1933 onwards, when the party line was being enforced more and more rigorously and Stalin's reign was becoming increasingly repressive. Rumour had it that Stalin himself had quite enjoyed the play when he saw it at the MAT in 1929, regarded its contents as innocuous, and had himself authorized its wider performances.

It was ultimately premiered on 26th October 1926, and achieved great acclaim, becoming known as "the second *Seagull*", as the first performance of Chekhov's *Seagull* at the MAT in 1898 had inaugurated the theatre's financial and artistic success after a long period of mediocrity and falling popularity. This was a turning point in the fortunes of the MAT, which had been coming under fire for only performing the classics and not adopting styles of acting and subject matter more in keeping with modern times and themes. The play was directed by one of the original founders of the MAT, Konstantin Stanislavsky, and he authorized a thousand-rouble advance for the playwright, which alleviated somewhat the severe financial constraints he had been living under.

The play received mixed reviews, depending almost entirely on the journal or reviewer's political views. One critic objected to its "idealization of the Bolsheviks' enemies", while another vilified its "petit-bourgeois vulgarity". Others accused it of using means of expression dating from the era of classic theatre which had now been replaced in contemporary plays by styles – often crudely propagandistic – which were more in tune with the Soviet proletarian ethos. The piece was extremely popular, however, and in spite of the fact that it was only on in one theatre, Bulgakov could live reasonably well on his share of the royalties.

At this time another Moscow theatre, the Vakhtangov, also requested a play from the author, so Bulgakov gave them *Zoyka's*

*Apartment*, which had probably been written in late 1925. It was premiered on 28th October, just two days after *The Days of the Turbins*. The theatre's representatives suggested a few textual (not political) changes, and Bulgakov first reacted with some irritation, then acknowledged he had been overworked and under stress, due to the strain of the negotiations with OGPU and the censors over *The Days of the Turbins*.

Various other changes had to be made before the censors were satisfied, but the play was allowed to go on tour throughout the Soviet Union. It is rather surprising that it was permitted, because, in line with party doctrine, social and sexual mores were beginning to become more and more puritanical, and the play brought out into the open the seamier side of life which still existed in the workers' paradise. Zoyka's apartment is in fact a high-class brothel, and the Moscow papers had recently reported the discovery in the city of various such establishments, as well as drug dens. The acting and production received rave reviews, but the subject matter was condemned by some reviewers as philistine and shallow, and the appearance of scantily clad actresses on stage was excoriated as being immoral.

The play was extremely successful, both in Moscow and on tour, and brought the author further substantial royalties. Bulgakov was at this time photographed wearing a monocle and looking extremely dandified; those close to him claimed that the monocle was worn for genuine medical reasons, but this photograph attracted personal criticism in the press: he was accused of living in the past and being reactionary.

Perhaps to counteract this out-of-touch image, Bulgakov published a number of sketches in various journals between 1925 and 1927 giving his reminiscences of medical practice in the remote countryside. When finally collected and published posthumously, they were given the title *A Young Doctor's Notebook*. Although they were written principally to alleviate his financial straits, the writer may also have been trying to demonstrate that, in spite of all the criticism, he was a useful member of society with his medical knowledge.

*Censorship* — Bulgakov's next major work was the play *Escape* (also translated as *Flight*), which, according to dates on some of the manuscript pages, was written and revised between 1926 and 1928. The script was thoroughly rewritten in 1932 and only performed in the USSR in 1957. The play was banned at the rehearsal stage in 1929 as being not sufficiently "revolutionary", though Bulgakov claimed in bafflement that he had in fact been trying to write a piece that was more akin to agitprop than anything he'd previously written.

*Escape* is set in the Crimea during the struggle between the Whites and Reds in the Civil War, and portrays the Whites as stereotypical villains involved in prostitution, corruption and terror. At first it seems perplexing that the piece should have been banned, since it seems so in tune with the spirit of the times, but given Bulgakov's well-known old-fashioned and anti-Red stance, the play may well have been viewed as in fact a satire on the crude agitprop pieces of the time.

The year 1929 was cataclysmic both for Bulgakov and for other Soviet writers: by order of RAPP (Russian Association of Proletarian Writers) *Escape*, *The Days of the Turbins* and *Zoyka's Apartment* had their productions suspended. Although, with the exception of *Zoyka*, they were then granted temporary runs, at least until the end of that season, their long-term future remained uncertain.

Bulgakov had apparently started drafting his masterpiece *The Master and Margarita* as early as 1928. The novel had gone through at least six revisions by the time of the writer's death in 1940. With the tightening of the party line, there was an increase in militant, politically approved atheism, and one of the novel's major themes is a retelling of Christ's final days, and his victory in defeat – possibly a response to the atheism of Bulgakov's time. He submitted one chapter, under a pseudonym, to the magazine *Nedra* in May 1929, which described satirically the intrigues among the official literary bodies of the time, such as RAPP and others. This chapter was rejected. Yevgeny Zamyatin, another writer in disfavour at the time, who finally emigrated permanently, stated privately that the Soviet Government was adopting the worst excesses of old Spanish Catholicism, seeing heresies where there were none.

In July of that year Bulgakov wrote a letter to Stalin and other leading politicians and writers in good standing with the authorities, asking to be allowed to leave the USSR with his wife; he stated in this letter that it appeared he would never be allowed to be published or performed again in his own country. His next play, *Molière*, was about problems faced by the French playwright in the period of the autocratic monarch Louis XIV; the parallels between the times of Molière and the Soviet writer are blatant. It was read in January 1930 to the Artistic Board of the MAT, who reported that, although it had "no relevance to contemporary questions", they had now admitted a couple of modern propaganda plays to their repertoire, and so they thought the authorities might stretch a point and permit Bulgakov's play. But in March he was told that the Government artistic authorities had not passed the piece. The MAT now demanded the return of the thousand-rouble advance they had allowed Bulgakov for *Escape*, also now banned; furthermore the writer was plagued by demands for unpaid income tax relating to the previous year. None of his works were now in production.

*Help from Stalin*

On Good Friday Bulgakov received a telephone call from Stalin himself promising a favourable response to his letter to the authorities, either to be allowed to emigrate, or at least to be permitted to take up gainful employment in a theatre if he so wished. Stalin even promised a personal meeting with the writer. Neither meeting nor response ever materialized, but Bulgakov was shortly afterwards appointed Assistant Director at the MAT, and Consultant to the Theatre of Working Youth, probably as a result of some strings being pulled in high places. Although unsatisfactory, these officially sanctioned positions provided the writer with some income and measure of protection against the torrent of arbitrary arrests now sweeping through the country.

*Yelena Shilovskaya*

Although there was now some stability in Bulgakov's professional life, there was to be another major turn in his love life. In February 1929 he had met at a friend's house in Moscow a woman called Yelena Shilovskaya; she was married with two children, highly cultured, and was personal secretary at the MAT to the world-famous theatre director Vladimir Nemirovich-Danchenko. They fell in love, but then did not see each other again for around eighteen months. When they did meet again, they found they were still drawn to each other, divorced their partners, and married in October 1932. She remained his wife till his death, and afterwards became the keeper of his archives and worked tirelessly to have his works published.

Over the next few years Bulgakov wrote at least twice more to Stalin asking to be allowed to emigrate. But permission was not forthcoming, and so Bulgakov would never travel outside the USSR. He always felt deprived because of this and sensed something had been lacking in his education. At this time, because of his experience in writing such letters, and because of his apparent "pull" in high places, other intellectuals such as Stanislavsky and Anna Akhmatova were asking for his help in writing similar letters.

While working at the MAT, Bulgakov's enthusiasm quickly waned and he felt creatively stifled as his adaptations for the stage of such classic Russian novels as Gogol's *Dead Souls* were altered extensively either for political or artistic reasons. However, despite these changes, he also provided screenplays for mooted films of both *Dead Souls* and Gogol's play *The Government Inspector*. Once again, neither ever came to fruition. There were further projects at this time for other major theatres, both in Moscow and Leningrad, such as an adaptation of Tolstoy's novel *War and Peace* for the stage. This too never came to anything. In May 1932 he wrote: "In nine days' time I shall be celebrating my forty-first birthday... And so towards the conclusion of my literary career I've been forced to write adaptations. A brilliant finale, don't you think?" He wrote numerous other plays and adaptations between then and the end of his life, but no new works were ever produced on stage.

Things appeared to be looking up at one point, because in October 1931 *Molière* had been passed by the censors for production and was accepted by the Bolshoi Drama Theatre in Leningrad. Moreover, in 1932, the MAT had made a routine request to be allowed to restage certain works, and to their surprise were permitted to put *Zoyka's Apartment* and *The Days of the Turbins* back into their schedules. This initially seemed to herald a new thaw, a new liberalism, and these prospects were enhanced by the dissolution of such bodies as RAPP, and the formation of the Soviet Writers' Union. Writers hitherto regarded with suspicion were published.

However, although *Molière* was now in production at the Leningrad theatre, the theatre authorities withdrew it suddenly, terrified by the vituperative attacks of a revolutionary and hard-line Communist playwright, Vsevolod Vishnevsky, whose works celebrated the heroic deeds of the Soviet armed forces and working people and who would place a gun on the table when reading a play aloud.

Bulgakov was then commissioned to write a biography of Molière for the popular market, and the typescript was submitted to the authorities in March 1933. However, it was once again rejected, because Bulgakov, never one to compromise, had adopted an unorthodox means of telling his story, having a flamboyant narrator within the story laying out the known details of Molière's life, but also commenting on them and on the times in which he lived; parallels with modern Soviet times were not hard to find. The censor who rejected Bulgakov's work suggested the project should only be undertaken by a "serious Soviet historian". It was finally published only in 1962, and was one of the writer's first works to be issued posthumously. It is now regarded as a major work, both in content and style.

*Acting*    In December 1934 Bulgakov made his acting debut for the MAT as the judge in an adaptation of Dickens's *Pickwick Papers*, and the performance was universally described as hilarious and brilliant. However, though he obviously had great acting ability, he found the stress and the commitment of performing night after night a distraction from his career as a creative writer. He was still attempting to write plays and other works – such as *Ivan Vasilyevich*, set in the time of Ivan the Terrible – which were rejected by the authorities.

At about this time, Bulgakov proposed a play on the life of Alexander Pushkin, and both Shostakovich and Prokofiev expressed an interest in turning the play into an opera. But then Shostakovich's opera *Lady Macbeth of Mtsensk* was slaughtered in the press for being ideologically and artistically unsound, and Bulgakov's play, which had not even gone into production, was banned in January 1936.

*Molière*, in a revised form, was passed for performance in late 1935, and premiered by the MAT in February 1936. However, it was promptly savaged by the newspaper *Pravda* for its "falsity", and the MAT immediately withdrew it from the repertoire. Bulgakov, bitterly resentful at the theatre's abject capitulation, resigned later in the year, and swiftly joined the famous Moscow Bolshoi Opera Theatre as librettist and adviser. In November 1936, in just a few hours he churned out *Black Snow* (later to be called *A Theatrical Novel*), a short satire on the recent events at the MAT.

*Play on Stalin*    In mid-1937 he began intensive work on yet another redaction of *The Master and Margarita*, which was finally typed out by June 1938. Soon afterwards, he started work on a play about Stalin, *Batum*. The dictator, although in the main disapproving of the tendency of Bulgakov's works, still found them interesting, and had always extended a certain amount of protection to him. Bulgakov had started work in 1936 on a history of the USSR for schools and, although the project remained fragmentary, he had gathered a tremendous amount of material on Stalin for the project, which he proposed to incorporate in his play. It is odd that this ruthless dictator and Bulgakov – who was certainly not a supporter of the regime and whose patrician views seemed to date from a previous era – should have been locked in such a relationship of mutual fascination.

Although the MAT told him that the play on Stalin would do both him and the theatre good in official eyes, Bulgakov, still contemptuous of the theatre, demanded that they provide him with a new flat where he could work without interruption from noise. The MAT complied with this condition. He submitted the manuscript in July 1939, but it was turned down, apparently by the dictator himself.

Bulgakov was devastated by this rejection, and almost immediately began to suffer a massive deterioration in health. His eyesight became worse and worse, he developed appalling headaches, he grew extremely sensitive to light and often could not leave his flat for days on end. All this was the first manifestation of the sclerosis of the kidneys which finally killed him, as it had killed his father. When he could, he continued revising *The Master and Margarita*, but only managed to finish correcting the first part. He became totally bedridden, his weight fell to under fifty kilograms, and he finally died on 10th March 1940. The next morning a call came through from Stalin's office – though not from the leader himself – asking whether it was true the writer was dead. On receiving the answer, the caller hung up with no comment. Bulgakov had had no new work published or performed for some time, yet the Soviet Writers' Union, full of many of the people who had pilloried him so mercilessly over the years, honoured him respectfully. He was buried in the Novodevichy Cemetery, in the section for artistic figures, near Chekhov and Gogol. Ultimately, a large stone which had lain on Gogol's grave, but had been replaced by a memorial bust, was placed on Bulgakov's grave, where it still lies.

*Illness and Death*

After the Second World War ended in 1945, the country had other priorities than the publication of hitherto banned authors, but Bulgakov's wife campaigned fearlessly for his rehabilitation, and in 1957 *The Days of the Turbins* and his play on the end of Pushkin's life were published, and a larger selection of his plays appeared in 1962. A heavily cut version of *The Master and Margarita* appeared in a specialist literary journal throughout 1966–67, and the full uncensored text in 1973. Subsequently – especially post-Glasnost – more

*Posthumous Publications and Reputation*

and more works of Bulgakov's were published in uncensored redactions, and at last Western publishers could see the originals of what they had frequently published before in corrupt smuggled variants. Bulgakov's third wife maintained his archive, and both she and his second wife gave public lectures on him, wrote memoirs of him and campaigned for publication of his works. Bulgakov has now achieved cult status in Russia, and almost all of his works have been published in uncensored editions, with unbiased editorial commentary and annotation.

## Mikhail Bulgakov's Works

It is difficult to give an overall survey of Bulgakov's works, which, counting short stories and adaptations, approach a total of almost one hundred. Many of these works exist in several versions, as the author revised them constantly to make them more acceptable to the authorities. This meant that published versions – including translations brought out abroad – were frequently not based on what the author might have considered the "definitive" version. In fact to talk of "definitive versions" with reference to Bulgakov's works may be misleading. Furthermore, no new works of his were published after 1927, and they only began to be issued sporadically, frequently in censored versions, from 1962 onwards. Complete and uncut editions of many of the works have begun to appear only from the mid-1990s. Therefore the section below will contain only the most prominent works in all genres.

*Themes*    Despite the wide variety of settings of his novels – Russia, the Caucasus, Ukraine, Jerusalem in New Testament times and the Paris of Louis XIV – the underlying themes of Bulgakov's works remain remarkably constant throughout his career. Although these works contain a huge number of characters, most of them conform to certain archetypes and patterns of behaviour.

Stylistically, Bulgakov was influenced by early-nineteenth-century classic Russian writers such as Gogol and Pushkin, and he espoused the values of late-nineteenth-century liberal democracy and culture, underpinned by Christian teachings. Although Bulgakov came from an ecclesiastical background, he was never in fact a conventional believer, but, like many agnostic or atheistic Russian nineteenth-century intellectuals and artists, he respected the role that the basic teachings of religion had played in forming Russian and European culture – although they, and Bulgakov, had no liking for the way religions upheld obscurantism and authority.

Some works portray the struggle of the outsider against society, such as the play and narrative based on the life of Molière, or the novel *The Master and Margarita*, in which the outsider persecuted by society and the state is Yeshua, i.e. Jesus. Other works give prominent roles to doctors and scientists, and demonstrate what happens if science is misused and is subjected to Government interference. Those works portraying historical reality, such as *The White Guard*, show the Whites – who were normally depicted in Communist literature as evil reactionaries – to be ordinary human beings with their own concerns and ideals. Most of all, Bulgakov's work is pervaded by a biting satire on life as he saw it around him in the USSR, especially in the artistic world, and there is frequently a "magical realist" element – as in *The Master and Margarita* – in which contemporary reality and fantasy are intermingled, or which show the influence of Western science fiction (Bulgakov admired the works of H.G. Wells enormously).

Bulgakov's major works are written in a variety of forms, including novels, plays and short stories. His first novel, *The White Guard*, was written between 1922 and 1924, but it received numerous substantial revisions later. It was originally conceived as the first volume of a trilogy portraying the entire sweep of the post-revolutionary Civil War from a number of different points of view. Although this first and only volume was criticized for showing events from the viewpoint of the Whites, the third volume would apparently have given the perspective of the Communists. Many chapters of the novel were published separately in literary journals as they appeared. The ending – the dreams presaging disaster for the country – never appeared, because the journal it was due to be printed in, *Rossiya*, was shut down by official order, precisely because it was publishing such material as Bulgakov's. Different pirate versions, with radically variant texts and concocted endings, appeared abroad. The novel only appeared complete in Russian, having been proofread by the author, in 1929 in Paris, where there was a substantial émigré population from the Tsarist Empire/USSR.

The major part of the story takes place during the forty-seven days in which the Ukrainian Nationalists, under their leader Petlyura, held power in Kiev. The novel ends in February 1919, when Petlyura was overthrown by the Bolsheviks. The major

*The White Guard*

protagonists are the Turbins, a family reminiscent of Bulgakov's own, with a similar address, who also work in the medical profession: many elements of the novel are in fact autobiographical. At the beginning of the novel, we are still in the world of old Russia, with artistic and elegant furniture dating from the Tsarist era, and a piano, books and high-quality pictures on the walls. But the atmosphere is one of fear about the future, and apprehension at the world collapsing. The Turbins' warm flat, in which the closely knit family can take refuge from the events outside, is progressively encroached on by reality. Nikolka Turbin, the younger son, is still at high school and in the cadet corps; he has a vague feeling that he should be fighting on the side of the Whites – that is, the forces who were against both the Nationalists and Communists. However, when a self-sacrificing White soldier dies in the street in Nikolka's arms, he realizes for the first time that war is vile. Near the conclusion of the novel there is a family gathering at the flat, but everything has changed since the beginning of the book: relationships have been severed, and there is no longer any confidence in the future. As the Ukrainian Nationalists flee, they brutally murder a Jew near the Turbins' flat, demonstrating that liberal tolerant values have disintegrated. The novel ends with a series of sinister apocalyptic dreams – indeed the novel contains imagery throughout from the Biblical Apocalypse. These dreams mainly presage catastrophe for the family and society, although the novel ends with the very short dream of a child, which does seem to prefigure some sort of peace in the distant future.

*The Life of Monsieur de Molière* is sometimes classed not as a novel but as a biography. However, the treatment is distinctive enough to enable the work to be ranked as semi-fictionalized. Bulgakov's interpretative view of the French writer's life, rather than a purely historical perspective, is very similar to that in his play on the same theme. The book was written in 1932, but was banned for the same reasons which were to cause problems later for the play. Molière's life is narrated in the novel by an intermediary, a flamboyant figure who often digresses, and frequently comments on the political intrigues of the French author's time. The censors may have felt that the description of the French writer's relationship to an autocrat might have borne too many similarities to Bulgakov's relationship to Stalin. The book was only finally published in the USSR in 1962, and is now regarded as a major work.

Although he had written fragmentary pieces about the theatre before, Bulgakov only really settled down to produce a longer work on the theme – a short, vicious satire on events in the Soviet theatre – in November 1936, after what he saw as the MAT's abject capitulation in the face of attacks by Communists on *Molière*. *Black Snow: A Theatrical Novel* was only published for the first time in the Soviet Union in 1969. There is a short introduction, purporting to be by an author who has found a manuscript written by a theatrical personage who has committed suicide (the reason for Bulgakov's original title, *Notes of the Deceased*; other mooted titles were *Black Snow* and *White Snow*). Not only does Bulgakov take a swipe at censorship and the abject and pusillanimous authorities of the theatre world, but he also deals savagely with the reputations of such people as the theatre director Stanislavsky, who, despite his fame abroad, is depicted – in a thinly veiled portrait – as a tyrannical figure who crushes the individuality and flair of writers and actors in the plays which he is directing. The manuscript ends inconclusively, with the dead writer still proclaiming his wonder at the nature of theatre itself, despite its intrigues and frustrations; the original author who has found the manuscript does not reappear, and it's uncertain whether the point is that the theatrical figure left his memoirs uncompleted, or whether in fact Bulgakov failed to finish his original project.

*The Master and Margarita* is generally regarded as Bulgakov's masterpiece. He worked on it from 1928 to 1940, and it exists in at least six different variants, ranging from the fragmentary to the large-scale narrative which he was working on at the onset of the illness from which he died. Even the first redaction contains many of the final elements, although the Devil is the only narrator of the story of Pilate and Jesus – the insertion of the Master and Margarita came at a later stage. In 1929 the provisional title was *The Engineer's Hoof* (the word "engineer" had become part of the vocabulary of the Soviet demonology of the times, since in May and June 1928 a large group of mining engineers had been tried for anti-revolutionary activities, and they were equated in the press to the Devil who was trying to undermine the new Soviet society). The last variant written before the author's death was completed around mid-1938, and Bulgakov began proofreading and revising it, making numerous corrections and sorting out loose ends. In his sick state, he managed to revise only the first part of the novel, and there are still a certain number of moot points remaining later on. The novel was first published in a severely cut version in 1966–67, in a specialist Russian literary journal, while the complete text was published only in 1973. At one stage, Bulgakov apparently intended to allow Stalin to be the first reader of *The Master and Margarita*, and to present him with a personal copy.

The multi-layered narrative switches backwards and forwards between Jerusalem in the time of Christ and contemporary Moscow. The Devil – who assumes the name Woland – visits Moscow with his entourage, which includes a large talking black cat and a naked witch, and they cause havoc with their displays of magic.

In the scenes set in modern times, the narrative indirectly evokes the atmosphere of a dictatorship. This is paralleled in the Pilate narrative by the figure of Caesar, who, although he is mentioned, never appears.

The atheists of modern Moscow who, following the contemporary party line, snigger at Christ's miracles and deny his existence, are forced to create explanations for what they see the Devil doing in front of them in their own city.

There are numerous references to literature, and also to music – there are three characters with the names of composers, Berlioz, Stravinsky and Rimsky-Korsakov. Berlioz the composer wrote an oratorio on the theme of Faust, who is in love with the self-sacrificing Margarita; immediately we are drawn towards the idea that the persecuted writer known as the Master, who also has a devoted lover called Margarita, is a modern manifestation of Faust. Bulgakov carried out immense research on studies of ancient Jerusalem and theology, particularly Christology. The novel demands several readings, such are the depths of interconnected details and implications.

*Days of the Turbins*

Apart from novels, another important area for Bulgakov to channel his creative energy into was plays. *The Days of the Turbins* was the first of his works to be staged: it was commissioned by the Moscow Arts Theatre in early 1925, although it seems Bulgakov had already thought of the possibility of a stage adaptation of *The White Guard*, since acquaintances report him making drafts for such a project slightly earlier. It had an extremely complex history, which involved numerous rewritings after constant negotiations between the writer, theatre, secret police and censors. Bulgakov did not want to leave any elements of the novel out, but on his reading the initial manuscript at the Moscow Arts Theatre it was found to be far too long, and so he cut out a few of the minor characters and pruned the dream sequences in the novel. However, the background is still the same – the Civil War in Kiev after the Bolshevik Revolution. The family are broadly moderate Tsarists in their views, and therefore are anti-Communist but, being ethnically Russian, have no sympathy with the Ukrainian Nationalists either, and so end up fighting for the White Guards. Their flat at the beginning is almost Chekhovian in its warmth, cosiness and air of old-world culture, but by the end one brother has been killed in the fighting and, as the sounds of the 'Internationale' offstage announce the victory of the Communists, a feeling of apprehension grips the family as their world seems to be collapsing round them. The final lines of the play communicate these misgivings (Nikolka: "Gentlemen, this evening is a great prologue to a new historical play." / Studzinsky: "For some a prologue – for others an epilogue."). The final sentence may be taken as representing Bulgakov's fear about the effect the Communist takeover might have on the rest of his own career.

The Soviet playwright Viktor Nekrasov, who was in favour of the Revolution, commented that the play was an excellent recreation of that time in Kiev, where he had also been participating in the historic events on the Bolshevik side – the atmosphere was all very familiar, Nekrasov confirmed, and one couldn't help extending sympathy to such characters as the Turbins, even if they were on the other side: they were simply individuals caught up in historical events.

At around the time of the writing of *The Days of the Turbins*, another Moscow theatre, the Vakhtangov, requested a play from Bulgakov, so he provided them with *Zoyka's Apartment*, which had been first drafted in late 1925. Various alterations had to be made before the censors were satisfied. At least four different texts of *Zoyka* exist, the final revision completed as late as 1935; this last is now regarded as the authoritative text, and is that generally translated for Western editions.

*Zoyka's Apartment*

The setting is a Moscow apartment run by Zoyka; it operates as a women's dress shop and haute-couturier during the day, and becomes a brothel after closing time. At the time the play was written, various brothels and drug dens had been unearthed by the police in the capital, some run by Chinese

nationals. Bulgakov's play contains therefore not only easily recognizable political and social types who turn up for a
session with the scantily clad ladies, but also stereotypical Chinese drug dealers and addicts. Zoyka is however treated with
moral neutrality by the author: she operates as the madam of
the brothel in order to raise money as fast as possible so that
she can emigrate abroad with her husband, an impoverished
former aristocrat, who is also a drug addict. In the final act the
ladies and clients dance to decadent Western popular music,
a fight breaks out and a man is murdered. The play ends with
the establishment being raided by "unknown strangers", who
are presumably government inspectors and the police. At this
point the final curtain comes down, so we never find out the
ultimate fate of the characters.

*The Crimson*
*Island*
In 1924 Bulgakov had written a rather unsubtle short story,
*The Crimson Island*, which was a parody of the crude agitprop
style of much of the literature of the time, with its stereotypical heroic and noble Communists, and evil reactionaries and
foreigners trying to undermine the new Communist state, all
written in the language of the person in the street – often as
imagined by educated people who had no direct knowledge of
this working-class language. In 1927 he adapted this parody for
the stage. The play bears the subtitle: *The Dress Rehearsal of
a Play by Citizen Jules Verne in Gennady Panfilovich's theatre,
with music, a volcanic eruption and English sailors: in four acts,
with a prologue and an epilogue.* The play was much more successful than the story. He offered it to the Kamerny ["Chamber"]
Theatre, in Moscow, which specialized in mannered and elegant
productions, still in the style of the late 1890s; it was passed
for performance and premiered in December 1928, and was a
success, though some of the more left-wing of the audience and
critics found it hard to swallow. However, the critic Novitsky
wrote that it was an "interesting and witty parody, satirizing
what crushes artistic creativity and cultivates slavish and absurd
dramatic characters, removing the individuality from actors
and writers and creating idols, lickspittles and panegyrists".
The director of the play, Alexander Tairov, claimed that the
work was meant to be self-criticism of the falsity and crudeness
of some revolutionary work. Most reviews found it amusing
and harmless, and it attracted good audiences. However, there
were just a few vitriolic reviews; Stalin himself commented that
the production of such a play underlined how reactionary the

Kamerny Theatre still was. The work was subsequently banned by the censor in March 1929.

*The Crimson Island* takes the form of a play within a play: the prologue and epilogue take place in the theatre where the play is to be rehearsed and performed; the playwright – who, although Russian, has taken the pen name Jules Verne – is progressive and sensitive, but his original work is increasingly censored and altered out of all recognition. The rest of the acts show the rewritten play, which has now become a crude agitprop piece. The play within *Crimson Island* takes place on a sparsely populated desert island run by a white king and ruling class, with black underlings. There is a volcano rumbling in the background, which occasionally erupts. The wicked foreigners are represented by the English Lord and Lady Aberaven, who sail in on a yacht crewed by English sailors who march on singing 'It's a Long Way to Tipperary'. During the play the island's underlings stage a revolution and try unsuccessfully to urge the English sailors to rebel against the evil Lord and Lady. However, they do not succeed, and the wicked aristocrats sail away unharmed, leaving the revolutionaries in control of the island.

Bulgakov's play *Escape* (also translated as *Flight*), drafted *Escape* between 1926 and 1928, and completely rewritten in 1932, is set in the Crimea during the conflicts between the Whites and Reds in the Civil War after the Revolution.

The Whites – who include a general who has murdered people in cold blood – emigrate to Constantinople, but find they are not accepted by the locals, and their living conditions are appalling. One of the women has to support them all by resorting to prostitution. The murderous White general nurses his colleagues during an outbreak of typhus, and feels he has expiated some of his guilt for the crimes he has committed against humanity. He and a few of his colleagues decide to return to the USSR, since even life under Communism cannot be as bad as in Turkey. However, the censors objected that these people were coming back for negative reasons – simply to get away from where they were – and not because they had genuinely come to believe in the Revolution, or had the welfare of the working people at heart.

Molière was one of Bulgakov's favourite writers, and some *Molière* aspects of his writing seemed relevant to Soviet reality – for example the character of the fawning, scheming, hypocritical anti-hero of *Tartuffe*. Bulgakov's next play, *Molière*, was about problems faced by the French playwright during the reign of the autocratic monarch Louis XIV. It was written between October and December 1929 and, as seen above, submitted in January 1930 to the Artistic Board of the MAT. Bulgakov told them that he had not written an overtly political piece, but one about a writer hounded by a cabal of critics in connivance with the absolute monarch. Unfortunately, despite the MAT's optimism, the authorities did not permit a production. In this piece the French writer at one stage, like Bulgakov, intends to leave the country permanently. Late in the play, the King realizes that Molière's brilliance would be a further ornament to his resplendent court, and extends him his protection; however, then this official attitude changes, Molière is once again an outcast, and he dies on stage, while acting in one of his own plays, a broken man. The play's original title was *The Cabal of Hypocrites*, but it was probably decided that this was too contentious.

*Bliss and Ivan Vasilyevich*

A version of the play *Bliss* appears to have been drafted in 1929, but was destroyed and thoroughly rewritten between then and 1934. Bulgakov managed to interest both the Leningrad Music Hall Theatre and Moscow Satire Theatre in the idea, but they both said it would be impossible to stage because of the political climate of the time, and told him to rewrite it; accordingly he transferred the original plot to the time of Tsar Ivan the Terrible in the sixteenth century, and the new play, entitled *Ivan Vasilyevich*, was completed by late 1935.

The basic premise behind both plays is the same: an inventor builds a time machine (as mentioned above, Bulgakov was a great admirer of H.G. Wells) and travels to a very different period of history: present-day society is contrasted starkly with the world he has travelled to. However, in *Bliss*, the contrasted world is far in the future, while in *Ivan Vasilyevich* it is almost four hundred years in the past. In *Bliss* the inventor accidentally takes a petty criminal and a typically idiotic building manager from his own time to the Moscow of 2222: it is a utopian society, with no police and no denunciations to the authorities. He finally returns to his own time with the criminal and the building manager, but also with somebody from the future who is fed up with the bland and boring conformity of such a paradise (Bulgakov was always sceptical of the idea of any utopia, not just the Communist one).

*Ivan Vasilyevich* is set in the Moscow of the tyrannical Tsar, and therefore the contrast between a paradise and present reality is not the major theme. In fact, contemporary Russian society is almost presented favourably in contrast with the distant past. However, when the inventor and his crew – including a character from Ivan's time who has been transported to the present accidentally – arrive back in modern Moscow, they are all promptly arrested and the play finishes, emphasizing that, although modern times are an improvement on the distant past, the problems of that remote period still exist in contemporary reality. For all the differences in period and emphasis, most of the characters of the two plays are the same, and have very similar speeches.

Even this watered-down version of the original theme was rejected by the theatres it was offered to, who thought that it would still be unperformable. It was only premiered in the Soviet Union in 1966. Bulgakov tried neutering the theme even further, most notably by tacking on an ending in which the inventor wakes up in his Moscow flat with the music of Rimsky-Korsakov's popular opera *The Maid of Pskov* (set in Ivan the Terrible's time) wafting in from offstage, presumably meant to be from a radio in another room. The inventor gives the impression that the events of the play in Ivan's time have all been a dream brought on by the music. But all this rewriting was to no avail, and the play was never accepted by any theatre during Bulgakov's lifetime.

In January 1931 Bulgakov signed a contract with the Leningrad Red Theatre to write a play about a "future world"; he also offered it, in case of rejection, to the Vakhtangov Theatre, which had premiered *Zoyka's Apartment*. However, it was banned even before rehearsals by a visiting official from the censor's department, because it showed a cataclysmic world war in which Leningrad was destroyed. Bulgakov had seen the horror of war, including gas attacks, in his medical service, and the underlying idea of *Adam and Eve* appears to be that all war is wrong, even when waged by Communists and patriots.

*Adam and Eve*

The play opens just before a world war breaks out; a poison gas is released which kills almost everybody on all sides. A scientist from the Communist camp develops an antidote, and wishes it to be available to everybody, but a patriot and a party official want it only to be distributed to people from their homeland. The Adam of the title is a cardboard caricature of a well-meaning but misguided Communist; his wife, Eve, is much less of a caricature, and is in love with the scientist who has invented the antidote. After the carnage, a world government is set up, which is neither left- nor right-wing. The scientist and Eve try to escape together, apparently to set up civilization again as the new Adam and Eve, but the sinister last line addressed to them both is: "Go, the Secretary General wants to see you." The Secretary General of the Communist Party in Russia at the time was of course Stalin, and the message may well be that even such an apparently apolitical government as that now ruling the world, which is supposed to rebuild the human race almost from nothing, is still being headed by a dictatorial character, and that the proposed regeneration of humanity has gone wrong once again from the outset and will never succeed.

*The Last Days*    In October 1934 Bulgakov decided to write a play about Pushkin, the great Russian poet, to be ready for the centenary of his death in 1937. He revised the original manuscript several times, but submitted it finally to the censors in late 1935. It was passed for performance, and might have been produced, but just at this time Bulgakov was in such disfavour that the MAT themselves backtracked on the project.

Bulgakov, as usual, took an unusual slant on the theme: Pushkin was never to appear on stage during the piece, unless one counts the appearance at the end, in the distance, of his body being carried across stage after he has been killed in a duel. Bulgakov believed that even a great actor could not embody the full magnificence of Pushkin's achievement, the beauty of his language and his towering presence in Russian literature, let alone any of the second-rate hams who might vulgarize his image in provincial theatres. He embarked on the project at first with a Pushkin scholar, Vikenty Veresayev. However, Veresayev wanted everything written strictly in accordance with historical fact, whereas Bulgakov viewed the project dramatically. He introduced a few fictitious minor characters, and invented speeches between other characters where there is no record of what was actually said. Many events in Pushkin's life remain unclear, including who precisely engineered the duel between the army officer d'Anthès and the dangerously liberal thinker Pushkin, which resulted in the writer's death: the army, the Tsar or others? Bulgakov, while studying all the sources assiduously, put his own gloss and interpretation on these unresolved issues. In the end, Veresayev withdrew from the project in protest. The play was viewed with disfavour by critics and censors, because it implied that it may well have been the autocratic Tsar Nicholas I who was behind the events leading up to the duel, and comparison with another autocrat of modern times who also concocted plots against dissidents would inevitably have arisen in people's minds.

*The Last Days* was first performed in war-torn Moscow in April 1943, by the MAT, since the Government was at the time striving to build up Russian morale and national consciousness in the face of enemy attack and invasion, and this play devoted to a Russian literary giant was ideal, in spite of its unorthodox perspective on events.

Commissioned by the MAT in 1938, *Batum* was projected as *Batum* a play about Joseph Stalin, mainly concerning his early life in the Caucasus, which was to be ready for his sixtieth birthday on 21st December 1939. Its first title was *Pastyr* ["The Shepherd"], in reference to Stalin's early training in a seminary for the priesthood, and to his later role as leader of his national "flock". However, although most of Bulgakov's acquaintances were full of praise for the play, and it passed the censors with no objections, it was finally rejected by the dictator himself.

Divided into four acts, the play covers the period 1898–1904, following Stalin's expulsion from the Tiflis (modern Tbilisi) Seminary, where he had been training to be an Orthodox priest, because of his anti-government activity. He is then shown in the Caucasian town of Batum organizing strikes and leading huge marches of workers to demand the release of imprisoned workers, following which he is arrested and exiled to Siberia. Stalin escapes after a month and in the last two scenes resumes the revolutionary activity which finally led to the Bolshevik Revolution under Lenin. Modern scholars have expressed scepticism as to the prominent role that Soviet biographers of Stalin's time ascribed to his period in Batum and later, and Bulgakov's play, although not disapproving of the autocrat, is objective, and far from the tone of the prevailing hagiography.

Varying explanations have been proposed as to why Stalin rejected the play. Although this was probably because it portrayed the dictator as an ordinary human being, the theory has been advanced that one of the reasons Stalin was fascinated by Bulgakov's works was precisely that the writer refused to knuckle under to the prevailing ethos, and Stalin possibly wrongly interpreted the writer's play about him as an attempt to curry favour, in the manner of all the mediocrities around him.

One Western commentator termed the writing of this play a "shameful act" on Bulgakov's part; however, the author was now beginning to show signs of severe ill health, and was perhaps understandably starting at last to feel worn down both mentally and physically by his lack of success and the constant struggle to try to make any headway in his literary career, or even to earn a crust of bread. Whatever the reasons behind the final rejection of *Batum*, Bulgakov was profoundly depressed by it, and it may have hastened his death from the hereditary sclerosis of the kidneys which he suffered from.

Bulgakov also wrote numerous short stories and novellas, the most significant of which include 'Diaboliad', 'The Fatal Eggs' and *A Dog's Heart*.

*Diaboliad*

'Diaboliad' was first published in the journal *Nedra* in 1924, and then reappeared as the lead story of a collection of stories under the same name in July 1925; this was in fact the last major volume brought out by the author during his lifetime in Russia, although he continued to have stories and articles published in journals for some years. In theme and treatment the story has reminiscences of Dostoevsky and Gogol.

The "hero" of the tale, a minor ordering clerk at a match factory in Moscow, misreads his boss's name – Kalsoner – as *kalsony*, i.e. "underwear". In confusion he puts through an order for underwear and is sacked. It should be mentioned here that both he and the boss have doubles, and the clerk spends the rest of the story trying to track down his boss through an increasingly nightmarish bureaucratic labyrinth, continually confusing him with his double; at the same time he is constantly having to account for misdemeanours carried out by his own double, who has a totally different personality from him, and is a raffish philanderer. The clerk is robbed of his documents and identity papers, and can no longer prove who he is – the implication being that his double is now the real him, and that he doesn't exist any longer. Finally, the petty clerk, caught up in a Kafkaesque world of bureaucracy and false appearances, goes mad and throws himself off the roof of a well-known Moscow high-rise block.

*The Fatal Eggs*

'The Fatal Eggs' was first published in the journal *Nedra* in early 1925, then reissued as the second story in the collection *Diaboliad*, which appeared in July 1925. The title in Russian contains a number of untranslatable puns. The major one is that a main character is named "Rokk", and the word "rok" means "fate" in Russian, so "fatal" could also mean "belonging to Rokk". Also, "eggs" is the Russian equivalent of "balls", i.e. testicles, and there is also an overtone of the "roc", i.e. the giant mythical bird in the *Thousand and One Nights*. The theme of the story is reminiscent of *The Island of Doctor Moreau* by H.G. Wells. However, Bulgakov's tale also satirizes the belief of the time, held by both scientists and journalists, that science would solve all human problems, as society moved towards utopia. Bulgakov was suspicious of such ideals and always doubted the possibility of human perfection.

In the story, a professor of zoology discovers accidentally that a certain ray will increase enormously the size of any organism or egg exposed to it – by accelerating the rate of cell multiplication – although it also increases the aggressive tendencies of any creatures contaminated in this manner. At the time, chicken plague is raging throughout Russia, all of the birds have died, and so there is a shortage of eggs. The political activist Rokk wants to get hold of the ray to irradiate eggs brought from abroad, to replenish rapidly the nation's devastated stock of poultry. The professor is reluctant, but a telephone call is received from "someone in authority" ordering him to surrender the ray. When the foreign eggs arrive at the collective farm, they look unusually large, but they are irradiated just the same. Soon Rokk's wife is devoured by an enormous snake, and the country is plagued by giant reptiles and ostriches which wreak havoc. It turns out that a batch of reptile eggs was accidentally substituted for the hens' eggs. Chaos and destruction ensue, creating a sense of panic, during which the professor is murdered. The army is mobilized unsuccessfully, but – like the providential extermination of the invaders by germs in Wells's *The War of the Worlds* – the reptiles are all wiped out by an unexpected hard summer frost. The evil ray is destroyed in a fire.

*A Dog's Heart* was begun in January 1925 and finished the following month. Bulgakov offered it to the journal *Nedra*, who told him it was unpublishable in the prevailing political climate; it was never issued during Bulgakov's lifetime. Its themes are reminiscent of *The Island of Doctor Moreau*, *Dr Jekyll and Mr Hyde* and *Frankenstein*.

*A Dog's Heart*

In the tale, a doctor, Preobrazhensky ["Transfigurative", or "Transformational"] by name, transplants the pituitary glands and testicles from the corpse of a moronic petty criminal and thug into a dog (Sharik). The dog gradually takes on human form, and turns out to be a hybrid of a dog's psyche and a criminal human being. The dog's natural affectionate nature has been swamped by the viciousness of the human, who has in his turn acquired the animal appetites and instincts of the dog. The monster chooses the name Polygraf ["printing works"], and this may well have been a contemptuous reference to the numerous printing presses in Moscow churning out idiotic propaganda, appealing to the lowest common denominator in terms of intelligence and gullibility. The new creature gains employment, in keeping with his animal nature, as a cat exterminator. He is indoctrinated with party ideology by a manipulative official, and denounces numerous acquaintances to the authorities as being ideologically unsound, including his creator, the doctor. Although regarded with suspicion and warned as to his future behaviour, the doctor escapes further punishment. The hybrid creature disappears, and the dog Sharik reappears; there is a suggestion that the operation has been reversed by the doctor and his faithful assistant, and the human part of his personality has returned to its original form – a corpse – while the canine characteristics have also reassumed their natural form. Although the doctor is devastated at the evil results of his experiment, and vows to renounce all such researches in future, he appears in the last paragraph already to be delving into body parts again. The implication is that he will never be able to refrain from inventing, and the whole sorry disaster will be repeated ad infinitum. Again, as with 'The Fatal Eggs', the writer was voicing his suspicion of science and medicine's interference with nature, and his scepticism as to the possibility of utopias.

*Notes on a Cuff*   From 1920 to 1921, Bulgakov worked in a hospital in the Caucasus, and during this time he produced a series of journalistic sketches detailing his experiences in the region, a series which he continued when he moved to Moscow and was employed in the literary section of Glavpolitprosvet (Central Committee of the Republic for Political Education). The principal theme is the development of a writer amid scenes of chaos, disruption, politics and bureaucracy. These pieces, now collected under the name *Notes on a Cuff*, were published in various publications, and an offer was made to publish an anthology of the sketches in Paris in 1924, but the project never came to fruition. The collection was only published in full in Russia in 1982.

*A Young Doctor's Notebook*   *A Young Doctor's Notebook* was drafted in 1919, then published mainly in medical journals between 1925–27. It is different in nature from Bulgakov's most famous works, being a first-person account of his experiences of treating peasants in his country practice, surrounded by ignorance and poverty, in a style reminiscent of another doctor and writer, Chekhov. Bulgakov learns by experience that often in this milieu what he has learnt in medical books and at medical school can seem useless, as he delivers babies, treats syphilitics and carries out amputations. The work is often published with *Morphine*, which describes the experience of a doctor addicted to morphine. This is autobiographical: it recalls Bulgakov's own period in medical service in Vyazma, in 1918, where, to alleviate his distress at the suffering he was seeing, he dosed himself heavily on his own drugs and temporarily became addicted to morphine.

## Select Bibliography

*Biographies*:
Drawicz, Andrzey, *The Master and the Devil*, tr. Kevin Windle (New York, NY: Edwin Mellen Press, 2001)
Haber, Edythe C., *Mikhail Bulgakov: The Early Years* (Cambridge, MS: Harvard University Press, 1998)
Milne, Lesley, *Mikhail Bulgakov: A Critical Biography* (Cambridge: Cambridge University Press, 1990)
Proffer, Ellendea, *Bulgakov: Life and Work* (Ann Arbor, MI: Ardis, 1984)
Proffer, Ellendea, *A Pictorial Biography of Mikhail Bulgakov* (Ann Arbor, MI: Ardis, 1984)
Wright, A. Colin, *Mikhail Bulgakov: Life and Interpretation* (Toronto, ON: University of Toronto Press, 1978)

*Letters, Memoirs*:
Belozerskaya-Bulgakova, Lyubov, *My Life with Mikhail Bulgakov*, tr. Margareta Thompson (Ann Arbor, MI: Ardis, 1983)
Bulgakov, Mikhail, *Diaries and Selected Letters*, tr. Roger Cockrell (London: Alma Classics, 2013).
Curtis, J.A.E., *Manuscripts Don't Burn: Mikhail Bulgakov: A Life in Letters and Diaries* (London: Bloomsbury, 1991)
Vozdvizhensky, Vyacheslav, ed., *Mikhail Bulgakov and his Times – Memoirs, Letters*, tr. Liv Tudge (Moscow: Progress Publishers, 1990)

Other books by MIKHAIL BULGAKOV
published by Alma Classics

*Black Snow*

*Diaboliad and Other Stories*

*Diaries and Selected Letters*

*A Dog's Heart*

*The Fatal Eggs*

*The Life of Monsieur de Molière*

*The Master and Margarita*

*The White Guard*

*A Young Doctor's Notebook*

# ALMA CLASSICS

ALMA CLASSICS aims to publish mainstream and lesser-known European classics in an innovative and striking way, while employing the highest editorial and production standards. By way of a unique approach the range offers much more, both visually and textually, than readers have come to expect from contemporary classics publishing.

## LATEST TITLES PUBLISHED BY ALMA CLASSICS

To order any of our titles and for up-to-date information about our current and forthcoming publications, please visit our website on:

# www.almaclassics.com